M000085188

Bye-Bye	*Flying Out with the*
Jane Ransom	*Wounded*
(fiction)	Anne Caston
	(poetry)

In 1997, the jurors selected Trace Farrell's novel, *The Ruins,* and Nancy Shoenberger's collection of poems, *Long Like a River.*

TRACE FARRELL

NEW YORK UNIVERSITY PRESS
New York and London

NEW YORK UNIVERSITY PRESS
New York and London

This book is fictional. Names, characters, places, and incidents are invented or used fictitiously. Any resemblance to actual people, places, or events is purely coincidental.

Partial support for this work was provided by the King County Arts Commission Hotel/Motel Tax Revenues.

Library of Congress Cataloging-in-Publication Data
Farrell, Trace, 1959–
The ruins / Trace Farrell.
p.   cm.
ISBN 0-8147-2685-2 (acid-free paper)
I. Title.
PS3556.A7723R85   1998
813'.54—dc21   98-10683
                              CIP

New York University Press books are printed on acid-free paper, and their binding materials are chosen for strength and durability.

Manufactured in the United States of America
10 9 8 7 6 5 4 3 2 1

ACKNOWLEDGMENTS, etc.

Among other things, a book's what finally doesn't budge when you've shooed what you can from the page. Thanks to my editor, the intrepid Barbara Epler, for a hand in the shooing; and to Chris and Mar for a timely haven in which to shoo.

A heavy debt is owed, as well, to Marianne Faithful for her hysterical schtick on the demise of Harry Nilsson (on which La Stupenda's account of "the gay dog Doug" is based).

Goethe's the wag behind the first verse of the lullaby on p. 146; the insights on green apples and uncounted heads belong to Machiavelli.

In the end, of course, I have to hand it to Tom-Tom.

CHAPTER ONE

*In Which Our Hero's Knees—Dicey, a
Hazard in the Best of Times—Have
Never Been Worse . . .*

1—

Tom grunts like a girl as he hurdles a black-spotted sow
barreling straight for him down the narrow cobbled lane
. . . swerves violently round two roaring guttersnipes,
hung like hams from the big red fists of a leering police
matron . . . vaults a row of battered metal folding chairs
laid out with bundles of colored wire, used computer
geegaws and papers of rusted needles—lands hard on
both tender heels and whistles to cover the small involuntary cry that escapes him. He pulls up wincing, mincing like a crab. On either side two wharf hands bellow:

"*Porca madonna!*"

"*Guarda! Aiee—*"

Huh? Tom looks up and a thirty-pound watermelon,
monstrous in the flickering gaslit drizzle of rain, sails elegantly not an inch before his own dripping nose. He rears
back—*ungh!*—then grabs to save it. Slick fingers goose

the glamorous green butt. Too late! A hollow thunk; a sharp wet crack. Like magic, children swarm from under empty produce crates and overturned dollies to cast themselves, spitting and snarling like monkeys, upon the bright red, black-eyed fruit: "*Crackerjack!*" No small booty in a neighborhood of weeping mutton and green potatoes.

Tom pauses, impressed by their bravado. Himself high-browed, gaunt-cheeked, small-chinned; with rheumy spaniel eyes set close above the bridge of a long, deferential nose, and a calamitous thatch of ruddy curls, flared as a fruit bowl, crowning his tapering, pear-shaped torso (tragic legs; broad, delicate feet). Tom's pluckless exterior belies a keen admiration for the defiant self-servers of the world. He clucks, is tapped from behind—spins— then backs away, appalled, before two abruptly looming, yellow-slickered dock bulls.

"Whoah!" He tugs a penitent red forelock. *An accident!* "I didn't, that is, I'm really—" No use. He fakes left, cuts right; a pretty cheat, bum knees and all. The yellowbacks spit, cursing the tactical squeak of rubber sneakers on wet cement, the flagrant white flash of fugitive heels, rising and falling, away and further away, down the long dark tunnel of night. Close call!

The crooked lane is tight as a hen's ass, snot-slick with rain and perilously lit. Tom hugs his ribs and hightails it anyway; the impact of each striking heel drives jagged bolts of blue lightning clear to his plump, pumping hips. *Rickets,* is why. Wrung like rags in the tenderness of their

growing years, our hero's legs came through conspicuously calcified in their misfortune: sockets taut, exquisitely bowed, he warps with the weather like a sensitive
guitar.

"Alas," Tom would be the first to agree, born to a
caste of humble shoeshines obliged for generations to
make ends meet by the dogged, day-long tuck of their
typically inadequate knees. And yet, adds he (the sort of
green apple that favors a comforting lie, as they say, to the
uncomfortable truth): "It could be worse!"

Tom knew, for instance, a certain butcher, born with
no eyelids, who depended on a spray bottle of boiled
water to spare his eyeballs' drying out. The fellow's wife
covered his face with a damp rag at night as she could not
bear to wake and see her husband's eyes—"like two
boiled onions!"—staring at the ceiling while he snored.

And then there was Rosie. A real heartbreaker, Tom's
ravishing baby sister; only innocent as an egg. Talk about
luck! She'd been hours each day lighting candles at the
parish church, her hair an apricot cloud bound clumsily
with dirty blue string, and despite her devotions—or *because?*—brought home a virgin belly miraculously
abloom with child. Oh la! (a coral blush stained her perfect cheeks). And what was Tom to think? Tubercular Father Ratskin, from whose blunt, nicotine-stained fingers
the meek parishioners weekly received God's inescapable
dispensations, didn't blink an eye.

"Mysterium tremendum!" he drew hard on the stale
weed of a smoldering Pall Mall. "Penetrated by a heav-

enly incubus while telling her beads." The priest's voice rattled with furtive yellow phlegm. "Happens all the time!" He dropped one proprietary hand to Rosie's slender neck and squeezed, his gaze trailing a haggard ash gone to rest upon the child's precocious, blue-marbled bosom. Tom shuffled his feet; Father Ratskin glared— "*Scram!*"—turned, and with a convulsive hitch of his long black skirt, shepherded the waddling and obedient Rose up the aisle. And that was that. Tom watched them disappear inside the priest's dim and airless sacristy; eyeballed, uncertainly, the zipped lips of the plaster saints; and finally left, only knocking wood for the less inscrutable liabilities of punk knees.

• • •

At the end of the lane Tom's side stitches, forcing him to walk. *Was* it weather made things worse? Honestly, he can't remember a less promising spring. Five minutes ago it rained; the backed-up sewers ebb and flow, awash with iridescent oil slicks, unsinkable filter tips, and the floundering headlights of stalled automobiles, mopeds, and careening bicycles. In five minutes more it will rain again. People push past Tom in ancient oilskins, or makeshift tarps of torn and dirty plastic, sick and tired of being wet—no surprise!—their ruby-lobed cabbage ears shoved deep into yawning collarbones, their dripping hoods and hunched shoulders reflecting the interminable red, green, and amber of the corner traffic lights. Rude carts insinuate themselves amongst the indifferent crowd; ragamuffins prowl the gutters in packs, slapping parked cars with freezing hands to set off a chorus of wailing security alarms; broken-tailed cats slip sourly along the damp walls, pausing now and then to stare with wide, accusing eyes at the mess of humanity surging by.

Tom draws bead on a rusty vinyl awning bellied low with rain; steals sideways between the wearily kissing chrome of checked traffic and ducks in, shuddering the water from his back like a finicky sparrow.

Are all chips vendors junkies? *Any port in a storm,* Tom reckons. This one's surprised holding a mustard dispenser to his whorled gray ear with evident wonder, his mouth opening and closing in astonishment. Well? Tom taps at the window and the old man jumps. His red-rimmed, caramel eyes roll in their sockets like loose marbles; his face is a wad of blue-black wrinkles, white stubble and brilliant gold teeth as he points at Tom, slaps his skinny thigh and hoots, his bald head wobbly as an egg on end. Tom nods, accepts a cracked cup of pale pink tea, and to pamper his knees squats gingerly upon a splintered orange crate; the slats give uneasily. He twirls his tea bag counter-clockwise, lifts it up and observes the drops that fall from it back into the cup, sinks the bag once more into the steaming pink water. Across the sidewalk thin filaments of rain attach themselves to a bucket of Chinese chrysanthemums and a child's rubber galoshes, as if to catch the colors up and dangle them over the gleaming pavement, the yellows a bit higher than the reds. Tom squints and the blue-white headlamps of cars swim like platinum fish.

"But, oh!" (and oh! here we go again). "Why here? Why on earth *Q*—?"

This is Tom's cross to bear, his bone to chew, the hard yellow pea that won't let him rest. He's had his head turned, is the problem, by tales overheard while plying his trade. Bent over the caulked boots of sailors, the cracked leather thongs of itinerant saints, the gaudy two-tones of fast-talking traveling salesmen—our hero listens, and marvels at what he hears.

> . . . *three skinny boys, yellow as snakes, with glittering smiles they dangle like bracelets before the faltering guardians of your desire* . . .

> . . . *tomahawks, uranium, absinthe, you bet! Snake oil for amethysts, marigolds for tin!*

> . . . *beyond a frozen, pitiless bivouac of pitched bones and blood-daubed caribou hide—and in all directions, for miles—the silent drifts like God's dream of angels, or death* . . .

> . . . *a naked girl with tattooed breasts, wrestling a puma!*

> . . . *what isn't light is stone, what isn't stone is sea, and an army of blue mountains standing at your back* . . .

> . . . *ruby slippers, glass coffins, poisoned pancakes— and the geese!*

> . . . *across the water is Africa* . . .

Tom's head spins, and no wonder. In *Q*—, a tired, bristling city of crumbling brickyards, contaminated needles, coal barges and abject fog, the days come and go in a flat, lurid tide, noon and midnight like sullen twins, so indifferently does light distinguish itself from darkness. Encrustations of oil and soot eclipse the shattered street lamps, hissing neon, and storefront windows; grease the puddled streets, the bald, glabrous tires of carts and lorries. A dank, funereal smoke hangs in the air everywhere—down among the slimy docks beetling out over the viscous yellow river; choking the crowded market stalls where half-dressed chickens flap by their heels from loops of rusting wire; and in the open ulcered squares, pearled, like vast laboring brows, with gobbets of blood-marbled sputum and the brought-up bile of bellies dizzy with cheap yellow ale. The damp fetor clings to people's hair and skin, and to the filthy matted hides of the cart horses dragging their haphazard loads of pig iron, draff, recyclable glass and busted furniture. Crows, pigeons, and starlings slouch along the gutters, their feathers a bootless debauch of grease and grit, their black eyes bulging with ill will.

Phew! One day spent in this town is too much—one hour! Tom hugs his tea and nods with understanding at the botched, beset faces of the people slogging by—the stooping, soot-masked furnace tenders; doomed insurance adjusters clutching taut black umbrellas; restless crews of saffron-robed Hare Krishnas, their shaved heads stubbly under backwards baseball caps; teen moms pushing preemies in strollers with torn tops; apocalyptic fags in patent leather drag; tiny Asians in tall rubber boots; old people with no homes who slept on the smothering ash heaps beside the river for warmth and woke with cinders in their eyes to stare at the muddy dawn of another uncharitable day. Our hero shivers, his curved spine rattling like a child's stick against the aluminum chips wagon, and lets his eyes close as the gaslights sputter overhead like dying stars and *still* it rains, vertical ladders of water rising up out of the streets, leaning on nothing at all, going nowhere.

"Yet only read the papers!" Tom rouses himself, set in his ways for one so young, *"—it could be worse!"* Worse indeed. Rogue viruses, religious terrorism, cross-tribal atomic sniping, the stratosphere in smithereens.

Grandma's Favorite Devoured by Deceiving Wolf!
Stepmother's Slave Rescued after Lifetime of Forced Labor!
Oh la!

"On the other hand," Tom allows, nodding drowsily, "it wouldn't take much to brighten things up a bit." For just a moment, eyes fluttering like little birds beneath sweetly lowered lids, Tom yields, cradled and consoled, to a small private rapture (wholly invented) of *Better Days*. Warm breezes tumbling about like flossy, sun-licked kittens, and a cloud of hummingbirds beating the air to stiff, luminous peaks. There would be hands, bodiless and soft as butter, to tease the rough kinks from one's sullen curls; and a bower of round-cheeked yellow roses, shaking their skirts at the leering sky; and the so-porific drone of wasps, swinging dizzily among ripe, un-reachable apples. A white rabbit's pink, quivering nose . . . and something nice, *nice* to eat . . . and thickets of tall grass to nap in, and oh!—ecstasy of the golden carrot!

When Tom's eyes open it's raining buckets and the junkie's out in it, aghast: seven pigeons press toward him along the gutter, shoving with tender urgency like old people for a bus. The frightened vendor backs away, one arm thrown up across his stunned, streaming face. Tom shakes his head, tucks several pennies beneath a tin of pal-lid lard, and steps out from beneath the dripping tarpau-lin. The crowds, anyway, have thinned.

• • •

At the next intersection it's the letter of the law for Tom—a dauntless stickler, *natch*—who bides his time at the deserted crossing shifting his weight from one peev-ish knee to the other while the traffic signal deliberates. Meanwhile his idle belly, nettled by the indeterminate pink tea, is arranging a conniption.

Not surprisingly, Tom's never managed to eat prop-erly. Sure he's mouse-poor, motherless, and (beyond the niceties of boiling water) never risen much to the occa-sion of *cuisine;* all more or less to be expected. But it's not strictly a lack of resources that frustrates him; the fact is, Tom's saddled with a nervous stomach. What *he'll* say, presented with a not unappetizing crust of gravy, the flac-cid skin from a kind man's pudding: "Mmm? Oh! *ha ha*—no really . . . I'm, I couldn't—I've *eaten,* yes! You go ahead though, go on! I'll just . . ." and he backs away from the innocent morsel, hands palming the air as though you'd pulled a knife on him. Modesty, is it? Or pride? Bad breeding? (There is more to any hero than meets the eye, and Tom, for all his youth and inexperience, is no exception.) Still, you wonder how he manages; these so-called growing years. . . . Furthermore, and what's worse, people are insulted. *We're all rats on the same sinking ship*, goes their thinking. *Who's he to powder his nose?*

Needless to say, his belly's none too happy about it either. Tom has a special—indeed, an *inspired*—relationship with his hunger, which he perceives as very like a glowering, one-eyed dachshund one used to see dragged through the market in a fancy cart by an otherwise destitute bum. Heaven knows, that shabby old man was *born* dreadful to look at—his tiny eyes peered warily from the face of a bloated and blistering seal—and could scarcely provide for his own material needs, much less those of an ill-tempered bitch named "Kevin." Nevertheless he doted on his snarling, darling mascot, his horrid little cyclops, his *Kevver;* and would swaddle it in his own stinking rags, kiss the tip of its torn ear, beg for its ungrateful sake first, and promise it brighter skies, silver linings, pots of gold, a plump and steaming phoenix rising from old, cold ashes. *Just around the corner, little princess, over the next rainbow and we're there* . . . Now and then the nasty little princess would narrow her one gummy eye, lift her lip and snap traitorously at the earnest, uneasy bum, who invariably believed (poor wretch! heartless Kevver!) that he had it coming.

Our Tom assumed the same tender, futile guardianship toward his own perpetually dissatisfied belly. He fed it hope in humble crumbs; he made excuses for its bad manners; he flattered and indulged it; he did what he could. When it showed its teeth he clucked and promised it anything—fish fingers, malted milk balls, hot cross buns, chicken à la king.

Now Tom's stomach, unappeased since this morning's hasty and wholly insufficient gruel, rattles the cage of his ribs in high dudgeon while the rain streams down the collar of his hoodless mack, and the crossing light is predictably on the fritz. Overhead a wrought iron sign complains of rusty hinges; Tom looks up: The Groaning Board. Turning around, he admires the big, blowzy edifice, five stories high, its beam-built frame haphazardly stuffed with stucco, mortar, lath, and straw. Neon silhouettes of implausibly endowed barmaids animate the steamy, street level windows; the entire structure lists right. Oblivious, now, to the abruptly green and insistently flashing *Walk!* signal behind him, Tom whistles to distract his belly and fingers the pennies at scant liberty inside his pocket. *Mm-hmm, mm-hmm . . .*

When the double-wide doors of the public house burst open, discharging a great friendly belch of laughter and curses and the mingled odors of scorched grease, mildew, and corrosive perfume, our hero surrenders.

Tom darts in, automatically shaking the water from his unruly red crest, before the heavy doors swing shut behind him with a great whack like a clap of thunder and a godawful *whoosh* of air.

2—

Gracious! Transfixed by the abrupt fluorescence of furious orange bulbs—hundreds of them, bare and hissing from long black wires that criss-cross the high exposed beams of the hall—Tom hesitates, then creeps forward, his feet testing the unfamiliar threshold of damp clay and rushes, his hands cagey as spiders along splayed walls festooned with spit and vomit. The place is vast and, though unheated, the stale air nevertheless steams with the congregate squalor of wet dogs and woolen underclothes, the morbid reek of indoor plumbing, and the rank collective gorge of countless indefatigable gobs—bared, carious teeth closing on plump sausages and meaty white shoulders; withered lungs sucking greedily at fat cigars and windy gossip; ambitious tongues lashing away at pert earlobes and promising assholes and the overlooked bottoms of unattended gravy boats. The commotion is *de luxe*.

"Pretty kettle of fish!" thinks Tom, looking round a little wildly. Here a fairy's strapped to a table, blowing air like a laboring porpoise while a tattooed hoyden sets steel rings through his pierced and bleeding nipples. There by the bar a turtlenecked highbrow in a wheelchair with bent spokes puts a cigarette out in the palm of his own hand, glaring at a skinny girl who looks away, flicking her lips with the fat black whisk of a greasy braid. Not far from them an immense tub of a woman in a tired blue hat has her elbows out around a platter of meat sandwiches; her tiny eyes gaze wearily around the crowded room. Oh, a lively spot, all right! Lame dogs, ulcerated pigs and rickety kids with ticks in their seams, run hell-bent and shrieking, snapping and squealing, up and down the narrow aisles. Walleyed pigeons sidle along the overhead beams, indifferent to the sizzle and pop of shattering orange bulbs. In one corner a little goat bleats mildly, head in a sack, twat impaled on the red hot poker of an amorous schoolboy. Frowzy chickens browse among the dirty straw pallets of deadbeats and pilgrims, penny-a-flop, snoring round an unlit stove. Rats run like eels beneath the long communal tables, while fat cats sneer over filched sprats; and it's nobody's business if here and there a wink's met with a nod, a likely pocket's picked, a ripe crotch experimentally squeezed.

A small gray mouse, confused, runs halfway up Tom's sopping leg. "Sweet!" he thinks (*a little velvet sack with claws*), then kicks it off and edges closer to the dining hall. Waitresses in shapeless paper caps struggle past him with platters of bashed neeps, mingle-mangle, and red flannel hash. Barmaids' arms terminate in tankards of beer and ale, like enormous glass knuckles, or tall flagons of boiled wine, fumey with gentian and juniper. Fresh loaves grow limp under fat, perspiring arms; from bagging apron pockets comes the covert, beguiling clink of ash trays and bottles of sauce. Not bad, not bad at all! Tom's belly lifts its pointed muzzle, dances on its hind feet and moans. *Well,* our boy reasons, *he that allows A cannot deny B*—and so on. In other words, one thing leads to another. Tom therefore fills his lungs, tucks his chin, and plunges into the teeming hall.

"Sorry, s'cuse me . . . oh pardon! Ugh! I mean—"

Tom's dogged as a dowser's stick, nosing his way among patrons no more mindful of him than the nits in their ale. He finally squeezes in between a huddle of Chinese cooks sipping cognac from thimble-sized tea cups, and two wan girls in flaking black lipstick who turn their backs at Tom's friendly nod. Well! A pig-tailed chef offers him the bottle; flattered, self-conscious, our fledgling hero demurs with a flurry of mute, inscrutable gestures. The cook shrugs and Tom reaches for the menu, a single sheet of greasy foolscap folded and stuck between a red glass candle globe netted in white plastic and an empty napkin dispenser.

And now, the moment he's been waiting for!

Naturally he's short on dough and doomed, as a consequence, to a saucer of dry groats, a shy measure of cider (if he's lucky). Nevertheless Tom has grave instincts for the *ceremony* of dining and will give all possibles an extravagant going-over before placing his final order. He shrugs off his mack and unfolds the soiled paper.

Has Your Bed of Roses Gone to Seed?
Is Your Ivory Tower Besieged?
Has the Spice in Your Life Lost Its Zing?

Never Fear, Fret, or Bemoan Your Fate!
The Ruins
Will Gladly Engage All Those in Sincere Pursuit
of
Prosperity, Prestige, and a Promising Future . . .
Does This Mean You?
No Experience Necessary!

Imagine . . .
Gainful Employment!
A Glamorous Environment . . .
Your Big Chance!

Don't Pass Up This Rare Opportunity!
Join Us and Leave Your Troubles Behind!

The paper itself, once thick and creamy, is now dog-eared and spotted with sauce, limp and nearly torn across the middle from repeated folding. Ah, but the bold, gold, elegantly bossed script! Back-slanting languidly, glinting come-hitherly! Mmm-mmm-*mmm!* Our hero's fingers brush the face of it. Tantalized, provoked, he lays one hand upon his abruptly galloping heart.

In the meantime a waitress has arrived and, noting Tom's preoccupation, takes this opportunity to sort furiously among a fistful of loose yellow receipts—amending one with the licked tip of a ravaged red pencil; crushing another to a grimy yellow nugget—her darkly muttering

lips parting to reveal two rows of childish, milk-white
teeth.

"Unh huh, that—that was . . . uh oh! Oh!—what?"

Slope-shouldered and ostensibly boneless, with tiny
hands and a transparently anxious brow, she put Tom in
mind of the little gray mouse, and seemed frail for the
job. Her pointed chin shone like the petal of a flower; her
wide mouth—an artless, unrouged pink—blurred at its
edges. Her nose, on the other hand, was the sharpest
he'd ever seen (a little chapped around the nostrils, as
though recovering from a cold). She had bright black,
slightly protruding eyes, unabashed as buttons, with vigorously arched brows in marked contrast to the cloud of
feckless, fuzzy hair drawn back from her face into a dubious knot at the back of her head. Her bosom, as revealed
by the flagrant plunge of her uniform neckline, stared
one in the face, frankly flat as the bottom of a pan, chaste
as whey. On the other hand, there was a delicate commotion at the base of her throat—a flicker, a serene
churn—as though it were *there* her heart lodged, just
below the skin, and not hidden behind the hard, bony
confines of the ribs.

Tom gazes politely somewhere to the left of the girl's
sternum, intending, when she has concluded her paper-
work, to inquire as to the strange and remarkable handbill he'd discovered in place of a menu. As it happens, the
girl sinks slowly—still biting her big soft lips, totting up
numbers and exclaiming under her breath—down upon
the bench beside him. Tom bends over to collect several

dingy receipts she's let slip to the floor; but even as he delivers these before the waitress's distracted eye, his own gaze steals back to the luminous golden letters of the broadsheet lying open on the table.

The Ruins . . .

Some kind of joke?

Prosperity! Prestige!

"No," Tom reasons, "that's no joke!"

All right then, was it a club of some kind? An agency? The thing read like a solicitation, but expressed a disregard for experience or credentials. A training program? An apprenticeship? Ah, the future! Indeed, that certainly rang a bell! It was no picnic, after all, to have been born a two-penny shoeshine with lousy knees; Tom had often asked himself if there weren't, perhaps, *another way.* In any case, there was only so much can-do a fellow could muster; as things stood it was all he could manage just to pacify his churlish belly and keep a thatch over his head. The here-and-now consumed him, no blame there; and it was only in "the future" that he was able to discern, however remote, the faint glimmer of a different, *better* life. Something, for example, up off his knees.

Well then? Heart in his throat and decidedly half-cocked, our hero slaps his hand flat against the table top, sending a litter of yellow receipts fluttering to the floor; the waitress looks up. For a brief moment both their mouths are open to exclaim; then each indicates with a

polite nod for the other to go ahead. Then it's "no, pardon *me,*" and "no, no, you were saying?"; then a volley
of "please, I insist"—"no *you*"—"no no"—"well"—
"*well* . . ." They break off. Tom's hands meet precisely in
his lap; the girl's mouth nips to one side of her face, a
wince of impatience to the other.

"Well I was just going to—"

"I guess you'd like to—"

Oh for the love of—! Again they break off, eyes narrowing with suspicion. When Tom frowns the waitress
surrenders, throwing up her hands with a contrite yelp.

"Oh I *am* sorry—jeez! And now you're mad? Well
look, it's nothing, I won't say another word. Cross my
heart! You just go ahead!"

Tom softens. "Oh, as for that—mad! No, not at all.
Fellow like me? The fact is, well, no, I am a little tired, to
be sure, and of course I might order a bite to eat—oh,
nothing elaborate, mind you, a little snack, and only
when it's convenient for you, naturally . . ." The waitress
nods briskly and pulls a yellow receipt book from her
apron pocket. "*No!*" Tom nearly snatches the girl's pencil from her hand; then sits back, surprised and embarrassed by his own lathered nerves. He manages a neutral
s'cuse me, then fixes his eyes down the table where a seedy
pigeon pecks casually at a plate of battered cod.

"The thing is, really, I'm a little—well, *very* curious, I
must say, about this, this little circular, or whatever, that
was left on the table. 'Spect you've seen it! Some kind of

advertisement? I don't know, exactly. *The Ruins*, it says. I was hoping you could, uhmm, fill in the picture?"

The waitress, when Tom peeks, sits smiling right at him, blithe and indulgent, her bland brown head on its slender stem bobbing up and down, up and down, a few ashy tendrils spilling dreamily from the bun at her nape, down the smooth ivory palisade of her neck, to be crushed inside the sweat-stiffened collar of her uniform. Her dark eyes gleam like chocolate drops in a warm oven. Tom meets her tender gaze, then turns his head carefully to one side, alarmed and uneasy. He clears his throat, shifts a little on the bench, looks up with a wary smile and then immediately down again. No doubt about it, the girl's *beaming;* and if there's anything Tom finds dismaying it's the recklessly spilled milk of human kindness. His heart crouches, his own gaze panning left and right, playing for a dodge.

The Future! The Future!

Of course! Our hero's eye is caught and recalled by the pitched, precipitous storm of burnished upper case letters and bold exclamation points punctuating the paper clutched in his hand. Now *headlong* (the human angle of urgency) and in high relief, the fearless golden fingers charge to the fore, signaling his path: The Future! Tom's stomach rears with excitement, its cold nose shoving hard at his timid heart. *Come on, show some up-and-at-em!* Well. He dips his head, tugs with one hand at an obstinate cowlick, and with the other pushes the fateful bill marginally closer to the waitress's bent elbow, balanced gravely on its point in a puddle of spilled sauce.

"What I mean is, this, uh, brochure, as it may be—"

"You've run a bit off the rails, haven't you?" What! Tom lifts his head, startled. The waitress nods, still beaming. "Mmm-hmm, mmm-hmm. Just look at your eyes!" He looks away in confusion; she continues.

"You work too hard, I'm sorry to say; and don't eat properly, to boot. *No hobbies,* am I right? Tell me the truth," she says, "when was the last time you took yourself down for a nice stroll along the water, say, to feed the ducks or gather flowers, or just watch the lazy river go rolling by? Well? That's the ticket, you know—that's what the doctor ordered!"

She spoke in an eager, admonishing whisper, as though recalling Tom to an intimate secret. He is taken aback by the familiarity of her reproach, and by her fervent eyes; and is uncertain of an appropriate response. To begin with, he can't remember having once *seen* a duck on the river *Q*—.

"And besides," he thinks, "it's a career I'm after, not a vacation! Who is this so-called doctor? What's this kid talking about? And . . ." Tom pulls up short, despite himself, "—is she correct?" He frowns. It's true he can't remember the last time he took a day off, just for himself, as she put it. But? Distracted, perplexed, he indicates her arm.

"You—there's some gravy under your elbow!"

"Oh, no," the waitress leans toward him with a little shake of her soft, disheveled head. "You can't tell me anything; it's as clear as day. Believe me, I know what I'm talking about. White clouds sailing before the breeze, pink cheeks . . . and porridge!" she winks, "—with *butter!*"

Tom blushes, tips his head sideways and fusses with his cuffs; inside, his stomach trots in tight, suspenseful circles round the fence of his ribs.

"And as for the Ruins," she continues. Tom holds his breath. The girl sits up very straight, removing her elbow from the sticky pondlet; she hardly glances at the sheet of paper lying beside them.

"Wouldn't care to know what they eat at the Ruins, I guess. *Hmm?*"

Tom frowns, again impatient; but the girl presses her hands together, leans one cheek against the upraised fingers and lets her eyes fall closed in a kind of swoon. "*Grieves on show-frow!*"

(Huh? But say, her accent *is* convincing.)

"Singing thrushes, that's what, fattened on grapes, then boned and stuffed with *fwah graw* and truffles and served in a frilly paper case on chopped veal jelly. Jeez, can you imagine?" She opens her eyes and mugs an extravagant gulp. "Or listen: *triple-chocolate torte with brandy-soaked currents, toasted almonds, and loose cream.*" Surrendering to bliss, her voice drops an octave—"pecan-olive *roo-la!*"—then begins to rise. "Little black olives and roasted pecans minced together with garlic and fresh rosemary and honey, rolled up in puff pastry and baked to savory perfection . . . Or how about a nice filet of sole braised in French vermouth with lemons and capers? Flaming raspberry *creeps*? Poached celery hearts *oh grotten*? Lobster mayonnaise! And still, take it from me, that's not the half of it!"

Easy, easy! Tom glances around, shy of making a scene; but the girl's zeal goes unnoticed in the general din. She leans toward Tom and he, helplessly, toward her.

"Imagine pink crystal chandeliers pirouetting above your head like ballerinas on a stage. Tiny winter roses smelling of strawberries and chilled champagne. A huge marble portico gazing out over plunging cliffs to a ravishing wine-dark sea . . ." A wine-dark sea? The girl sighs. "The waitresses there wear frilly black dresses with white chiffon sleeves." Her voice is reverent. ". . . like big puffy wings." She thrusts her own arms out before her, burns and half-healed scratches lurid in the harsh light, and they both stare down at them, transfixed by the image of puffy white chiffon. Tom's eyes lift uncertainly and meet hers, ecstatic. His voice falters.

"It's . . . it's a restaurant, then. Is that it?"

The waitress claps her hands together with a loud report, squeezes them between her knees and laughs merrily. "A *restaurant*? Oh I should say not, the idea! Oh no, not just a *restaurant*. It's far more wonderful than any old *restaurant*! Let's see . . . what? A *restaurant*! Look—" She lowers her voice confidentially. "There's a life-sized mechanical elephant. *In the ballroom!*"

No!

The waitress nods. "So you see, it's . . . well, *very special*. Very, very exclusive, you understand. Not just anyone can go there. No, you must be someone very important, you must be a *member*. And to become a member you must be invited! There are *rules,* yes! it's quite marvelous, I assure you. And furthermore," she gives Tom's wrist a little, knowing tap, "it's not just a place to eat. They have, oh, cocktail parties, and fabulous, you know, *events*, and—well, all that. Oh it's something all right. You can't begin to imagine."

The girl's humble, nail-bitten hands, no bigger than a child's, flutter to rest in her lap; her gaze drifts with the serenity of an inviolable meringue high above the unsavory melee in which they sit. Ah, the innocence, the idealism of youth! Does she not *see* the toddler in his unblushing altogether, pissing down the gapped hatch of a pie-eyed, snoring sailor? Or the Pekinese bitch hauled up on a nearby table to be humped by an enormous mastiff, their tense feet scrambling for purchase amidst piles of greasy plates and puddles of spilled beer? Pigs grub among a pile of used nappies; the tattoo artist swabs an infected navel; the man in the wheelchair's got the girl on his lap, one hand trawling the irresistible channel of her yawning thighs (his other a screen before her bold, bored eyes). Why, it's enough to, *well!*

"Yes," the waitress muses, "it's really something . . ." One well-chewed fingertip scratches methodically at a spot of unidentifiable matter stuck to the edge of the table. "So *very* swank."

Tom himself is admittedly impressed. Champagne roses? Lobster mayonnaise? An *elephant*? Mouth-watering, spellbinding—a vision! But . . . was it real? Could it truly exist? He observes, once more, a muffled tremor just beneath the skin where the girl's collarbones meet in a pale, spreading V like the wings of a gull. Her forefinger rises and is blandly received by two rows of small, even teeth which promptly seize and go to work on the already savaged nail.

Does Tom consider her a reliable source of information?

Our hero, as it happens, believes not only in people but in the unforeseeable bumps and grinds of chance that throw people, places, and events together in surprising and occasionally fortuitous combinations. For this reason, and no other, he leans—ever a gentleman!—leans closer still. Gravely he removes the finger from her pink, parted lips. He speaks with care, swallowing down hard against his rising urgency. His stomach whines and he places the flat of his hand against it, pressing firmly.

"And so it seems—according to this flyer—it seems one might find employment with this, um, establishment, wouldn't you say? *Join us*, it says, and if . . ." Tom pauses, his mind awhirl. "Uh, what's your name?"

Their eyes meet, Tom's slightly puckered, straining; the girl's wide with amiable surprise. She'd started to gather up the little slips of yellow paper but now stops, impulsively covering Tom's hand, which has been lying, trembling, upon the impassive broadsheet, with her own.

"I'm Ada!"

Tom nods unheeding. "Uh-huh, well then, uh, Abby? Tell me, do *you,* uh, do you believe it's true?" They stare at one another, his thoughts beginning to spin with the irresistible vertigo of personal destiny; she sympathetic, oblivious, benign.

Heavens! There is a shrill curse (a chorus of whoops), and Ada jumps, tearing her gaze from Tom's opaque trance to glance round the riotous hall.

"True?" she echoes distractedly. "True? Why, of course it's true, um—uh . . ." She clears her throat, a question mark.

Blinking, our hero bows. "I'm Tom."

"Tom," she repeats, acknowledging the introduction with a warm, brief smile, "it's *Ada*"; then redirects her attention to the surrounding chaos. Goodness, she really should be getting back to work! Behind her the girls in black lipstick have their tongues down one another's throats.

"But, true? Of course, why wouldn't it be true? Naturally it's no piece of cake. *Yow!*" (A spectacular crash.) "Place like that! They'd want an enormous, um, staff, don't you think? Cooks and dishwashers and janitors and florists and—*hey you guys!* Maybe plumbers? And, well, wine stewards and things. Etcetera. Only imagine! Well, order must be kept, mustn't it? Arrangements and order and—*hey, look out!* That's no joke!"

The fiercest racket seems to be coming from a knot of broad-backed men several aisles away. Ada climbs up on the bench, craning her neck to see what could account for the hullabaloo.

"What on earth?" She stops abruptly and looks down at Tom with a little gasp. Then back to the men. Then Tom, again. Confused. "Jeez, what are you saying? Is it, are you thinking of giving them a try? Applying at the Ruins?"

Is the girl astonished, impressed (or a little offended, perhaps!) by the prospect of Tom engaged at the fabulous Ruins? Her black gosling eyes seem to bulge—with pleasure? Alarm? Tom instantly regrets his probable indiscretion and back-pedals hastily, wondering if he might not be exceeding himself, after all. How could one expect the Ruins to be interested in someone like himself? And yet it says right here: *No Experience Necessary.* The only qualification seems to be . . . sincerity? *In Sincere Pursuit.* Well? Isn't that just about hitting the bent nail on the rusty head as regards our Tom? On the other hand, could it really be so simple as that? "We-ell," he begins doubtfully.

The girl starts, covering her mouth with one grubby hand. "Oh! What in the world am I thinking, going on and on like this and here you sit, practically starving, and dripping wet and tired besides, poor lamb! I'll just run and get you something right away. First things first, I always say!" She climbs down from the bench, clutching a Chinaman's head. "But what will it be? What would you like, hmmm? Let's see now, there's a pretty fair fribble—or maybe the goosed fool? Say! *How about a big ol' sausage?"*

Oops! Her last suggestion rings out with unexpected volume, the room having gone suddenly, inexplicably quiet a moment before, and they both look up, startled and wondering. Dogs and kids are collared and hollered at to *sit,* or are kicked yelping beneath tables and benches. Women wink and prod their hair. Men put out their cigars in saucers of ketchup and silently hoist empty tankards to signal for more beer. Everyone turns in his seat to face the far end of the hall, hardly visible from where Tom and Ada sit. Say, what's happening? Ada?

Look out! The hodgepodge of fugitive receipts explodes once more as the waitress leaps to her feet; our hero, recalled from his woozy conjuring, jumps. *Ada!*

"Dang!" Diving for the wayward yellow papers, Ada responds to Tom's unspoken query in a breathless, broken croak, her upper body more or less beneath the table. "I'm—I . . . it's the, you know, the *show!* Egh! The Talent, you know? *La Stupenda!*—whoops! You don't suppose they come for the food, ha ha! Oh, excuse me! No, no, it's—it's . . . do you know her?" A small hand shoots up from below the table, fingertips pursed then flung open in a gesture of acclaim. "*Stupenda!* And listen, it's no secret *she's* somebody at the Ruins." Ada's face, pink and laughing, emerges at last from beneath the table. Her hair, now completely undone, makes a large frizzy halo around her head. She clambers back over the bench, stuffing the bundle of captured receipts deep inside her apron pocket.

"Tell you what! Don't even bother to decide. I'll just trot to the kitchen and see what looks yummy, shall I? And in the meantime you sit back and enjoy! Believe me, you've never seen anything the like of our L'Ultima . . ." Ada turns and is nearly down the aisle before Tom can utter a word, then spins round again. "Did I say L'Ultima?" She claps a hand to her brow and rolls her eyes— *"La Stupenda!"*—waves at Tom and is sucked into the crowd for good.

Well, whatever!

The fact is Tom hardly hears, hardly sees her go, his blank, besotted eyes having already sneaked back (like ditched kittens; like mercury to it's source) to the gold embossed circular lying on the table. *The Ruins, The Ruins.* His heart squirms like a worm on a hook.

Join Us and Leave Your Troubles Behind!

Sounds great. But wait a minute! *Does* Tom have troubles? He considers. Surely there was no denying his knees were getting worse. Day after day, for twelve or more hours at a stretch, Tom squats at his place against a damp, dirty wall (his official and legally reserved place, one might add, for which he was required to pay, at brisk intervals, exorbitant property, sales, business, and self-employment taxes). The last in his family of generations born to the trade, our Tom was subject, alas, to both occupational and strictly personal despair. After all, it's a cutthroat, competitive market! The block crawled with shoe shines, many of whom, Tom privately deplored, *had no business in the business.* No technique, no eye for detail! And yet, through unscrupulous marketing practices, they were slowly and surely eating away at Tom's already negligible livelihood.

So Tom had composed a medley of catchy phrases to attract the attention of passersby (his favorite: I Could Take a Shine to You!). Business slumped. What were fancy slogans compared to prize drawings and glass collectibles? Tom shook his head. By day's end he was lucky to hear two coins clink together in his pocket, and stumped home on knees griping of poison daggers and ground glass.

Oh yes, our hero had his problems all right; still, he was the last person to malinger. This was his world? His slice of the pie? So be it. Tom had not made his bed, but would lie down and make the best of it anyway. A stoic!

And yet there was a part of him that yearned—that had, in fact, been yearning for some time now—for something nobler, something that might really challenge the untapped resources he suspected in himself. Something, that is to say, upon which to test and prove his spirit. Modest by nature, Tom nevertheless believed himself capable of more than had as yet been his glamorless lot. He knew well enough he could out-shine any jockey on the wall; and yet, he fussed, surely there were other, more inspired means by which to make one's mark? Beauty and truth in other forms? Enlightenment bearing upon higher relations? Something (we are obliged to labor the point) *up off his knees*—which will not, he fears, withstand the punishing demands of his present career much longer.

To cut to the chase, the spice in Tom's life *had* lost its zing. *Ducks!* Tom snorts. *Doctors? What I need are first principles, a new beginning. My Big Chance!*

3—

At the other end of the hall something, indeed, was taking place. There was still no sign of Ada, but the Groaning Board was, if possible, even more thronged than before.

Gang 'way! Coming through!

Waitresses cursed and exclaimed at the crush; fathers swung overwrought tots to their shoulders; women subdued pigs and dogs beneath their booted feet, chickens between their knees. Tom, eyes pricking from the drifting clouds of tobacco, kerosene and kitchen smoke that mingled and obscured the air (and from his own weariness and excitement), knelt upon his bench to peer over the countless heads and backs that crowded the space between where he was seated and what appeared to be a small platform or stage set up on the other side of the room.

Just then the constellation of overhead bulbs dims to a murky orange nebula. Next: the sullen metallic hiss of an invisible snare, the spastic crash of tin cymbals. And finally everyone sits up straight and cranes his neck to behold the vision slowly materializing against the far, opposite wall.

And lo! The stage itself has disappeared! Obscured by a vaporous drift of swelling, upwelling, luminous pink clouds that lurch in the air like sea whuffle, and appear to boil, roiling up from either side of the platform to meet, overhead, in a throbbing pink arch, the whole spectacle crowned to marvelous effect by a great diadem of inexhaustible white lights that spiral and churn, exerting a steady and ineluctable upward traction as they rise, finally vanishing into the darkness like sparks from a fire— up, up, up . . .

In the midst of this flushed, vertiginous scene, floats a stocky figure swathed entirely in blue. La Stupenda? Tom, squinting from across the room, has an impression of high, imposing hair; of pale, muscular arms opening and closing with the languid precision of butterfly wings; and of two neatly polished blue shoes in which supple little feet kick coyly, desultorily at the air, as though the ascending diva in fact reclined upon the fluffed pillows of a providential updraft and need only go through the motions of staying aloft. Indeed she rose, or seemed to rise, by small, swaying, effortless degrees; higher and higher through the shuddering pink swoon of softly parting clouds and seething, inextinguishable stars.

"Can you beat that!" marvels Tom, "*And* she sings?" But while the snare drum continued its toneless rattle, punctuated by an irregular flourish of cymbals, Tom—surrounded by sighs, whispers, and muffled cries of delight—was unable to make out the tune. Crudely amplified, La Stupenda's voice distinguished itself in Tom's ear as a corrosive fizz of bright sputtering pops, tarnished incidentals, and a vicious lisp. One was persuaded nonetheless, and even at that distance, by the divine composure of her languorous blue eyes. The movements of her shapely head and well-modeled arms were, if somewhat wooden, appealing in their simplicity and grace. Her leisurely kicking feet left a spreading wake of ruffled, incandescent light.

Tom rubbed his eyes. Was it enchantment or fatigue that cast such a beguiling aura round that unlabored tableau, lending its forms and colors an enthralling if somewhat inexplicable vibration and buoyancy? It was as though one gazed through the lens of an extraordinary kaleidoscope, round whose periphery the colors reeled and eddied and fumed, yet never once disturbed the pure and imperturbable progress of the central figure. Fantastic! Tom blinked several times in quick succession and felt his knees soften, his belly curl at last into a tired, submissive ball. Strange, he'd never felt so weak, virtually prostrate. On the other hand, a positive mental attitude made up for a lot: his fingertips rested shyly upon the fateful handbill, his invitation—one might say *summons*—to a future toward which he found himself ever more inclined.

And was there, after all, any reason to resist?

Eyes fixed somewhat dully upon the distant blue diva, Tom drifted, surrendering to the fabulously whorled images impressed on him by the exultant waitress.

What were capers, anyway? For starters, Tom pictures tiny, sequin-bright fish, leaping gaily in a saucer of sunny lemon juice. He imagines gazing into the wise, sad eyes of the elephant in its sumptuous ballroom. Glamorous women in strapless gowns of watered silk, crisp taffeta, and unspeakable black velvet . . . the flawless chime of crystal stemware (*ting-a-ling!*) against the drawn-out *hiissss* of sweetbreads frying in clarified butter . . . the dizzying scent of monstrous, parrot-beaked orchids, of long-waisted tulips, blue heraldic iris, and thick-stemmed, fleshy gardenias. He sees mink stoles slithering to a cloakroom floor, their glass eyes gleaming in the dark; cocktails abob with little white onions and maraschino cherries and fat greasy olives, three to a swizzle.

And wine-dark seas?

You bet!

But then again, what *were* sweetbreads? What was *chiffon?* And did the men wear it as well? And would Tom, himself, feel comfortable in white puffy sleeves? Well? But after all, maybe he should go home and sleep on it.

Sure, sure, but first look, just look! At the other end of the hall, over the heads, beyond the wildest dreams of this rough, incorrigible mob, whirls a ravishing pink tornado—sublime! And La Stupenda its blue, unblinking eye . . . Just look!

Tom shakes himself, good lad, and pinches his arm, but nevertheless succumbs *(that's it)* to the mesmerizing to-and-fro, to-and-fro, of the airborne diva. He blinks the sting from his eyes; breathes the black, hot, murmuring air of the crowded room; yawns fiercely—once, and then again—and then, with a wordless quake of revelation and alarm *(go on!)* feels his timid heart slip its moorings. *And?* And . . .

Ahoy, then! Cast all lines! Square the yards!
He's off!

Like a little boat, our hero—trembling at the helm, his hunger to heel with alert, vigilant eyes—weighs anchor and sets his sails for the blue, uncharted waters of *the Future!*

•   •   •

Tom feels . . . something: a fresh and unaccountable breeze *(that's right!)* lifts the hair from his forehead. *Does he snort?* He snorts like a startled colt at the pungent, unfamiliar draughts of salt and tar. His fair, faintly freckled skin reddens from the prick of hot sun and cold spray. *Nice?* Indeed, it *is* pleasant. He lets one hand trail among the blue-green, cresting little waves, stations the other with bashful authority upon the straining tiller, but leans forward to whisper reassuringly into his companion's anxious, swiveling ear.

Easy boy, easy. Nose to the wind, that's it, and keep your eye on the horizon. It's a world of opportunity out there! Are you seeing it, old chum? Are you sniffing it out, do you hear it calling? Listen! A silver bell struck with perfect, regular restraint . . . the clean chime of knife meeting fork . . . wet lips parting with a careless smack . . . and somewhere secret the gurgle and sigh of aroused, ecstatic juices. That's right! And what would you say to a nicely grilled lamb chop? So tender you might not bother to chew, it melts on your tongue like a pat of sweet butter, a perfect swoon . . .

Ah! Tom leans back, eyes fluttering naively before the blue, importunate sky, the glittering waves. He lets his head rest against the gunwale; his jaw slides. A little breather, that's all! The sun feels fine and warm, like nothing he's ever known. *Why resist?*

And so, as it happens, our hero sprawls, witless and eager as the little boat rocks *to and fro, to and fro;* while at the same time a wild, ingratiating song bestows itself in brazen whispers and promises unfurled like silk ribbons in the breeze. Shameless, how it tickles, teases, and fingers the strings of his heart. *Plays with abandon upon his bare chest and belly, the moist drum of his inner ear, his naked toes, so that . . .*

Bare chest and belly? Wait a minute!

—so that, eyes struggling to open at last, oh la! Tom is astonished to find himself naked as a baby, his scandalously exposed member standing up straight and proud as a chubby pink mast! Good heavens!

Astounded, Tom covers his lap with both hands, twisting on his bench from one side to the other in violent

mortification (in the process driving a large splinter deep
into his bare right buttock). But—thank goodness!—in
every direction, as far as the eye can see, there is only the
glittering crest and break of glassy, indifferent waves. Not
a smirk from a single porpoise, no insect's insinuating
hum, nor even a rude gull's harsh, accusing cry. His companion whines edgily, nudging a speculative nose between Tom's tightly squeezed legs, but the horrified lad
slaps him away, for once unobliging. Where are his
clothes! What is the meaning of this! Where *is* he? Why
will his—*you know!*—not lie down properly?

All right! Don't get excited! There's no one about.
Only the bland, blue, painted-out sky; the anonymous
kiss-kiss of breezes as they come and go; the silken, ar-
rhythmic slap of blind waves against the sides of the boat;
and the sidelong glare of his offended mascot.

Tom stiffens uneasily, but does not pull away, as the
conciliatory air wraps an arm around his red, stinging
neck, presses its mouth against his ear, and . . . again Tom
does not hear so much as *feel* a low-pitched, beguiling
song enter him with the slow, clinging, whorled progress
of pink smoke; the smoldering edge of some peremptory
sweetness leaving a black, acrid residue all over the inside
of his head. It was unfamiliar, foul, irresistible. Would he
stop it if he could? Tom crosses his legs, clenches his
fists—but gives in nonetheless; furrows his brow against
the brash sky, but (what! was he made of steel?) falls back
against the tiller all the same, permitting his fearless
member, his one-eyed sailor, to pop up once more, stal-

wart in the breeze. The little boat rocks *to and fro, to and fro,* and a brusque muzzle pries open the unwilling fist of his right hand, laying out the squeamish palm with long wet strokes of its inexorable tongue. Tom whimpers as his imagination, in previous times a humble, predictably inert faculty, now wells up, rearing in awkward, powerful jerks of ambition and desire, growing taut (indeed, atremble!) with one buxom image after another.

The weight, my god, and the blind swing of an elephant's rampant trunk—and the tantalizing lip of a porcelain platter, bedewed with drops of sauce suprême. The tremor and the hasty drip of burning twelve-inch tapers; illumination of a cleft yam, oozing butter; a rum-soaked savarin, split through the middle and fattened with cream and crushed macaroons; the excruciating discharge of a ripe fig between one's tongue and the roof of one's mouth. Sticky pistils, bulbous yellow stamens; and the surrender, petal by petal, of a pale blossom's chaste defenses . . .

Tom feels the flutter of white chiffon against his vaulting ribs, a slim finger of sweat descend his belly, down, down . . .

As the temperature rises, flames tickling the tiny, swollen veins, steam rising from a full, from an overspilling plate!

His fingers splay, distended by the vehement *lick, lick, lick* of the long tongue across his reddening palm; the mouth against his ear breathes in, breathes out, in hot, sibilant, accelerating commands. He sees himself—

Ta-da! Impeccably dressed in stiff black and soft, shimmering white, he parts a sea of ferocious platinum coifs and proceeds to the center of the room, carrying aloft (as though it were nothing at all, a mere feather!) a massive silver tray from which arises, trembling, a tapering twelve-layer confection of marzipan, meringue, and sticky caramel syrup. Bravo! Smiles of approval and tasteful linen blots to well-greased, exquisitely rouged lips, while hands, glittering with sapphires, emeralds and diamonds, come together in a round of well-deserved applause. A real spectacle! He sees himself dining on late, elegant suppers of partridge wings and truffled eggs and an assortment of imported, liquor-filled chocolates. A tall flute of blushing champagne stands beside his plate; a circle of attentive, admiring underlings nods eagerly as he assigns tasks; doting chefs ply him with tender little morsels reserved especially for him. He sees himself sleeping dreamlessly between pressed linen sheets, waking fresh and looking like a million, grateful for another opportunity to make his mark (a flawless, incontestable mark!) in his chosen field. Self-respecting! Well fed! One hell of a fine fellow—

"Aaegck!"

There is a squeal, a snarl, a prodigious crash, and our enchanted hero's ship of dreams capsizes without warning. *Ta-da!* It's the end of the show and the Chinese cooks have shot to their feet for a big round of applause. *Up* goes their end of the bench; *down* without ceremony goes our bewildered Tom. His eyes fly open and white chiffon, partridge wings and pink champagne dissolve—

poof!—in the unspeakable smut and smoke and sudden uproar of the Groaning Board.

But!

But nothing! Bum smarting; an abandoned dumpling squashed beneath the palm of one hand—there's a kick and a curse as someone stumbles over Tom's outstretched legs. He scoots under the table to save his knees and collect his wits while those around him stamp their boots and pound their empty steins in speechless admiration. What a finale! As the lights come up they turn to one another, exclaiming loudly.

"Oooh, the voice of an angel, that one."

"She's a dirty girl, a real bawd, but what legs!"

"I believe she's tired tonight, her voice cracked desperately on several high notes."

"Doesn't she dance well? I was to have danced, you know. Well I was!"

"Flawless technique, classic repertory!"

"*Saving All My Kisses for My One-Eyed Sailor.* When's the last time you heard that!"

"There is Nature. There is Art. And there is La Stupenda!"

"The sticky little bun. The dirty, delicious girl!"

"Ma? How does she fly like that? *Ma!*—can I fly?"

Time to go. Mothers take up hats and sleeping babies, exchanging perfunctory goodnights in fierce, forlorn voices. Men stand about restlessly, jingling the loose change in their pockets, smacking their lips and eyeing the waitresses' behinds as the girls bend quickly and uneasily to their tasks, sensing an incalculable peril left in the wake of La Stupenda's performance. The man in his wheelchair has fallen asleep, pitched forward across the legs of the maiden still on his lap, her fingers now tenderly stroking the dirty gray numbers inscribed at the nape of his neck. The fat woman stares thoughtfully at her platter of uneaten crusts. A kitten mews, unheeded, from inside a forgotten paper carton. Someone hollers for a whore.

Tom lingers more or less beneath the table. He'd been moved (let's face it, *bowled over*) by La Stupenda's stellar performance. Sure, sure, maybe he'd been too far away to see or hear much. But say, he'd seen plenty! Personality, poise, allure? La Stupenda had it all. A real professional, an *artist!* Tom marvels at the stroke of luck that brought him to this place, this very night! If only he could peer directly—through thickets of bewitching, black-lacquered lashes, to be sure!—into those twinned sapphires, those prize dahlias, those *blue-blue* eyes. Imagine what wisdom (and what tips for success!) one might discern there. No wonder children flung roses at her feet, young women aspired to her confidence and chic, men puffed and preened.

Tom's own chest ached with longing; his knees began to prick. Oh, that he could ever hope for that sort of reputation and esteem! All right, he was as good a shoeshine as he knew how to be; he could not fault himself there. But where would that get him? No, no, when all was said and done, he simply *had* to try something new; put his lowborn, insignificant past behind him—good-bye and good riddance—and step boldly into the future.

Was he desperate?

Determined! And here, still clutched in his sticky right hand, was the very ticket to an incomparable, practically unimaginable destination: The Ruins! In the blackness beneath the table, Tom's sensitive fingertips trace the lines of embossed script. *Gainful Employment. A Glamorous Environment.* What did he have to lose? Surely this might very well be *his* "Big Chance"!

OK! It was settled.

Galvanized by his decision, Tom begins to crawl on hands and tender knees beneath the rows of tables, the aisles being as yet too thronged to admit him. "I'll go right home," he promises himself, happily sketching out a plan of action. "I'll get a good night's sleep, and in the morning spruce myself up—a bite to eat—and then, well, it's off to make my fortune! And no funny business! At the Ruins I'll simply speak my piece. Not too proud, but not too humble, either. Oh they'll see right away I'm on the up-and-up—an honest kid with an honest dream, nothing the matter with that! And then, well, surely they'll have something for me, p'raps right away. A 'starting position', as they say, something—"

Out of the clamor above his head, Tom's ear picks up a vaguely familiar voice, candid, conciliatory, frankly imploring. Ada? She seems to be explaining something to someone who isn't, apparently, listening. Tom pauses.

"*No!*—that is, please don't. Listen, don't be offended, nothing personal! It's just that—*ungh*. Oh don't! If you'd only try to see *my* position! That is, of course, my job is to serve, but—*mmnph*—I beg you! It's really a question of, oh, propriety and, *jeez!* Mutual respect!"

Tom drops his cheek to the floor and peeks out, but can see no further than a pair of cheap white patent leather ankle boots, soles separating, with broken zippers up the instep; and right behind—blunt brown toes to scuffed white heels—two huge, hobnailed boots, stolid as tree trunks. The little white feet balance weakly on their toes, wobbling, neither standing nor rising. They dangle rather apart, heels swinging to the outside, and a regular little jolt seems to go right through them, lifting them altogether off their toes to flutter for a moment in the air. Tom is immediately reminded of La Stupenda's fabulous ascent, of her elegantly slippered feet and the discreet, exquisitely languid little kick, kick, kick, as she rose, with consummate *sang-froid*, above the maelstrom of roiling pink clouds.

"*Unhh . . . unhh!*"

Tom oughtn't to interrupt Ada at her work, but he does wish to say good-bye (and thanks a million!) for her inside dope on the Ruins.

"Excuse me! Um . . . Ada?" The two smaller feet continue to lift and drop, lift and drop, with perhaps more impetus than before.

"Is that, *oh!* Tom?" Ada's disembodied voice jumps queerly. "Tom *(really, you mustn't!)* where *(ungh)* are you?"

Convulsed with increasing urgency, the white boots dangle entirely in the air now. Can Ada be rehearsing an act of her own? Tom shakes his head. No one, and certainly not little Ada in her peeling, patent leather boots, could match the splendor and sheer ingenuity of a professional like La Stupenda. An *artist*, a poet of *Life!* Tom wonders if, as Ada implied, La Stupenda actually does frequent the Ruins? The possibility both disturbs and excites him. Tom is anxious to leave now (and for morning to come *speedio!*) that he might embark upon his new career with no further delay. After all, when opportunity knocks!

"Say, Ada? Yes, it's me, Tom, and I only wanted to tell you—"

"Tom! I need *(no, don't!)* come up!"

"Huh? Well yes, I know you're pretty busy now Ada, but I just wanted to say good-bye and to—"

Ada's voice breaks in again and her little feet scrabble at the air for purchase as momentum continues to build. "Tom! *(ungh, ungh!)* Oh jeez, I'm a little—"

He got the picture! Things were clearly hectic (and organization, Tom chuckled, not one of the girl's strong points). To make matters worse, the customer in hob-nailed boots, planted at her heels, begins to sound off rather obviously in short, excited huffs of impatience. *What the heck!* Tom thinks. Surely she's doing the best she can! Feeling sorry for his overburdened friend, Tom determines to be brief.

"Listen, Ada! You've been awfully kind, so I just wanted you to know, well, I *have* decided to follow up on that ad. You know, the Ruins! And since it was you who sort of helped me think it through, I thought, well, like I said, I just wanted you to know, and to thank you—and, well, and say g'night?" Tom cocks his head, waiting for a reply. What, actually, is going on up there? He pokes uncertainly at one twitching white toe. Just then Ada's voice flutters down to him, a little weary?

"That's wonderful, Tom, I'm sure you'll be a great success. *Oh!* And maybe—*whoah, oh-oh!*" Here Ada's voice breaks down completely; Tom strains to understand her words. ". . . maybe we'll see each other again some-time."

Right-o! Tom nods, turns to continue his route beneath the tables; then stops, turns back, and reaches up to place his last few coins (a tip, howsoever meager!) on top of the stool beside Ada's wafting knees. He shakes his head fondly; she was no *Stupenda*, so pure, and lighter than air! But she was good-natured and obliging and Tom wished her well. Besides, tomorrow he would embark on a promising new future, rising out of a luckless, lackluster past toward a horizon flush with possibility.

"The emptier my pockets," he justifies his extravagance, "the higher I'll soar."

And so, his heart made light by the leaven of undivinable doom, our budding young hopeful proceeds—on hands, on querulous knees—down along the dirty aisles, the loose and illimitable squalor of the Groaning Board.

CHAPTER TWO

The Consummate Martooni

4—

Tom crosses his legs with gloomy discretion, eyes fixed upon a mute star of light that—poised upon the bobbing black toe of one flawlessly polished shoe—struggles like a bird to keep its perch.

Recalling the steps that brought him, howsoever uncertainly, not just to the Ruins but indeed to the coveted post of *maître d'hôtel,* Tom marvels, of course, at his lucky stars (and two glorious weeks were only the beginning). Still, he feels something, well, unreliable in the ground beneath his feet. He is oftentimes confused, even dismayed, and not naturally encouraged by an uneasy sense of sliding ever-so-gradually backwards down a glassy yet nearly imperceptible slope. Egh! No wonder he clings to that singular star of light, hovering bravely o'er the toe of his nervously rising and falling foot! *And* ponders, furthermore (while Jones screams into the telephone receiver) what keeps him, Tom, from expressing the inner freedom *he* feels?

• • •

Hmm, well, surely it all started chirpily enough . . .

Pshaw! In fact dawn squatted over the city (that proverbial "next morning") like a disdainful cat doing its business. All strategic imperatives aside, our hero had risen early, all right, his well-intended repose worried to a threadbare stupor by the tireless fingers of his own anticipation and dread.

Well, if a pimple, say, should've come up on my nose! Or some other horror make me out a clown! Details y' know, it's no joke!

Up, he puttered earnestly—a blithe whistle, if you please; took a limp whisk to his mud-stiffened trousers and wriggled his fingers gamely through the ruddy and incorrigible locks that sprung from his head like rusted corkscrews. He thought of the pasty seller around the corner ("Sav'ries and sweets! Veg for them't don't!"); and then, wistfully, of the two or three coins he'd left for his waitress the night before. "Well," said he, then boiled some water in a dented tin and *would* sip it gratefully all the same—when a cow kicked impatiently at the rotting plywood wall of an adjacent shed. Tom jumped and pulled on his mack with a dainty wriggle at the damp. "Ha ha!" he sang out forlornly. "Never fear, never fear. I'm off, see! Ready 'n rarin' . . ."

48

And in fact, without a backwards glance—the future, after all, lay before, not behind him—Tom threw open the door and plunged dutifully into the noxious, mouse-gray drizzle of a questionably new dawn.

> *There's nothin', says I, can keep a feller under*
> *If up is where he's meant to be!*

● ● ●

Midday finds our boy jacked down on throbbing haunches under the battered metal awning of a burnt out newsstand: quite, quite lost. Seamless clouds weep a steady, arguably septic dolor; and there isn't a bit more light at noon, Tom reckons, than there'd been at dawn, only a thick glaze that magnifies the wet streets like boiled jelly. Diffidence and dashed hopes encumber the bright, laboring wings of our hero's improvidently launched dreams. Alas, he doesn't blink an eye (or know a snake until it's bit him) when a long yellowish rat streaks across the toes of his shoes, dragging a swatch of mackerel skin still gleaming with anchovy paste and sauce *homard*. Finally—

Like magic, a lucky break!

Not five feet away, curdling in sodden strips against a creosotey pole, the poster's golden script is unmistakable, identical to that gracing the gravy-stained handbill tucked inside his shirt; and in fact Tom's belly wriggles with joyful recognition before his scrupling eyes are convinced by that which they behold.

But I knew. Of course I knew!

In any case it is an *aroma*—unspeakably lush, labored to the point of virtual deliquescence, decidedly fetishistic—that really settles the matter and persuades Tom that he has, indeed, arrived.

Struggling to his feet, Tom takes the intersection blindly—captivated by the singularly outrageous smell—to an unmarked warehouse on the opposite corner. Painted, none too recently, a flat, gelatinate brown, with narrow, soaring, multipaned windows that begin several feet above Tom's head and surround the building like a high, old-fashioned collar. Flatly abutting the sidewalk is a broad, impassive metal door, lavished with the same liverish enamel as the adjacent walls; and beside that, blooming from a bare wire, a cracked plastic button.

Hmm, but just suppose I nip around back?

Down a dumpster-lined alley to two enormous loading docks, their steel doors shuttered down to a scant inch shy of the snubbed concrete lip. The lane here is perilous with a rancid hash of vegetable peelings, boiled yellow bones and broken glass. Tom takes four concrete steps to his right, goes down on one knee, and bends, with no mortal shame, to spy beneath the short rubber skirt of the first hanging door.

I say! That's not—

Not a pretty picture, is it? Broadish bum over-easy, loose tresses trailing in the muck, squint-eyed . . . Thus, to his disadvantage, is our hero disclosed when the massive steel door abruptly, and with a bloodcurdling shriek, furls up, revealing all at once the bright and coiling penetralia of a thriving exogastric metropolis: a vast, ear-splitting, vortical, gorgeous, godforsaken disaster going off full bore in all directions at once.

My destiny!

Flabbergasted, Tom lifts his head from the squalid cement, stands and slowly brushes the coffee grounds and broken eggshells from his corduroyed knees. An air horn withers the air behind him and he crouches, fawning with automatic contrition. Flashing crimson back-up lights charge him at high speed from the rear bumper of a reversing panel van, and Tom only just manages to leap out of the way as the vehicle brakes to a cursory stop. At once both back panels fly open and a score of young men and women tumble out and begin, brigade style, to unload the contents of the van's interior; at the same time, from somewhere within the warehouse, another line has formed. Tom watches, fascinated, as in a flash (indeed before he can distinguish that coming in from that going out) the van is emptied, reloaded; there is a last-minute inspection while the workers stand at somewhat ironic attention; a brisk shout to the driver—and they're off. When the door of the loading dock begins to rattle down, Tom quails—

As though one made such a decision every day!

—makes up his mind and lurches inside as the warehouse door crashes to.

After all, it was meant to be!

Indeed it *was* a swell and unqualified anarchy: a teeming universe of slender, sturdy, smooth-haired men and women, cracked crystal punch bowls and dented plastic snowmen; sloe-eyed carpenters in white dust masks and loose jeans; barbaric silver coffee urns chained to their litters like pagan gods; garbage pails of fetid yellow roses and leftover cement; leaning towers of peeling plastic champagne buckets, swaying like stacked hats; a large bog of sullenly disintegrating particle board; tall metal racks of cooling *tartes Tatin;* green plastic garbage bags with slowly splitting seams, oozing a mess of clotted cream, mutilated lemons and crushed aluminum cans. A bank of washing machines and dryers throbs along one wall, belts and bearings squealing; a vacuum cleaner roars; pneumatic hammers *ca-thunk;* wine glasses ring; torrents of water thunder in unattended steel sinks; a cluster of severe-looking musicians squeak and tootle and blat; a doorbell peals incessantly; a fat Staffordshire bull terrier trots underfoot, retching and wheezing to itself.

I confess it was a bit daunting at first, but right off the bat I believe they all respected me for what I was—

No one so much as glanced at Tom, even as he let himself be more or less carried into the melee. In the vast, crowded kitchen—around a central island of gas burners and chopping blocks—chefs and scullions and bakers and line cooks steeled knives, skinned eels, grated nutmeg, clarified jellies, raised clouds of white flour, quartered lambs, blanched and deglazed and—

Oof!

Tom nearly had his nose flattened by the back-wallop of a well-swung cleaver, when an invisible hand fisted his coif and hauled him back in the nick. He found himself cowering before a pair of smoldering hazel eyes, which took him in sharply, narrowed—winked, thank goodness!—and with a cheerful shove he was on his way again.

Down a long insensible utility hall, at the far end of which (past a gray pony calmly eating the tinsel from a tawdry festal wreath) a door opened onto a cramped and badly lit back room. Here a hastily assembled satellite kitchen was presided over by a harum-scarum young woman with stringy hair and overbearing horn-rimmed glasses.

"So, count the plates yet?" she hollers, and fixes me with a rude stare. Well I—

And he, until this point deliciously anonymous, if not invisible amidst the fantastic clamor, is abruptly and terrifyingly conscious of himself as a strictly uninvited guest. He clears his throat but she gives him the back of her head, grunting as she pencils impatient calculations on the white-papered work table. "It's sixty up front which leaves us . . . okay, thirty-five. That's soup plates in the warming oven, platters out—sneak the Rouen saucers back in the end for dessert, *and so on!"* She straightens, claps an eye on Tom and barks again, "Got that?" Someone hollers *Richard!* and she cuts on one sneakered heel to tackle the terrier, aggressively nosing a large tub of marinating veal. "You're next, Toulouse!"

Richard? Toulouse? But . . . goodness! Duck and run?
On the other hand, how difficult can it be to count plates?
I'm not the first and, as they say, I shan't be the last—

(In fact, virtually unschooled, it's a slow boat past
ten.)

Still! One crosses a bridge when one comes to it, hey?

Of the many crates of unsorted china, Tom selects one
and hoists it onto the table beside him. Thirty-five plates
was what she wanted, thirty-five plates was what she
would get, more or—

The overhead lights hum excitedly, sputter, and go
out; and in the subsequent clap of darkness two hands
slip quietly over Tom's own—he gasps. Strong, dry, capable hands, they sit lightly upon his like jockeys on
horseback. The padded tip of the left forefinger strokes
Tom's knuckle reassuringly; but as he shies sideways from
the table the strange hands grip him sternly, holding him
in place.

Uhm? says I. Hello?

But the hands are already steering his own from the
crate of plates to the table and back again, counting out
quick neat methodical stacks of ten, ten, ten, and then
five—ten, ten, ten, and then five. All over the room
voices curse and cry. Dozens of folding chairs slide to the
floor with a resounding crash; two trays of sherbet glasses
sail blindly into a closed door; a plastic gallon tub of *béarnaise* chooses this moment to hurl itself from the
precipice of an unattended tabletop. Tom, his belly convulsing at every report, finds his hands beginning to

relax, nonetheless, beneath the firm, unflappable hands of his invisible accomplice.

Nothing to it, really. S'matter of fact—

In the midst of this chaos a door flies open and a smug, unctuous voice calls out: "Not to fear! One moment! Yes, now then, is that not enchanting?" A host of pillar candles is lit, sluicing the room in a syrupy yellow light. Tom whirls to apologize, explain. No one there. On the table, however: the sorted china, in luminous stacks of ten, ten, ten, and five.

As I say! That is, nothing to it!

Tom turns back, dumbfounded, to find a tiny, black-bearded, balding man with high burnished cheeks regarding him with a smile. A class of genteel elf with a slight permanent stoop; his figure describes a brief, elegant curve from his avid face, thrust just so solicitously forward, to the neat axis formed by his fastidiously kissing heels. One black, cavalier brow breaks in a simulation of wonder, to which Tom responds with a timid grin.

"What this! Can it be that in the riot of darkness one brave soul has managed to create an island of meaning, an oasis of order, a paradise of plates? You!"

Me? But his eyes cut to the pushy girl in glasses.

"The ambiguous *Richard!* In five minutes—no, make that four!—this *lac de béarnaise* will be gone if you must lap it up with your tongue! Now *shoo!*"

The amused, speculative face turns again toward our hero. A slightly upturned nose just verged on snoutishness; while the angle of his cheeks, no less swank than the black waxed beard or the sport of his well-groomed brow, perfectly confirmed the romantic tilt of his lustrous, black Tartar eyes. Explicitly he stared up at Tom while continuing to address the room at large.

"My friends—feckless, fainthearted, overtaken by darkness! But see what was left in our midst? A hero, a paragon of plates! He counts! He stacks! What, do you think, can he *not* do?"

The room is silent but for the accusing drip of ill-fated *béarnaise*. In the flickering yellow light impenitent faces glitter with lively skepticism.

"*Imbeciles!*" the supple voice rises nastily: an implausible bray. "*Pigs!*"

Tom licks his dry lips and opens his mouth; but the suddenly grinning elf throws both hands in the air and spins (to a merry, approving roar); then quickly presses a demure and perfectly manicured finger to his curving lips.

"It's like this, my dears," he resumes in a tender, conspiratorial voice. "Not a moment to lose, in fact! We must work together on this. Which means that *you*, dear Richard, get lapping! The rest of you no-goodniks follow the shining example set by our unexpected visitor . . ." he turns and wrinkles an inquiring brow. "Your name, my friend?"

Heavens, this isn't at all what I expected. Also, I wasn't sure about the plates—but what could I do? Oh, says I, oh it's Tom—

"What's that? Tom? Excellent! *Tom.* An all-American name. In fact! Ringing of naiveté, industry, and hope." His pink palms come together with a terrifying *crack.* "Now hop to it, cottontails, or we'll all land in the stew!"

Everyone jumps at once. Several photographers' lamps, ransacked from another room, cast a lurid light across the pocked walls and quick, flashing hands of the now gleefully bustling workers. Foodstuffs begin to arrive on long, stainless steel gurneys, accompanied by a brisk hazel-eyed chef, and another woman, with whom she is engaged in quiet, friendly conversation.

"Ladies!" the bald man exclaims, and with a lavish bow draws each by the arm to where Tom hovers uncertainly beside his miraculous china.

"I present . . ." his voice jells with pleasure, "*Tom!* Tom, you've no doubt met—"

"Mitzi, you can call me!" One hazel eye winked.

"And of course the matchless Conchita—devastating as usual, my dear."

Ooh! she gave a fella the unnecessaries!

Conchita was in fact devastating, her sallow skin powdered to an impeccable matte, her thin lips rouged a furious black-red. And the fascinating sickle of that swart, ruby-studded ear! That tawny hair drawn back in classically severe waves from a low, opaque forehead! And that short, muscular neck! Straight umber brows made a contrasting and nearly unbroken line across truly breathtaking eyes of pale Argentine gray, so sheer they reminded Tom of the unblinking, sightless eyes of statues.

Tom's toes curl and he turns in a hurry to Mitzi, whose regal cheekbones, stippled eyes—round and hooded as a frog queen's—generous mouth, and frizzy gray-brown hair (wound into a crown of braids, a girlish touch Tom finds quite charming) strike him as far more reassuring and approachable. Tall and raw-boned, with sturdy hips and freckled, long-fingered hands, she looks at Tom in an affable and approving way, as though by the candid meeting of their eyes they made a kind of pact, and would henceforth proceed as allies.

We'll fox 'em! she seemed to say. You wait, we'll fox 'em—

Conchita interrupts, "So dithis Tom," growling in her throat, swallowing back her words even as they rise (moreover brandishing an elusive and terribly intriguing lisp).

"We've been waiting for you, 'aven't we, Ugo?"

Ugo's profile is faintly mocking as he stands with arms folded, head bowed and upper body curved over the floor as though examining his shoes. "Ye-ess," he agrees. "Time was running out!"

"But he's here now," Mitzi breaks in, "and that's what counts. I expect he came as soon as he was able." She grins at Tom encouragingly.

What's that? Waiting for me! But surely there'd been a mistake! Expecting someone? Well, all right. But listen, some other Tom! Why I'd only cropped up—and counting plates, no less! And before I could . . . but say, for all I knew, I might be speaking to the owner right there! Heavens, maybe Ugo?

In a panic to set things straight, Tom began, post-
haste, to deliver a cringing little speech he'd memorized
on his way to the Ruins that morning.

*Cringing! Listen, if that's a joke it's a pretty poor one!
In the first place there's nothing the matter with watching
your p's and q's, as they say. We needn't all be high on our
horses. Not like some fancy talkers just waiting for a chance
to blow their own horns, when—*

5—

Abruptly the three people standing before Tom freeze.
Conchita's gaze drops like a flag and remains there, the
lowered violet lids trembling as though stirred by a quick,
secret breeze. Ugo cocks a perfectly pitched ear, scowls.
Mitzi winces, mimes a broad, horrified scream, and with
a final wink at Tom, takes cover in the anyway-over-
whelming wilderness of warming ovens and undercooks,
swarming ice buckets and bains-marie and—

La, then I heard it too!

Indeed, who could miss it? The voice, may we say, of
a highly tarnished scouring pad (take a moment, now, to
imagine it): in pitch insinuating as a dentist's drill, but
lavishly intoned, gassy as a five-day corpse.

"GAWD! Isn't it AWFUL? We LOVE it!"

Tom glances uncertainly at Conchita, whose gaze,
briefly lifted, discomfits him with its faintly suffocating
vacancy. The extraordinary voice dawdles in its approach,

whining in languid discontent, "Look, we've got to *kill* these cigars. Now *where* in the . . ." until there is a violent crash against a nearby door, a brief, foreboding pause, and the drawl throttles up like a petulant buzz saw, "Gawd *fucking* damn it!"

In a flash Ugo is not only pushing firmly at the door but laughing with gay and reassuring aplomb. "*There* we go! The door that's *pulled* from that side, *pushed* from this? Inconvenient, but changes take time—in fact!—and others have grown used to the, uh . . ."

The voice snarls. "Well *we* haven't gotten used to *the, uh*—and that ought to count for something since it's our door. *Our* door, you . . . you merely necessary worm! And we *hate* it like this. *Gawd!*"

La! my belly nearly disgraced me, right there and then! For of course it could only be (and indeed was!) none other than—

Indeed! The celebrated Jones, whose broadly yoked shoulders and blunt, tucked pelvis swiveled in notably nimble opposition; whose vast, admirably muscled belly was carried high, swaying peremptorily from side to side over abbreviated, yet also roundly muscled legs; and who, for all his impracticable, burst-barrel'd bulk, was nonetheless conspicuously light on his feet, moving with the rampant spine and delicately outheld arms of an old ballroom dandy. His platinum and vaguely astral hair explicitly haloed a livid complexion. Dainty, full-blooded lips; tiny lashless eyes so deep-set they seemed driven into his head like two lead pellets. Catching sight of Conchita, he simpered, his dry cheeks bulging with unexpected roundness. He was not, in any conventional sense of the word, handsome; and yet there was something in the bland animosity of those eyes beneath their snowy brows—and in the cruel, girlish curve of the oft-licked lips—and in the barbaric self-importance of that heedless, hair-raising voice—that one could not help but find fascinating and perhaps, even, irresistible. Just the sort of fellow, in short, with whom our hero could not say with any confidence he was "familiar."

This was it! My foot in the door! It was time to hop the threshold—or turn tail and resign myself to the cracked soles and dismal prospects of my former life (which seemed, I should admit, already a million miles behind me). Well! I was never more aware of myself, of my abilities and of the potential glory looming before and all around me—

Provoked, Tom's belly thrusts a cold disaffected nose between the slats of his ribs and begins, in belligerent tremolos, to pour out the bitter vials of its woe; his heart ricochets from one side of his chest to the other; and indeed our beleaguered hero felt (alas, not for the first time) as though he must simply burst into tears—or worse—the moment he opened his mouth.

Jones, in the meantime, wagged a short, malevolent finger beneath Conchita's flaring nostrils. "Conchita! How *could* you have left us with that vulgar little health inspector? The man was relentless! We had to promise him the *moon* and send him out the door with half a raspberry charlotte! Where do these people get their *nerve?*"

Conchita's reply is taut with restraint. "You didn't sign anyzing, did you Jonz?"

"Sign *anything?* The man was *uncompromising.* There was no getting him out of our hair." Jones sniffs. "That's what you get, Miss In*vi*sible. Don't speak! Call him in the morning, but right now we've got a party to throw."

Ugo cleared his throat and skipped forward to present Tom. "In fact!" But the massive white head is already rearing back; the tiny eyes roll once, wildly, before closing with unappealable doom; one arm supports the elbow of the other, the terminal end of which bristles with splayed and wriggling fingers as Jones enumerates the bones of his contention. His voice thickens with rising bile.

"Primo! One hundred perfectly revolting cigars. Where did you get them, children, a vomitoria? Two! Odette Fishbein-Brooke's *insufferable* low-fat diet . . ."

(Which as a matter of fact has always been kind of a—)

"—pain in the fucking *ass.* Three . . ."

Conchita's eyes catch Tom's and narrow speculatively. "Jonz?"

Ugo pulls Tom out from behind the table and interrupts once more, his voice beguiling. "See what we have, Jones, just see!"

Jones's hackles lift visibly; he raises the lid of a seething brow and shows them something quick and black that glitters there in the center of one eye, like a rat at the bottom of a dripping well. "Obsequious toad! Obscurantist! Don't play *games* with us!"

Conchita takes over, explaining in her burred, slurring voice. "Lizzen, Jonz, is *good* news; diz boy 'ere, dizziz *Tom*."

"Oh for the—!" Jones winced and fingered the front of his bulging yellow pullover, nevertheless appraising Tom with scrupulous care. "*Waalll.* What have we here? *Tom*, did you say? Now is that a *fact*? Tom. That's correct? *Tom* . . ." When Conchita and Ugo exchange uncertain glances, Tom feels suddenly afraid.

Chin in hand, Jones purses disdainful lips. "Oh he's *perfect*, isn't he perfect? But," he turns to his assistants, frowning. "That *hair*. Really! That hair is a sin. We wouldn't wish that hair on a yak." Conchita and Ugo snicker; Tom smiles weakly.

Still, things weren't going so badly; so far all was well.

Jones sniffed. "Anyway, who cares? Is this the time to stand around making nice? A hundred bellies will come barreling through these doors in a matter of hours. Are the wagons in a bloody circle? Has anyone even *bothered* to look for that awful pony?"

As for that! Without even thinking I says to him, "I know where the pony is!"

Jones stops, turns, slowly narrows his eyes at Tom and shakes his head in mock wonder. "Just *perfect!*" Then he whirls, tossing his arms into the air as Ugo had demonstrated only moments before. "All right, let's get cracking, kids! Conchita?"

They leave, and oh what I wouldn't give for a couch—la, a cupboard would do!—in which to bury my head, just for a moment, just to collect myself and consider, as they say, my options. But already Ugo has me by the arm and when we get to the door I push, like he said, but what do you know! The door won't give, when just a minute ago?

Ugo shrugs, smirks, pulls open the door and thrusts our uncertain hero into the dining Salon, letting the door fall closed between them. "Go on, go on! A moment's delay."

And then, oh, there it was! It was . . .

The inaugural moment,
yes!
Our hero's blind date with destiny!

• • •

Even now Tom's heart flip-flops only to recall that first wordless encounter. Without a doubt it was everything he had dreamed; indeed (as is often the case among the half-fed, the near-illiterate, the "disadvantaged") it was *more*. With nothing and no one to distract our dazzled lad and his fair one and only (the fresh and immediately all-consuming apple of his love-doped, doggish eye) those first delirious moments were inviolable—we won't say off the record; only discreetly veiled, as though under the protection of a spreading, luminously feathered, guardian wing. But *look*.

At either end of a vast rectangular room, perennial gas fires cavort discreetly within celadon green and pink checkered hearths; over their stately carved mantles loom ten-by-twenty-foot mirrors framed in peeling *fleur-de-lis*, the ancient glass an inspired corruption of tarnished silver and plain old dust. Tasseled hassocks and tapestry pillows accompany well-placed Italian armchairs in cucumber and lavender brocade, while a bargelike double-backed *chaise longue* in delirious saffron velvet puckers with dozens of padded satin buttons. Underfoot, illustrious Brussels carpets sprawl beneath stout porcelain swans and crocodiles upon whose obsequiously upraised beaks and snouts etched glass table tops glisten like perfect, imperishable dreams. Overhead, yard-wide violet ribbons swoop down from an imperial rosette at the center of a sixty-foot-high daffodil ceiling, to be caught up in colossal bows against the combed, pistachio walls—the wainscoting silverish beneath a sober wash. Portraits in oil (a tall, haughty girl in black bangs, one hand clasping a hoop; a cringing whippet, her craven belly sucked in as though upon a pearl; a moonlit marble portico, between whose columns gleams an indisputably *wine-dark sea)* engage the eye at regular intervals.

Flocked like debutantes, three dozen dining tables sport starched ecru linen (over snowy underskirts), upon which squads of heavily chased silver wink at the placid bottoms of hand blown Venetian stemware. From buxom table vases flirt pink magnolias, freckled lilies, and white freesia, while impossibly long-waisted apricot roses lean from green glass vases on marble-topped side tables whose cast bronze legs curve like the taut haunches of squatting satyrs. (Later would come pert, vanilla-scented carnations, frilled and threaded in shades of pink and white and burgundy; or tulips, whose prim yellow petals would be splayed, after one day in the warm room, like a Russian dancer's upended skirts; or cunning moss baskets brimful of wild primroses, violets, candyflower and fair narcissus.) Encircling sidechairs, striped in vivid poppy and olive silk, flex delicate brass feet against creamy marble and alabaster tiled floors, within whose border—an inlaid garland of desultory russet brambles—boastful robins lift their throats, greedy beaks abulge with tumescent golden worms.

Tom saw all this, and more! A multitude of exquisite and unforgettable details. He greeted each "sensation" with the artless, ecstatic delight of an unself-conscious child. Gawked at himself in the cloudy mirrors as though he were a stranger; marveled at the virtuosity of the counterfeit fires; painstakingly counted the gravely turning pink crystal chandeliers (and while so doing, allowed his fingers to tickle the black and ivory keys of a buttery yellow grand, chose *one*, and pressed it gently 'til the note struck—and striking, both raised and gilded his heart with its divine tone).

Ah! says I, and thought at once of the ineffable La Stupenda and her first-rate ascent into the rafters of the Groaning Board. Noble gestures! A song on her lips! And those shoes! Wasn't it she who'd mustered in me the confidence to quicken my own wings? Best-of-all-angels, I thought (no shame in my blush): I owe everything to you! To imagine that one day, perhaps here at the Ruins itself, I might confront that bright emancipator in person, gaze humbly into those celestial blue eyes, press my lips to that casual, incorruptible hand . . . At last she would know, and without my confessing a word, all that she must mean to me. A debt that can never be repaid, but oh, that one might be allowed to try!

• • •

"Deutsch!" someone spat, and Tom whirled at once, hands clasped before his crotch like a guilty choirboy.

Arms folded, head thrown back, Ugo glares at the florid chandeliers with undisguised contempt; then shrugs at Tom and in another flawless imitation of Jones's high, serrated gush sneers, "*Yazzss,* by all means, in the wurst, *faah*-bu-lous taste—"

My word, what nerve, and in this of all places!

"Not to worry!" quips Ugo. "A place for everything and everything in its—ah, here's the rascal now. Paulie!"

Tom's still cutting emotional glances left and right as Ugo leads him to a tall young man standing on the other side of an unfortunate pink marble fountain.

The fountain—the dear little goldfish!

Paulie's smugly tanned, pox-scarred face was wreathed in laughter. He wore a snug blue athletic suit, zippered to the middle of a soft, hairless chest; and in an excess of humor pressed both hands flat (diamond signet ring glittering from one outstretched pinkie) against a taut, muscular paunch. Bleached blond ringlets plunged somewhat deliberately over one brow; his round eyes were a startling blue in the flushed and cheerfully dissipated face. In all, one could not escape an impression of coarseness and lechery; but his transparent vanity, good humor, and cunning put a droll spin on character flaws in respect to which unheard-of allowances were more often made than merited.

So described, Paulie flung himself on little Ugo's neck, pressed his mouth against the other's ear and launched into an account the details of which elicited more than one admiring shake from Ugo's gleaming head. He doodled on the dainty shirt front; rubbed his thumb and forefinger together in a smooth, circular motion. Ugo smiled. *In fact, my friend, in fact!* With a final burst of laughter they both turned to face Tom (struggling politely not to overhear).

(Pig mask . . . saddle sores . . . a generous tip? I say!)

Ugo spoke sharply. "Tom, Paulie. Paulie leads on outside parties, stands second in the Salon. You'll find his experience valuable. More!" Paulie gave Tom a friendly nod, his blue eyes bright with curiosity. Ugo continued. "I'll leave you to it? Jones is frantic. Which means that Mitzi—" He sighed and nodded at Tom. "All right? Well, I—" There was a distant howl followed by Jones's festering squawk, and Ugo was off without another word. Paulie's big hands came together with unexpected authority as he turned, frowning, to survey the room.

"Okey-doke, here's the drill . . ."

6—

Several hours later Tom stared round himself in wonder and dismay. The matchless green walls are obscured now by looming and uneasily swaying papier-mâché cactuses whose flimsy cardboard foundations are camouflaged by handfuls of loose, moldering hay. French linens are re-placed by red and blue cotton bandannas, while a long central table boasts a luminous shroud of bright green plastic grass (the kind idling in window displays from one holiday to the next). Bales of hay sit in stolidly for the banished sidechairs; at each place setting a tin horseshoe is inscribed with a guest's name. There are two round hors d'oeuvre tables separated by a tiny corral in which the incarcerated pony slouches on one fat haunch, glar-ing from beneath the brim of a gaudy sombrero. Pasty looking helium balloons labor in batches overhead, bran-dishing posterboard blowups (flinty eyes, ten-gallon hat, cigar clenched between thin, colorless lips) of the guest of honor, Mr. Horst Dinwiddie. And in fact this gentle-man had already arrived, a somberly dressed man in a very large hat who stands in the center of the room, ges-turing gruffly with his smoldering cigar while Jones, hand on hip, hammers the air with his blunt, bored laugh. *Haw. Haw. Haw.*

Tom sighed and looked down at his borrowed shirt and knotted kerchief, felt for the diminutive dime store cowboy hat giddily perched atop his untamed crop, and couldn't help but chafe at the impression he must make. He turned and stared into the liquor-stacked bed of the small Conestoga to which he, designated bartender, had been assigned.

Cocktails? But I couldn't mix a cocktail to save my life! And frankly, even the smell of spirits . . .

"Don't worry, pal," Paulie assured him, tweaking the limp fleece of Tom's preposterous mustache. "These bubs drink like fish so pour big to keep 'em off your back and if they ask for something funny, make it up! Here's your bible." Paulie thrust a small, dog-eared book at Tom, slapped him on the back and moved to catch up with a plump waitress in chaps and spurs; as they hurried along he bent and whispered something in her ear and she pushed him away, laughing.

All right, it's only a matter of doing one's best, like the plates, hey? And anyway—

Tom sat down on a leaking styrofoam ice chest and dropped his face in his hands, heeding the mustache. It felt like weeks since morning, and already he could scarcely recall his former life as a shoeshine. Since arriving he'd learned to set a table for six courses and nine wines, shucked eight hundred oysters, and watched with terror over Mitzi's signature poached pears while she graciously instructed two reverent scullions in the proper way to dice a pepper. He'd been kicked twice while braiding the pony's tail, and discovered he had an allergy to furniture polish.

—who'd have guessed!

Conchita had him rolling hand towels for the Ladies';
Jones sent him to change his hair twice, in passing. The
upshot was, his head was spinning. What could be next?

"Martinis—yes or no? *Period!*"

Jones's voice sawed through the general hubbub like
a dull knife. "And we happen to know where you can get
the best martini in town! *Tom-Tom!*"

Tom-Tom? Martinis?

Jones piloted a flotilla of grim-visaged, glittering
guests toward the homemade Conestoga. Terrified, our
hero tore through his book, hurling ice, vermouth, gin
and olives together—alas, with less pomp than desperate
pretense. Jones got the picture at once, and bearing
down in undisguised wrath, yet threw his chin over one
shoulder to scold the procession loftily, "Yes or no? *Period.*"

Moments later they lifted frost-whiskered glasses in
which rakish olives lolled like fat green cherubs; by the
time they reeled from the wagon Tom had, by staggering repetition, made of the simple "martooni" an elegant science, and the mightily loosened guests were
begging Jones to saddle the pony for rides around the
Cloud Room. Lew Gottwald, three sheets to the wind,
made to thrust a large bill into Tom's hat band; the lad
drew back startled. Jones flapped a weary hand at them.
"Puh-*leeze.* Don't corrupt the boy! Now listen, have
you seen the Avocado Room? Don't speak! On our way

through the kitchen you'll sample the sauce . . ." As they tottered off Jones looked back over one shoulder, grimaced meaningfully and winked, "Swell martinis, Tom!"

Wha—? *Did Jones just wink at me?*

Tom caught his breath, smoothed his mustache and looked cautiously about the room. Hats cocked at jaunty angles, spurs whirling hilariously, waiters and waitresses circulated with trays of hors d'oeuvre; the musicians executed a haughty Mexican polka; the pony bared his teeth at a circle of half-swacked admirers. Paulie tapped his shoulder, glanced over the bar ("martinis, right?") and with a grin ran off to rustle more gin. Guests began to arrive in larger numbers, and Tom once again, despite the increasing din, heard Jones's unmistakable peal, "Martinis, what else? And we know just the place. *Tom-Tom!*"

· · ·

For dinner? There were pâtés in aspic, in pastry, in mousse . . . oyster croquettes Victoria . . . cherries in vinegar and savory date fritters . . . planked turbot *in toto*, glassy-eyed and fabulously shellacked with citron and herbs . . . wild duck in vintage port . . . purees of chestnut and artichoke heart . . . airy *paupiettes* of beef with pickled nasturtium buds . . . mock hedgehog, champagne sherbets and endive salad with partridge tongues . . . amber jelly, plain and fancy, and ripe cheeses rolled in caraway, capers, and minced pistachios . . . *tarte angoulousée, tarte d'Angleterre, tarte fanaïde,* and puddings! oh dear, puddings by the score!

Waiters flew in and out of both kitchens, flourishing hot plates and finger bowls, fresh napkins and clean forks. Now Tom circulated uneasily, a neatly bibbed bottle of Château-Latour in each dubious hand. Diligently—and like a tall, broad-bottomed bird—he made cantilevered attacks on each depleted glass he spied languishing among the unfamiliar currents of freckled or stiffly lacquered heads, smeared plates, and liver-spotted hands clutching cutlery with casual or predatory aplomb.

Then what? Inspired, I guess, by the farmyard theme, someone launched into animal impressions! And for the rest of the dinner the company resounded with what, er, can only be described as clucks, bellows, and high-spirited whinnies.

Mr. Trumbull Wanger grabbed Tom, thrust a greasy dinner plate into his hands and demanded to know where Jones kept the *feedbags!*—then threw back his head and roared. Before Tom could make up his mind to reply the man pushed him away, "Never mind, *caballero,* I found one myself!" and dropped his furious red face into the shelved, peninsular bosom of Candice Topping, at his side, who shrieked and wriggled as he rooted playfully between her dizzily-troughed breasts.

Well! I never in my life expected to . . . oh!

Tom jumped at a loathsome noise in his left ear, a horrible and rather insinuating utterance, coupling chuckle and snarl. He turned, cringing, but found no one; then turned back to find Jones glaring at him from across the table, his upper lip furled in a grotesque charade of deferential appeal.

"Yoo-*hoo* Tom-Tom! Mrs. Prosper Gosling here is absolutely *parched* and was just wondering if she was ever going to get that glass of Armagnac we promised her? How about you unload that plate and make yourself just a *lee*-tle bit useful? *Gawd!*"

Well! I started to remind Jones (with all due respect, of course) that unfortunately there was no Armagnac to be had. Indeed, I'd already looked twice and—

Jones cut him off. "And *don't* give us any of your tired excuses. Of *course* there's Armagnac in the house. Mrs. Prosper Gosling *adores* Armagnac and we *promised* her she could have it. What could be more simple! Now trot along, little piggy, and do as you're told . . ."

My jaw dropped. Little piggy? But wasn't I doing my best? And furthermore (though I'd never have dreamed of saying so out loud!) why should Jones promise people what couldn't be had? Flirting and prompting . . . Don't miss the chicken and dumplings! Save room for the banana-coconut cream pie! Is that fair?

Tom sought out Paulie, who punched him playfully in the ribs. "Don't make it so hard on yourself! Say *oui oui*—make 'em happy—then give 'em what we got. *They* won't know the difference."

All right then, so I did. And it was beef gâteau with pralines for chicken and dumplings, champagne ice for coconut cream. That's how it was—and just as he promised, no one said a word!

Courses arrived, loitered, and were relieved by subsequent courses. And if no one more than nibbled, there was notwithstanding a great deal of gush *about* food—other suppers, teas and brunches. All provided by Jones; indeed, in many cases featuring the exact dishes circulated that evening! And yet it was as though nothing in the world was or ever could be like *them*, like those *other* mouth-watering, sublime, unrepeatable dishes. Glasses were filled, drained, and replenished; the musicians threw back their heads, narrowed their eyes; the balloons sank gradually overhead; the celebrated Mr. Dinwiddie removed neither his hat nor the cigar from between his teeth.

• • •

In the end Tom found himself behind a monstrous tumbleweed, butt braced to the wall, knees scissoring, belly volcanic. It may have been "too much," after all, for our hero found himself, between shuddering breaths, entertaining second thoughts. *Heavens, why'd he come to this place, anyway? What was he looking for?* It was all quite sensational, a regular squall, and made his hands tremble and sweat. *Was he suave like Ugo? Could he tease and caper like Paulie? He certainly wasn't beautiful—he guessed that was why they pasted this mustache on him, and put him inside a goofy wagon where no one could see his rump-sprung trousers and humble shoes. Why sure!* At this our hero pulled off the disgraceful whiskers, loosened his kerchief, and—nearly weeping—rubbed his finger forlornly against the sleeve of his borrowed shirt. Chiffon?

Say, don't exaggerate! It wasn't so bad!

Crouched behind his tumbleweed, our hero quailed at the racket, the glare—a ferment of smeared lips and sagging, half-naked tits; luckless horseshoes and buckling cardboard cows; red cotton kerchiefs fluttering through the air like hens before a storm. He blinked, and the tables began to turn; he blinked again and oh, didn't the shiny plates spin! The chandeliers revolved overhead on their fraying ropes, while down below bellies jiggled and swelled, and butter balls, bright as suns, rose and fell, rose and fell. Martini glasses sailed end-over-end, and the sullen pony performed (were those *cartwheels?*) to a chorus of gratified bleats and honks.

Ugh! And everywhere the horrible snapping mouths, wet wrinkled beaks reaching for the worm! Bared circlets of amber-rooted teeth clacked and glittered round fat blind tongues. And how they flexed and writhed, flexed and writhed, those well-honed, eyeless probes whose unseen roots dropped deep into that lower infernal abyss, about which everything finally—

All right, too much!

. . . everything revolved!

• • •

"Tom-Tom!"

What? Jones! Oh . . .

Two strong hands pinned Tom to the wall just as his legs slid out from under him. Tom opened his eyes and met Paulie's wicked grin (the imitation of Jones's native caw was, like Ugo's, flawless). *Tom-Tom?* He gave Tom a little shake and Tom ducked his head, embarrassed and relieved. Paulie propped one forearm against Tom's chest and turned to survey the room.

"Listen Tom," he continued in his normal voice, "this might be a good time for you to grab a bite. Guess I kind of forgot about you, no offense! Anyway, skip back and see if they haven't got something left over. I'll cover here."

So I did and, well, you could have decked me with a feather when Mitzi laid it out. A feast! Oh, I'd ply some knife-and-fork now! People guess I have no appetite, but in fact it's simply a question of—

Ravenous, Tom yet would no more than marvel at his heaped and steaming plate. He rested on an overturned crate and reconsidered his previous despair.

After all, it was only my first day, and natural to feel a bit off. Nothing shameful in having to learn. And hadn't they taken my arrival for granted? Knew my name! And without blinking an eye set me to work. There's confidence!

Besides, was he prepared to walk away (he bent over his plate and inhaled blissfully) from *this*?

At last Tom picked up his fork, eased it beneath a tidbit of veal, and raised it to his mouth. His lips parted, his jaw dropped, his tongue guided the fork in, providing a warm wet altar for the helpless morsel. At once the juices in his mouth spurted into action: caressing the meat;

nuzzling the sauce from its naked flesh; suavely breaking down the veal's resistance with a host of persuasive enzymes. Tom's tongue practically squirmed now; his molars prepared to gnash. The roof of his mouth sank down upon the swooning and insidiously undone piece of meat, which could not but surrender to the slow, irresistibly penetrating embrace.

By jove, to grease my gills at last!

Suddenly the steel door burst open and Paulie cried from beneath a heap of furs: "They're off!"

Tom choked and rose hastily from his crate as left and right workers charged to the fore.

Oh, but perhaps they could put my dinner aside? Surely I wouldn't be long . . .

Ah, but the place was a shambles; the guests vague and hysterical, milling about with dim, glassy eyes, crying weakly for their coats, their cars, their servants— who, bustling and self-important, happily added to the flap.

"Well then, happy anniversary, Horst! Birthday? Hell, whatever!"

"You call this a three-quarter lynx! This is not Mr. Armond Frisson's three-quarter lynx! Where—"

"Midge Sprain Wilson! Where've you been hiding!"

"Now call us, darling—no, don't call us! Really, we'll call you . . ."

"Madam! Madam!"

"Say hello, but don't say it was me—

In the midst of this, Jones swept through the crowd, braying. "Kiss-kiss, kiss-kiss! *Fabulous*, wasn't it? Got everything? Gorgeous chinchilla—think it's *me*? Haw . . ." At the door, he suddenly threw up his hands and whirled. "Tom? *Tom-Tom!*"

I never did secure the Armagnac for Mrs. Gosling—did he know? Was this it? God, what did I do with that mustache?

Tom hurried, heart in his throat, to where Jones stood waiting beside the door. He thought longingly of the plate of food still waiting for him in the back room; would they let him eat before they made him leave? Jones indicated with a jerk of his chin the raccoon-eyed Vafa Herculani who'd been fingering Tom's sleeve a moment before.

"Tom-Tom! Don't believe a word that Abbysinian snake in the grass says. Married his money! Tired, tired, tired! And listen, we're counting on you to wrap up here, understand? You won't believe what's on the book for tomorrow, so first thing in the morning, Tom, get into that dining room and *kill* those chrysanthemums! All right? *Perfect!*"

And then he too was gone, the stout terrier trotting at his heels.

Me in charge! Why, I . . . Paulie!

A waiter, pulling on his own coat, shrugged. "He already left . . ."

Ugo gone too. "Off to the movies!" and whoosh. Conchita? And Mitzi with a wink between salad and dessert.

That left a few dawdling scullions and five or six wait-ers, all of whom were throwing off their spurs and taking their leave in the murky and querulous wake of their guests. Tom (still hovering beside the door) smiled pleadingly at them as they went, but in the end stood alone in a vacant and eerily suspended bedlam.

Anyone there?

Tom sighed, found a serving tray and began to circu-late, collecting sticky glasses and dessert plates, over-spilling ashtrays and dented cowboy hats. He wrestled the papier-mâché cactuses into the back storage room, stacked the bales of hay in the alley. He gathered the sur-viving balloons into one bunch and tied them to a sawhorse in the garage; broke down the pony's corral and hobbled him in the wine cellar; then started several loads of laundry. Picking the litter from a mountain of blue bandannas, Tom suddenly recalled his own deferred sup-per.

Perhaps? I hurried to the kitchen!

Dark and empty as a church, the sinks wiped dry, the concrete floor breathing cold. Tom's heart sank.

Oh, the lovely dinner—thrown out? Gobbled by another?

His belly laid back its ears and growled.

Still, maybe it was here, maybe . . .

But searching carefully, Tom found no dainties tucked amidst the barrels of sugar and oil, the blackened gas rings, the heavily chromed mixers and blenders, stacks of casseroles, custard cups and chafing dishes. And yet he was appeased and gratified simply to *be* in this safe, orderly place; to stand and not move a muscle in the chaste flicker of tiny blue pilot lights, dozens of scattered blue lights . . . and the beckoning red "ON" of one overlooked warming oven! Tom smiled dreamily, dropped the oven door and burned his fingers on the plate inside.

My dinner!

After several hours in a 350-degree oven, it was un-recognizable, the veal twisted as a dry shoe, the sauce fused to the plate. Tom shook his head. Darned shame.

But proof someone was thinking of me!

Tom turned and, on impulse, tugged at the door of one humming refrigerator. The sudden light made him wince, and only gradually was he able to make out the numberless unmarked tubs, damp paper cartons and anonymous packets with which the scoured aluminum shelves were crammed. Tom was tempted, stood with wide, fascinated eyes, but finally let the door close and the room return to shadows and scattered blue lights. As he turned to go, his eye fell upon a broken loaf of bread crowning an overstuffed garbage bag. How inviting it looked! Luminous, white as—

As white chiffon! Surely . . .

His stomach, aroused by the proximity of food, threw itself determinedly at Tom's wavering pride. He slowly grasped and tore a piece from the loaf—then another, and another. Standing in the dim, pristine kitchen, Tom devoured most of the loaf, chewing reverently.

Bread! Incomparable . . .

Wandering back to the dining room (heavenly once more in the nacreous light of a late-rising, lopsided moon), Tom sat upon the mammoth yellow sofa and placidly gathered his thoughts—so far as they went; then curled on one side, tucked the crumbling heel of bread beneath his chin, and fell fast, fast asleep.

CHAPTER THREE

Beauty, Truth, and a Call to First Principles

7—

And where, oh where did that put him now? (Sternum slipping, spine aslant, hips cocked awkwardly on the edge of his seat . . .)

Called on the carpet, is where we find our hero after two weeks of earnest, if inauspicious, service. Sitting in Jones's office, the pandemonic Maisonette, that's where! Waiting for Jones to conclude his telephone call; impatient (and who's to say not a little fainthearted?) to determine the object of their meeting. Or perhaps he's guessed the prognosis already, hm? And was only looking forward to a speedy confirmation of his condition? After all, our hero knows in his own heart what excuses are worth; and the fact is (his thin fingers pinch morosely at the crease of his checkered trousers), *the fact is,* after two weeks he just isn't cutting the mustard.

And whose fault was that? He was the one begged a challenge, bid illustrious opportunity Knock, Knock! And now, in some incalculable manner, the Ruins eluded him. Yes, *things happened*. Regrettable things. He does not see them coming and he cannot seem to prevent them from occurring again and again, no matter how he tries.

It may, for instance, be the flowers, about which Jones is apt to throw particularly virulent fits, snarling "do something, for gawd's sake, about those fucking artemisia!" Jones called them old whores, spoiled cunts, hemorrhages, stinking cankers—while Tom, his ears burning, wracked his brains over some new disguise for splayed roses and seedy mignonette.

Worse yet, *complaints had been lodged*. Oh, not against Tom himself, but against his staff; and wasn't that the same thing? Tom could not have imagined a more wayward company upon whom he was expected to rely: a feckless, indeterminate horde of lackeys hired, it seemed, despite diffidence and a poor understanding of their most rudimentary duties. In general, when not cavorting like kids, they stood about dim-witted as sheep; at the same time they were full of scorn for members and guests (who were, it was popularly believed, "unequal to the food"). For that matter, conceits of all kinds—cats, ladders, the counting of cups—entangled the simplest acts. And if there weren't occult reasons for why the sauce broke or how twelve dozen dinner napkins came to be stuffed up the kitchen chimney, it was easy enough to blame

Jones—a perfect alibi, in fact; for as it happened Jones was capable of issuing the most extraordinary, improvident commands, and moments later disowning what he'd only just decreed. In the end, nothing was accountable, and Tom was forever bearing the burden of impossible deadlines, unspoken "agreements," cross-grained and enigmatic personnel. (But if Tom knew and sympathized, to some extent, with the difficulties placed upon all by the thorny and indefensible intrusions of Jones; still, was it really Jones's fault the doorman—a smoldering Latvian dwarf—swilled a thermos of cognac every night?)

At the same time, they maintained that "outside the Ruins there is no salvation," and there was a peculiar mixture of satisfaction and apathy in their voices as they said this. Tom noted with surprise, however, that they did not despair, and responded to his own upsets and urgency with curiosity, at best. "That's just how it is," they assured him, as though explaining to a child. "That's just how Jones is." To be sure, they were stubbornly resistant to change, even when it promised an advantage. Practically without ego—and certainly no grasp of personal boundaries! (Tom's pressed tunics were forever disappearing from his locker; and a day did not pass when he was not astonished by a couplet of underlings, writhing in the corner.) Tom, a fusspot by nature, was still less appalled by their brazen indiscretions than by this tacit acceptance of "circumstances"—including a future!—of frankly the basest sort. And when it could all be arranged, Tom knew, so *differently*. After all, he fumed, this was their "big chance" too! Didn't they understand? Didn't they care?

He recalled again, and with undiminished chagrin, Conchita's face as she held out the letters of complaint. Those nerveless gray eyes in which nothing could be read! And those dry rouged lips that seemed at times—in their leanness and in the livid cast of their pigmentation— like those of a shrewd monkey, or a fox.

After that it was no time at all before Jones himself began to storm the rear of the house with lacerating regularity, denouncing the garde-manger's *bombe glacée;* looking daggers at an unassuming laundry-maid's starch; felling cakes with his bellow (and making a perfect federal case over the regular spectacle of Tom's intractable hair, which could never be maintained, really *ever*, to Jones's complete satisfaction). In short, aside from his precocious martinis, Tom had come to feel he could do almost nothing right. Possibly (there was a surly mutter from the region of his belly) the future held no more than shoe polish and mucid groats after all.

• • •

Jones cooed ominously "*Yazzss, yazzss,* you know we'd never deny you. *Yes or no?* Fabulous!" then slammed the receiver home. "Gawd! I *loathe* climbers." He sprawled, overhanging the armrests of his low-backed leather chair, like a prodigal chop overwhelming a scant bun. He sighed, and with the point of a sharpened pencil stabbed wearily at a profusion of luncheon tarts piled up before him—then cuffed the platter to the floor. When stout Toulouse lurched down from the daybed to investigate, Jones went still—then bent and *whizzsst* at him peremptorily, like a hog passing urine. Straightening, he glowered at a puddle of coffee gone cold in his cup.

Tom shifted uneasily in his chair, wishing not to heed these garish and, one earnestly hoped, involuntary behavioral spasms; and shuddered inwardly at what must surely come next. He was unprepared, therefore, and transparently taken aback by Jones's first words.

• • •

"Tom-Tom! You know we rely on you ab-so-*loot*-ly! Yes or no? Why, you deserve a medal!" (Did Jones smirk? Tom studied the floor.) "Don't speak! We all know the score. So! Can you imagine how it pains us, really *pains* us, to see you skulking about so, so . . . *Gawd!* Well, we just can't have it!" Jones waited, kicked peevishly at the litter of tarts; then, shuttering his eyes, buzzed silkily, "Tom-Tom! Tell us, what *is* the matter?"

And here our shamed, spitless hero—who'd bid his gaze (atremble with tears from the moment he entered the room) remain prostrate upon the impeccable toe of his shoe—at last looked up, rather more than less undone. *A medal?* La! He'd frankly prepared for the worst; now these expectations buckled in a most astonishing manner. He swallowed hard (glancing at the heap of broken tarts—then hastily away). Where to begin! Artless hick, how his stickling heart hemmed and hawed within his breast; at once fierce, and then again, so awfully, awfully needy.

The remorseful child in him wanted forgiveness, naturally enough—and another chance; wanted desperately to succeed, and believed, perhaps, it still might. But honestly, the complications brought to bear upon the situation rather exceeded his own ingenuity. It was as simple (wasn't it?) as that.

Tom hauled a bit at the slack in his spine and experimentally coughed; he prodded the brightly feathered spectacle of his *Big Chance* to the foreground of an otherwise motley lot of doubts. Jones, he assured himself, could only want the best for the Ruins; it stood to reason. And wasn't that all Tom wanted, as well? And say! Could Jones (who practically commanded him to open his heart!), mightn't he seem to have, well, a "soft spot" for Tom? Well?

8—

Thus it happened that Tom (his misgiving heart making cynically for the door) determined to make a clean breast of things. He *would* confide his hopes, his fears, to Jones—why, as a son to a father! Surely then, and quite naturally, Jones would grasp and moreover commend Tom's industry and zeal; exonerate his coincident despair; and immediately pledge himself, with every instrument of his agency, to a friendly, all-around reorganization of the Ruins. How could Tom lose?

"Okay, well, the thing is, Mr. Jones, I . . . I have a vision—" Tom looked up with shining eyes to find Jones scrutinizing a small crust of yellowish matter upon the tip of his extended right forefinger. "Uh—your um . . . your restaurant, you see—"

Jones flicked the withered dab at Toulouse, leaned back, folded his arms and said nothing. Rattled, Tom could not but envy the impression made by a pair of powerfully built knees, broadly splayed with swank negligence, their every tendon and ligament visibly abulge beneath the taut sheath of polyester trousers. Alas (and, goodness knows, out of the blue), this picture was followed by a private and horrifying vision of Jones on all fours among the scattered leek and mushroom tarts, elbows bent, belly brushing the ground, teeth buried to the gums in the pungent scruff of the mutely squirming Staffordshire. Fingertips kneading at the bridge of his nose, the confused lad fumbled, understandably, with his next words. "That is to say, this restaurant—for *me*, I mean . . ."

Jones swiveled in his chair to face Tom directly, forming a bullhorn out of both cupped hands.

"NOW HEAR THIS! *Mr.* Tom—are you listening?
THIS . . . is *NOT* . . . a *RESTAURANT!*"

Tom gawked, and Jones, satisfied, sat back in his chair and continued in a slightly less strident, though no less mocking, tone.

"Haw! The expression on your face would be a real holiday, if it weren't all so tired-making. Let's repeat, then, to dispel any lagging ambiguity from your grasping and heroically mismanaged mind: This is *not* a restaurant! A *restaurant*? Fegh! Can't imagine where you get these unnatural ideas. Well, are you with us thus far?"

Tom's pretty dream, half-revealed and astonished, withdrew instantly—like a tender white paw from a thundering highway—to a remote, unmarked burrow in the deepest forest of his sadly vindicated heart. He blinked. Not a restaurant?

"We advise you, Tom, to put the swift kibosh on whatever delusions you've cooked up in that rust-buggered kettle you keep for a head. The Ruins is *ours,* our so-called vision! A vision to which you seem not, without reservation, to subscribe. Quel bore! Let's then, if we must, take a look at the stickier points bollixing up your expectations and—" Jones bent stiffly, snatched a handful of broken tarts and began to hurl them in small, calculated pieces, at the unblinking Toulouse, "*Your . . . good . . . faith!*" He spoke with undisguised ennui.

"*Primo.* The people you so obstinately refer to as 'customers' in your quaint, unimaginative way, are *not*. Not customers. And certainly not—as you now and then sanctimoniously proclaim—not 'guests'. Number two. Your so-called *co*-workers? You've mistaken them as well. Further evidence of that mawkish solicitude that earmarks the rank amateur. *Terzo.* Imagine what you will, Tom-

Tom, the blindingly bald fact is you haven't a shred of self-knowledge. Period. *Ultimamente.* Given all this, then what—and we can only shudder to think—can you have arrived at regarding *us?* Some kind of 'boss', is that it? Is it? *Bawz!"* Jones glared at Tom, dropped his jaw and bleated like a lamb, *"ba-aw-awz!";* raised one eyebrow and sniffed. "Gawd!"

Tom, bewildered, his concentration beginning to bob, was yet again taken aback by Jones's next pronouncement which, for all its sour and mincing overtones, made an unexpected, if grudging appeal to his own more delicate sensibilities.

"What you must *get* and endeavor to hold firmly in your homespun, workaday paw, is that we at the Ruins— that means yourself, Dame Cynthia Tilt, that tubercular bum that stokes the furnace, you're getting this?—are simply One Big Family." He stopped, seemed glum, and peered at Tom, wiggling his fingers squeamishly in the air between them. "I suppose you had some sort of family before you, egh, fetched up here?"

Tom blushed and bit his lip, remembering for the first time since he'd arrived his beloved, misspent Rose: her round, fair, yet easily flushed face; round russet eyes, like two sunburned apples; winsome nostrils; chapped cameo lips (that irresistible overbite!); and those lively looping copper curls, in which one might espy (as one's fancy betokened) a thread of Spanish gold, of saffron, of flax. "And la," he recalled abruptly, "the poor belly, too! Pop-eyed! Rounder and rounder . . ." His heart beat anxious wings at the thought of her flagrant, inexpungable girth. Darling Rose! His little red hen! His lucky chestnut! His—

"Well just forget about them," Jones's voice cut in, "—whoever they were. Snip! snip! and the past is past. You have a new family now. *Period.* Still with us? In short, not a *riz-drah-uhn* . . ." he dangled the word disdainfully like a shot 'possum by its tail, "but in fact the best of all *homes,* and those of us here your *real* family—second to none. Fabulous, yes or no? *Merde!*" Jones's face closed up in a cautious, inclement fist. He sneezed (Tom felt an errant drop strike impersonally against his cheek), held a finger to each nostril and sniffed with languid puissance, then went on.

"Now then, like every ménage, we have our own special, *unspoken* little rules and what-not. Yaazzss, many, *many* little ways and what-nots. Naturally! This is the highest of households, *ne plus ultra!* Now, while some of these unspoken little what-nots may seem, to the outsider, obscure—*you* might say improvident—they're each of them, without exception, indispensible to the ball of wax. *Your* problem, Tom, is that you don't know the rules! Am I right? Don't speak! Let's take an example. Let's take, in fact, a particularly *dreary* example. Go ahead, you choose it."

Tom, who was still nowhere up to speed, tugged at an opportune cowlick. He simply had no idea what Jones was getting at.

"Uhm, well . . . I guess I'm not quite following you?"

"An *example*, for god's sake! *A fucking case in point!*" Jones's heels gnashed the floor like vehement molars. "Really, Tom, you're beginning to try our patience! No doubt you have *names* for these obstinate sticks up your tender, tiresome ass. Tell you what! If you can't remember 'em, just reach back, yank one out, and tell us what it says. For *gawd's* sake!"

Tom's ears burned and a woeful lump formed in his chest, crept into his throat and took unavailing refuge behind his already cowering larynx (a reluctant soldier at best, and notably unequal to the situation at hand). To think he'd imagined Jones harbored anything like a soft spot for him! *Obstinate sticks?*

Jones leaned coyly over the desk, chiding Tom with bland, buttery bonhomie.

"Just kidding, Tom-Tom! We forget you're new here, the 'baby' of the family, eh? Following our analogy! Now, nothing to be afraid of! Simply tell us one thing that's been troubling you, one thing you feel, oh, gets in the way, makes life *seem hard,* hmmm? Just any little thing."

Tom shifted in feeble resentment, still smarting from the sting of Jones's previous lashes.

"Okay, um, well I guess you could say the menu thing has been bothering me. You know, how the menu changes every night? But for some reason no one ever gets around to printing up new ones? Okay, sure, sometimes there's one or two, but other times—not one single menu!" Tom shook his head incredulously, and began, despite his initial doubts, to warm to his topic.

"You can't imagine how annoying that gets—and, gee, inconvenient! Now I've asked the office to *please* make sure and have them ready *before* we open, right? But I don't know, it's like they don't hear me or something, *or just don't care*. Which, come to think of it, is what *really* gets—"

Jones cut in brusquely. "*The menu thing*. Perfect. This is precisely what we're getting at. *Gawd.*" He paused, then leaned on both elbows and aimed a finger at Tom in dour contention.

"Ask yourself this, Tom. *Would* you—and in your own home!—hand out menus to your *family?*" He nodded significantly. "Go ahead, think it over. It won't be easy for someone of your, egh, resources."

Young Tom (but what did Jones mean: *resources?*) was clearly in the hot seat; his response was exploratory.

"Well, I mean . . . no! My *family*, you're asking me? N-no, I shouldn't think—"

"*Correctamundo.* Menu schmenu! What's good enough for family is *perfect* here. Get the picture? *Say* you do."

Tom frowned. The fact was, he *didn't* get it. The idea didn't really hold water, because—well, because . . .

"But these people!" he finally objected. "They're *not*, well, they're *not all the same*. They don't—they *expect*, I think—to be treated, well . . . *differently*. I—"

"Differently!" Jones marveled. "Say, don't pull your punches!" Rising, he began to wander the room, constellating the blue and gold Qum silk rug with the finally

94

irreclaimable remnants of his squandered luncheon. "It's
rather more complicated, more *insidious*, than that." He
stopped before a wall display of priceless Sèvres china, in
the center of which a life-sized bas-relief wolf disembow-
eled a wild-eyed ewe. "Tell us Tom, are you familiar with
the seven so-called 'deadly' sins?"

9—

Tom perked up and, sure of himself for once, responded
with imprudent bravado. "You bet! Pride, lechery, envy,
anger, covetousness, gluttony, and uh, sloth . . . that's
them."

"*You bet!*" Jones's voice mimicked Tom's with careless
derision. "*That's them! Ugh. That's them all right. The
trouble is, you swaggering little choirboy, the list is in-
complete—a ludicrous oversight—but do you think a
person could get anything changed in this world? Say
what you will, if we ran things our way . . ." Jones seemed
to drift, then spun on his heel. Arms pressed tightly over
his belly, he leaned toward Tom, his outlandish voice
ripped by urgency and what struck our hero's astonished
ears as genuine grief.

"Of all the evils and errors practiced by man, Tom, the
worst—*the very worst*—is ingratitude! Ingratitude and
ambition. Never forget! There are no human failings
more regrettable than these!"

Tom felt, and could not prevent, a rush of blood suf-
fuse his cheeks; there *was*, in fact, a distinct sob in Jones's

voice. Throwing himself into a brocade chair by the fire, Jones closed his eyes and folded his hands on his pot, elbows winging.

"The world," he lamented, "is not what it once was. No! And we gravely lament its decline. It's a fact that the primary agent of moral decay is, without contest, the almighty buck. Are you with us, so far? Mammon has evermore buttered the pans of illicit, unsavory pies." He sighed.

"Oh, it wasn't so bad when the shekels stayed tight in the hands of the dissolute few—one *knew* them. Popes, princes, now and then a smart whore. But the problem these days is that *everyone* has it. Chiropractors! TV hosts! Those weird kids in software? Republican *petite-noblesse* . . . And *why* they must bring their insensible bellies here . . . they don't know Spode from a hubcap. And cognac? They'll sip—if you *watch*—but they'd rather have beer.

"Well excuse me? It's tired-making! *We* know they're faking." Jones opened one eye, skewering Tom with his glance. "*Climbers* is all that they are, get the picture? Ungrateful, ambitious—*and* half of them queer."

Tom himself felt increasingly unfit, and reeled in his chair like a pie-eyed tailor. Jones's short, powerful index finger poked absently into the depths of a potted amaryllis, scattering crumbs of soil across the inlaid table, as he continued.

"Let's face it, your 'average man' is, by nature, a more or less spineless, sniveling lout. Weak-willed, hairsplitting. Not ashamed to tip his hat, lick your boots, or bug-ger his (obliging!) mother for the favor of a musty bun. You may have noticed. These make up the hoi polloi, 'the blunt monster with uncounted heads, the still-discordant wavering multitude.' *Gawd!"* Jones jerked his chin. "*That* one certainly knew his onions.

"*Bellies,* Tom. That's all they are, all they'll ever be! World without end, amen. *Just bellies.* Think about it."

Tom might have, but for the scarcely muffled, lugubrious sob that rose, immediately, from the region of his own belly. Jones, gazing into the flames, twirled his dirtied finger knowingly, dismissively.

"You too, of course. Don't try to hide it. It's written all over your face. *Belly.*" He glanced over one shoulder. "Why, what's the matter, Tom-Tom? You're looking very *withered prune.* Too graphic? For an old guttersnipe like you?"

"The *point* being that *given* the bun (or more likely having wrestled it from someone else), even an uncounted head might show a little gratitude, as would befit a strictly unmerited advantage. As it happens, this is rarely the case. While the bellies that *have-not* pull strings, drop names, and machinate, the bellies that *have* bite the hand that bestowed the bun. Climbers and ingrates, is what it amounts to. The only thing that differentiates them is what side of the table they're fated to work—server, or served. In the end, of course, it's all one trough." He paused.

"Now listen Tom, there are precisely two ways of combating the blunt monster: Law, and the Big Stick.

The first method is arguably proper to civilized men.
After all, a well-rendered law represents the *imminence* of
force, which is in general immeasurably more versatile
than the clumsy stick itself, more incisive, more—*gawd!*"
He paused to cast a cold, furious eye in the direction of
Toulouse, just awake and laboring immodestly at his
post-slumber ablutions.

"Fegh! Mankind is, as we've just agreed, inconstant,
and will succumb at once to the blandishments of cruelty,
luxury—ambition and ingratitude!—and every other sin
of expedience. They're almost never good voluntarily, oh
no, but must be *made* good by the threat of force,
poverty, shame—and by their own fear, in the absence of
which men submit to evil *tout de suite.*"

"But surely," Tom finally managed to speak, "one
can . . . can put oneself in another's place! And by so
doing—"

"You, Tom, are *delirious.* Don't speak! Simply shoo
that idea back beneath whatever rock you found it. Once
and for all, men do not choose to 'be good,' they choose
to be *fed.*"

"But virtue is teachable, isn't it? Men are morally, uh,
educable?"

"As a dog who learns to walk on its hind legs! As a rat
who, through a maze, sniffs out the cheese! The law, understand, merely serves as a corrective bit in men's
mouths."

"And if . . ." Tom could not help himself, "if the laws
themselves are bad?"

Jones heaved himself out of the chair (upsetting the potted plant in the process), and crossed to the daybed. Arms akimbo, he stood over the immersed pooch who, tongue toiling at his private parts, managed to roll one bleary eye up to meet his master's. Jones spoke to Tom, but his thoughts seemed to be closing in on something else.

"What *is* it with you and this 'bad-good' thing? Bad, good, right, wrong! Get this straight, little bean-counter: *all things of this world must remain true to the principles governing them at their inception. Ergo* men, who are born into sin, are not only more intelligible as a species, but really most comfortable with *themselves* with that provision kept firmly in mind. Besides, who are you to challenge tried-and-true principles?" Jones turned abruptly and went back to sit behind his desk.

"Anyway, we're not talking philosophy here, we're talking about how not to run a *riz-drah-uhn*. Now then, as to your perfectly cynical request, last week, for a 'coat check'—"

"But, but . . . isn't it possible to—to rule by . . . love?"

Tom by this time hadn't an inkling as to what they were talking about, and hardly knew himself what he meant by *love*.

"That is to say, well, must fear and fear alone be what makes men . . . behave?"

At this, to our hero's great surprise, Jones's face changed; a kind of resignation softened it to near ap-

proachability; and Tom's own fisted belly relaxed the tini-
est bit, untucking its nose from beneath its turned tail,
upper lip quivering indecisively.

"Love! Gawd yes! One would know you'd bring up
that old saw." Shoulders sagging (weary? Tom wondered), Jones nevertheless managed a schoolboy's flip-
pant simper and teased his sagging tenor up an octave.

"Is it better to be loved or feared? Well strictly off the
record, in our opinion that dull hash will never be settled.
Too many variables. We therefore suggest a more practical question: is it more *reliable* to be loved or feared?
Don't strain yourself, boy wonder! The answer, take it
from us, is *feared.* Less equivocal, less vulnerable to appeal. Results, Tom, are the bottom line here. And what
are we asking for, anyway? Obedience, a little respect . . .
this is the fatherland nest. Don't speak!"

10—

The telephone rang as, with one hand, Jones drew a tiny,
nickel-plated revolver from the disorder of his desk, took
unhurried aim, and fired three shots in quick succession
at the preoccupied Staffordshire. With his other hand he
lifted the receiver.

Tom (staggered by the gun's sudden appearance, he'd
immediately covered his eyes with both hands) heard the
shots, the single, astonished yelp. If he'd felt insubstantial
before, he was now in danger of completely slithering,

like an unoccupied set of clothes, down the front of his chair. Folding at the waist, he dropped his forehead to his knees.

"We're talking," Jones had insisted, *"about how not to run a restaurant."* So be it, but did he mean how *not* to run a restaurant? Or how not to run a *restaurant?*

Tom couldn't say, wouldn't dare. Indeed his heart (everlastingly abashed) hid its face at the memory of that private, princely, uncompromising optimism with which he'd assumed custody of the Ruins. Sure, he'd set his cap, and who wouldn't! A green lad's untarnished, inaugural conceit . . . He was tireless in his efforts not merely to fit in (which seemed the right approach), but likewise to impart the sort of dispassionate moral rectitude he'd felt incumbent upon someone in his position. And still, at the first signs of trouble, he'd played a modest hand. Drafting deceptively casual reports (together with elegant, inarguable reforms!), he'd recently impressed this notebook upon Ugo, and hoped, naturally, it was to discuss these ideas that Jones had summoned him this deadly, unforetellable afternoon.

Fair hope, your goose is cooked!

Three brisk bullets and this, *this* is what it had come to, no more: tough love, family values, and a dog bleeding to death on the daybed!

Jones's voice, all curdled milk and venom, ate a crooked path through Tom's thoughts. "Yazzss, yazzss

. . . whatever you want! Have we ever failed you?" He made disagreeable faces at the receiver—*yazzss*—then, bored, jerked the cord from the wall, dropped the whole apparatus down among the ravaged tarts, and turned once more to Tom, still jackknifed across his own checkered lap.

"Now, for the most part the system works. There is, however, as you yourself brought up with strictly witless foresight, this pesky . . . Oh for gawd's sake! You, Tom! What kind of insolence do you call that? Sit up this instant! *Gawd*. You have all the grit of a sick kitten!"

Tom forced himself into an upright position, his fingers leaving red marks where they'd pressed into his cheeks. And the gun? No sign of it. Hmmm, perhaps he'd been overreacting; could he have imagined the three neat bullets, the bodiless yelp? Blood throbbed behind his eyes, then *whoosh!* Ugh. People worked too hard; hysterics were the natural result. All the same, he didn't dare look over his shoulder. *Woo.* Sit up this instant! Well, perhaps there was something to be gained from this interview yet. Jones glared from the end of a long, dim, fuzzy tunnel, and Tom peered back: skeptical, rather nauseous. He groaned, shook his head, grinned sickishly. "Umm . . . I—excuse me?"

Jones closed his eyes, lips pursed in a tight, trembling bud, then burst out, "Just who the hell do they think they are, anyway? *Gawd! Gawd!* Ingrates! Know-it-alls! *Poseurs!*"

He bent awkwardly, picked up the telephone and—
with a weak overhand and a stertorous grunt—sent it ca-
reering, the receiver looping crazily at the end of its
springy cord, into the wall of hand-painted Sèvres. La!
The strident, discontinuous clamor of tumbling plates—
one discharging the other; their rollicking encounter
with a third, and so on—seemed briefly to appease and
unite, in some unspoken, unaccountable way, the two attentive bystanders. It was, Tom allowed, a surprisingly
agreeable sound.

As though reading his mind, Jones winked. "Divine,
isn't it? They simply don't make china like that anymore." He rummaged impatiently among the papers on
his desk. "*Yazzss*. The so-called gastronomical Elect!
Haw! Who sit at their tables, indifferent as oysters in an
oyster bed. What *they* do not know is that for wanting
too much, indiscriminately, they will find themselves in
the end with nothing at all. *We* are here to guarantee
that. Ah . . ."

He turned, one arm held stiffly away from his body,
and from the uncharitable pincer of thumb and forefinger dangled a slender, sky-blue notebook. "Lately
brought to our attention: *Policy and Procedures at the
Ruins*. Gawd! A list of strictly criminal bushwah. Don't
kid yourself, Tom . . ." Jones moved to a candelabra. One
by one he ripped each tidy page from its binding and
toasted it over the circlet of flames; then—as quickly as it
darkened, blazed—tossed each one aside to flare wistfully, and expire. In the end, he nudged one toe through

the scant gray ash. "Constructive criticism? *Anathema*. Don't let it happen again."

Our hero watched with groggy fascination as page after page of his lovingly composed report went fluttering to the floor on scorched, smoking wings. Would Jones *never* stop talking? Tom fought against a desire to close his eyes while Jones's voice tumbled like coarse grit in his ears, finally diminishing to an aberrant buzz, a dull fly sluggishly circling the room. ("Cheese parings and penny wisdom? *No* one gets out of here without dessert! Is that clear? If they order one, bring them *two*, and . . .") His head lolled against the back of his chair; he felt as though he were drowning—no, falling! *Falling!* ("Forget what you know! *Fat of the land,* try that on for . . .") His arms and legs began to prickle. It was pleasant, at first— and then not so pleasant. Forget what you know? *("Sauce is everything . . .")*

Alas, when our hapless lad shifts in his seat, the prickles in his arms and legs—lulled to a blunt tingle, a moment before—flash suddenly to life with the exquisite fury of tiny daggers. Tom's eyes fly open as he yelps "Ow! Oh, no!"

WHAT WAS THAT, YOU INSUFFERABLE PUNK?!

Instantly Jones was before him, had seized the front of his shirt in one colossal fist, and was hoisting him effortlessly up out of his chair. "That word!" Jones hissed, with a flourish that rattled the tacks in the terrified lad's arms and legs, ". . . is *not* part of the vocabulary here!"

Abruptly, Jones dropped him (Tom clutched at the chair to prevent a nasty spill), and turned his attention to the daybed where stout Toulouse indeed lay motionless in a sordid puddle of blood. Jones poked speculatively at the burst brown sausage, then reached down, lifted the dog by its scruff and turned back to Tom, eyebrows lifted in polite inquiry.

"We trust this has been a helpful chat? Not a *riz-drah-uhn* at all, is it? Gawd, the idea!" Jones crossed the room, Toulouse held absently before him like a cat put out with the milk, an exiguous trickle of gore scarcely defacing the blue and gold fantasia of the rug.

At the swinging door leading to the kitchen Jones paused, turned, lips puckered in labored vexation. "Now *will* you get this mess cleaned up? The Fel Belcombes— *him*, not *her*—claim, with perfectly savage insolence, to have scheduled a private party for this room. Liars! They'll be here in thirty minutes, with goodness knows how many mangy little parasites in tow. And *what*, pray tell, we'll feed them . . ." Tom heard a horrified gasp— *Toulouse!*—as the door swung-to behind Jones's broad, impassive back.

11—

Head shaking in wordless denial, our hero stood on weak, trembling legs. He took unvarnished stock of the wrack and squalor of smashed tarts, scorned ashes, and unspeakable carnage still roiling in the wake of Jones's stunning passage . . . and with a sigh began, mechanically, to tidy up.

Then stops, his thin wrists dangling like bell clappers in their starched cuffs. He stops! His cupped ears flush a shade of astonished pink. What *is* it?

Stiffly, self-consciously, Tom edges toward the standing french doors that frame the vacant dining Salon where plush, melon-green drapes are half-drawn, chandeliers dimmed to an erubescent glow. A final beam of afternoon light strays across the room, pensive as a young girl with downcast, calculating eyes (coyly fingering the cambered backs of diligently sucked spoons, the spent petals of exquisitely panting lilies, the overwrought knobs of polished grates and memorialized marble pates). A dozen camellia trees press against the walls like tall, bedazzled debutantes at their first ball; and at either end of the room each beckoning hearth's aflutter with canary and finch-yellow flames. Sure, the rugs were strictly lousy—claret-stippled, unkempt. But Tom himself had placed every chair round every table, *just so,* the taut silk of each upholstered seat suavely kissing the hem of a table's chaste, maidenly skirt. On each table the pouting lower lip of a single rose was blushingly proffered; and everywhere the air, lissome and honeycombed with light, sighed and stood and stretched itself with the warm, alluring curves of radiantly inspired flesh. *Well?*

Something trembled oh so feebly in Tom's agitated breast. A discrete spark? A diffident glimmer of . . . what?

Disaffection? Revolt? (Well, revolt *is* perhaps too muscular a word for what our hero experienced.) What, then? What?

Tom straightened, planted both fists atop his hips, and *tsk'd* out loud (his belly, suspicious, pricking one ear).

Why, this was no fatherland nest!

In the heat of the moment, Jones *could* certainly queer up a fellow's thinking. But in fact it was a miracle the Ruins (a priceless pearl! *ne plus ultra!*) had survived that madman's vision thus far. Did Tom exaggerate? Ha! Daily there were rumors of flagrant licensing violations, condemnatory health inspectors, puveyors storming the door. Jones flatly would *not* have a financial consultant, but ran through a brisk and illimitable series of junior accountants (each, by some remarkable coincidence, named Lou). Revenue officials leveled fine after fine— OK! His bristling creditors called him Mr. Johns, Jobes, or Joy. Jones never called them, and behaved with supreme indifference with regards to the manifold perils of his (as *they'd* say) "particulars."

He was blithe in general, as far as that went; and a day did not pass when the SS *Ruins* did not founder against some unforeseeable iceberg of Jones's creation. Something he'd *promised*—never intending to provide; something, as was often the case, more or less impossible to provide. (A certain poet laureate—dead, as it happened— for tea!) Tom negotiated each new provocation with tact and ingenuity, only thankful not to be squatting on a sidewalk in the rain. After all—

It could be worse!

But could it? The Ruins, Tom now realized, was in the hands of an extravagant, if charismatic, crackpot. Our hero trembled, dazzled by the new, illuminating secret in his heart: that for all Jones's peremptory huffing and puffing, it was actually he, Tom (the so-called *baby* of the family!) who really understood the place. So, it had only been a few weeks? Still, Tom was *sure* now that from the moment he was born (and indeed, perhaps before that!) the Ruins and he were conjoined in some unnamable, co-incident destiny. Dazed—at the portals of heaven, as it were—our dawdling hero gazed (rapt, reverent; and at last, he ventured to submit, *redeemable)* into the soulful, twilit interior of the unshuttered Salon. He felt, oh! He felt like, like . . .

Hmm, a champion? Sure, that's the idea! . . . After all, a guy had to draw the line somewhere. If he didn't go to bat for the Ruins, who would? Ugo? Ha ha! that slippery eel! . . . As for those others! . . . You had to admit, in a way Jones had hit the nail on the head when it came to human nature. Couldn't call this a trusty bunch . . . 'Mangy little para-sites,' hee hee!—not that they were all bad! Still . . . Time would tell! A champion was a champion!

When Tom's second waiter burst in loudly, his stun-ning blue eyes red-rimmed and laughing, lips poised to describe how he'd managed to arrive so late (again!), Tom waved him away with unprecedented insouciance, and with no further hesitation entered the Salon. (That Paulie! A regular wastrel whose wealthy mother had convinced Jones that all her boy needed was some "practical experience.")

Well, well, they'd see. A champion was a champion! Ruthlessly Tom inspected the tables, detailing a salad fork here, a salt cellar there, his blissful eye peeled to the arrant ways of water spots, tarnish, and lint. *Just so, just so.* By jove, how he admired—revered!—each and every detail, from the cunning brass key used to open the gas fires, to the imperial pink marble fountain plashing gravely at the center of the room. He *loved* the goldfish . . .

But a moment later, glancing from the Salon into the adjacent hall, Tom was arrested, as usual, by the fantastic and possibly vulgar taste displayed by a series of portraits lining those walls, each of which featured an animal whimsically portrayed in the trappings of upper crust society. There was a thin chinless zebra in top hat and tails; a dowager lobster in evening gown, lorgnette, and glittering tiara; an apoplectic bison at his cups; a frothy french poodle flaunting décolletage and an implausible pink bouffant . . . Tom found these caricatures facetious, even bizarre; and vowed, then and there, to have them removed—first thing!—after delivering the Ruins from Jones's lethal designs.

And just what did that mean, *deliver the Ruins?*

Tom took a deep breath, turned on his heel and walked straight into the indifferent withers of a mammoth hog. He clutched at his face (his *nose!* was it *bleeding?*), kicked furiously at the bronze trotter's cloven hooves and fumed. Alas, had that silly Ada's breathless disclosures only been confirmed with regards to this notorious titan: to an elephant Tom might have surrendered a place—but *this!* Not only did it loom, corpulent and vastly more complacent than any mere elephant; but it was daubed all over, rather farcically, in gold leaf, and moreover festooned with painted garlands of simpering wildflowers and glossily enticing fruits, with scurrying insects and pursuant, vaguely human-faced birds. An imperial lei of plump plaster sausages encircled its neck. Ingeniously designed, the razorback concealed a powerful motor, accessed through a hatch in its belly, which, when activated, empowered its enormous head to circle—eyes to roll, tail to corkscrew—round and round. Guests never failed to marvel at the leering colossus; the loud mechanical whine of its motor did not distract them in the least. Indeed there were any number of them who made a virtual ritual, each time they arrived, of sending Tom down among the pinched, grizzled teats to *plug 'er in* while they stood by snickering, or wagging their heads in besotted wonder.

The Pig, Tom instantly resolved, must go, along with the gallery of grotesques. A clean sweep was the thing—reforms! modern methods! Was this a place for lewdness, for capering beasts, for scandalous business practices, for dead dogs? The Ruins had promised him, from the first, his Big Chance. Now Tom vowed, with all the misdirected fervor and credulity of youth, to do everything in his power to defend that chance—to *save* the Ruins, and in so doing, *to save himself.*

CHAPTER FOUR

*In Which Tom Is Reacquainted with
Some Old Friends*

12—

Our hero took aim at his target anew, fired by the infatuation and zeal that spell success. It was not his job now, but his mission, his crusade, and like any fanatic he not only pledged himself, but labored frankly for the conversion of others. Mornings, polishing silver with his staff, he congratulated them generally, then spoke firmly, *very firmly,* of their obligations ("not a job at all, but a kind of *stewardship,* do you see?"), and of the opportunities he saw both to advance and exalt their lot.

"It's more than 'a place for everything and everything in its place,' though that would hardly go amiss, ha ha!" (Here the hoist of one studied brow and a wry, regretful nod.) "Kinks need ironing—well, I've got a slew of ideas on that score, let me assure you! But this is different, eh? It's got to do with—well, with *attitude,* and uh . . . *investment.* With an appreciation for—of the, um . . ."

Come to think of it, "attitude" wasn't what he meant at all. Indeed, Tom hardly knew himself what *precisely* he was getting at, and could only gesture vaguely at a nameless conviction that had overtaken his heart in those brief, invincible moments following his interview with Jones. *An air of . . . for the, uh—*

"Sublime?" Spoons and forks, murky with polish, hovered in midair while Tom, oblivious, continued to wrestle with his idea. "That might be it. *An air of the sublime.* Not just getting the job done, you see, but having the sense, no matter how apparently insignificant the task, that in fact . . . Look—" Tom leaned toward them over a clutter of smeared cutlery and they, poking one another self-importantly, leaned toward him. Tom spoke slowly, but with urgency. "This is our big chance. Without the Ruins people like us are, are . . . *without hope.* Do you know what I mean?" The bright encircling faces nodded, it seemed to Tom, with approval and encouragement. He nodded back, but wondered if he was making himself perfectly clear.

• • •

The next day he sought out Ugo.

"In fact, my friend, in fact! Tell them what you want from them—your prerogative, naturally. You must lay down the law."

They were standing in the Avocado Room, staring at a group of paintings from which one apparently was missing. Ugo speculated cheerfully.

"The question is—*the question is!*—who managed the heist? Paulie? No, hardly Paulie's style. Very delicate, very, hmm, yes . . . *delicate*." He glanced up at Tom, who couldn't honestly recall another painting there at all. "Fear not, my friend, you are above my suspicions. Still!" Ugo's brow arched with oriental precision. "Diplomacy, eh? Say, for example, Jones himself instigated the removal—to cover tonight's roast goose? Or our own humble salaries! In fact! Nothing new! A painting here, a case of cognac . . . What do we do? We close our eyes—half-close them!—and wait. We pretend not to notice. We play heads or tails with our paychecks. What else! In this case, we alter the grouping . . ." Ugo scampered up a stepladder, made a few adjustments in the arrangement of paintings, "—so! Business as usual! The painting is forgotten!"

Shocked, Tom burst out angrily. "But, but that's *exactly* what I wanted to talk to you about!"

Ugo looked down on him coolly. "Yes? A confession! *You* took the painting?"

"What? No! Of course not—"

"You know who did?"

"No, no—that's not what I mean at all! I don't know anything about the painting. I'm just saying, I mean—well, your attitude! But *attitude* is not . . . Oh! this is just the problem I was having before!" And Tom went on to describe his conversations with the staff, ending with: "I only want it understood that this is more . . . more than just a job! I myself feel—that is, pledge to *protect* the

Ruins from . . . from whatever might harm it," he finished weakly.

Ugo toyed with the point of his elaborately waxed beard. "Yes, well! Of course my friend, your commitment is clear. Commendable! And—in strict confidence, you understand—long overdue here." He shook his head meaningfully and repeated, "*Long overdue.*"

Tom was taken aback by Ugo's candid admission. "Well, thank you . . . that is, yes. I hope you know you can trust me, that I would never let, um, let you down . . ."

"*The Ruins,* let down the *Ruins!*"

"Well yes! Exactly—"

"For what, but the Ruins, do we toil? Eh, my friend?"

"Yes, yes, that's it exactly!"

"All one in one great concern! That's it?"

"Why Ugo, you understand *exactly.* Oh, you can't imagine how important this is to me—to all of us, I mean—I mean, to the *Ruins,* as you said . . ."

"*You* said! No need to 'imagine.' Behold your radiant face! Your, well, shall we call it *an air of the sublime?*"

"*Yes!* That's exactly what I'm trying to get across! *An air of the sublime.* If we all join together—"

"But every ship has just one helm? In fact! You take my meaning? Less a matter of seniority or rank than initiative. Inspiration! In short, my friend, how *very* welcome you are. But now, a little surprise! You'll see I've not been blind to your Augean labors. Come—"

Ugo hopped from the rung of his ladder and our hero, elated, intent on his own thoughts, followed him in the direction of the Maisonette. All down the bustling utility hall, the people they met—secretaries, dishwashers, laundry maids, electricians—greeted Tom enthusiastically, making big eyes and whispering in his ear.

"When the time comes, Tom . . ."

"—count on me!"

"We rely on you, Tom, *a thousand percent!*"

Tom, flattered by their sudden and vehement endorsement, smiled and touched his cap, not entirely persuaded by the display. *Could* he count on them? Even Ugo, even Conchita, seemed, well, "unpredictable." Try telling him it wasn't hard work understanding these people! He bit his lip, pushing past a small Filipino woman who clung to his arm, grinning and shaking her hips. Ugo waited at the door of the Maisonette. "After you, my friend . . ."

But—good heavens! What was this?

13—

A glad cry—a resentful grunt—and at once a slight young girl rose from a chair before the hearth, spilling Toulouse from her disorderly skirts.

Toulouse! but he—?

Tom stared. It was . . . was that *Ada?* He glanced uneasily at her feet, but the white patent leather boots were gone. Atop her cloudy head sat a hat with a scrap of veil.

"Ada?"

"That's right! Tom, it's me! Aren't you surprised? In fact, *I* can hardly believe I'm here—here! *The Ruins!*"

Tom glanced at Ugo, who immediately bowed—once for Ada; again, with an impudent wink, at Tom. "Miss Ada, Tom. Already acquainted? Very good, very good! Then I'll be off! One thing, Tom—*I have the utmost confidence in you.* Miss Ada, welcome! Tom will see to you now—can't go wrong if you follow his lead. In fact!" And, almost skipping, Ugo was gone.

Tom and Ada watched him leave, then turned to one another, Ada beaming as usual. The fact is, their original meeting at the Groaning Board now struck Tom as having happened in another life, to another person, even. He was terribly taken aback.

"You, you're . . . how are you?"

Ada continued to smile, glanced at the floor and then, timidly, all around her, taking in the clever, if slightly grotesque, antler chandelier—the leopard skin hearth-rug—the ebony inlaid side tables. She was clearly transported; her ivory skin glowed, her soft, ashen hair roiled about her head like smoke. "Jeez," she whispered, her round eyes shining, "it's really something, isn't it?"

At this Tom softened, if only slightly. He played no small part in the spectacle, after all, and struggled against an impulse to boast.

"Of course, silly. It's the Ruins, what do you expect?"

Ada, emboldened, now focused directly on him. She took in his spotless white tunic with the narrow black sleeves, the strict crease of his black-and-white checkered trousers, the jaunty black cap with its patent leather brim and stiff white band—and came at last to his hands, from which all traces of shoe polish had been erased.

"You're looking awfully well. Handsome—don't blush! My goodness, it's there for anyone to see! I'd say you've really found yourself, just as you dreamed. I'm so pleased for you, Tom." She paused, then sighed with pleasure. "And now I'm here too! Jeez, I can hardly believe it . . . like a fairy tale!"

"What," Tom asked uncertainly, "—what exactly are you doing here, Ada?"

She looked at him curiously, then burst out laughing. "What am I doing? What am I doing? You dope, I've come here to *work*, of course—just like you! After that night, you know, when we met, things just got harder and harder. Or maybe it was only me that changed. Oh, it got to be I couldn't stand the food, couldn't stand the customers, couldn't stand anything—you know? And I kept remembering that night, how *you* just . . . I don't know, just decided what you wanted—then went off to get it! It was so splendid and brave, well, I decided I couldn't live with myself if I didn't do the same. So," she flung out her arms, taking in the whole of her surroundings, ". . . here I am!" When Tom said nothing, only pushing carefully with his toe at a piece of lint, she innocently asked, "But aren't you glad to see me?"

Tom cleared his throat, shrugged, nodded feebly. The truth is, he really didn't know if Ada's presence here was what he'd call a *good idea*. Not that he wasn't happy to see her! Ada was a sweet girl, good-natured and kind, with a blithe smile and a willing nature—sure, he was glad to see her. It was just that, right now, things seemed so, well, *delicate*, here at the Ruins. Tom himself did not know exactly what he meant by "delicate"; but there was a feeling in the air, an indescribable "something" in the way people looked at him lately, that made him feel a very important thing could happen at any moment. Important for the Ruins and important for himself. It made him nervous and exultant at the same time—and he was determined to go through with it, no matter what.

Now Ada showed up. Which wasn't a bad thing necessarily, only . . . he hadn't expected it. And there was something about this girl that made him—oh, he didn't know. A little soft? That is to say, perhaps, a little "too nice." Naturally he wanted to be *nice*, but he had come to realize that his position at the Ruins was not always about being nice. Sometimes you had to be a little hard; sometimes you had to be a little demanding. He wasn't sure a girl like Ada would understand a thing like that.

"Are you . . . working in the laundry, then?" he asked hopefully.

"No! Can you believe it? The Salon, just like that! I told them I'd had some experience—of course, in a different sort of place altogether. But Mr. Jones and Mr. Ugo didn't mind that at all. Mr. Jones asked did I have any lip rouge, and Mr. Ugo said *that's that!* Then Mr.

Jones said for somebody to find *Tom,* and I thought to myself, I wonder if that's *my* Tom—I mean, you know, the Tom I met . . . that is to say, *you."* Ada frowned at her feet, rubbing the palms of her hands together dryly. "And in you walked." One last time she poked her arms out in either direction, but without conviction, eyes still fixed upon her feet. "And here we are!"

Tom, nodding his head throughout Ada's long explanation, went on nodding, paying no attention. So Ada had been placed in the dining room, under his supervision, without even consulting him? *Was he the maître d' or not!* And what did that *mean,* anyway? Half the time nothing—zilch! Except that *he* was the accountable one, *he* took up the slack, *he* went the extra mile. That was all right. But when would it mean *respect?* When would it mean having a say-so in how things were done around here?

Tom clucked impatiently and sat down on the daybed, fingertips pressed to his brow. Really, this was the last straw. Ada sat beside him, a little furrow shadowing the bridge between her round black eyes.

"But Tom, look at you! I should have guessed! Still working too hard—and not taking care of yourself! True? And why haven't they been feeding you, I'd like to know? A place like this! It's a crime! Why, you'll be down with the anemics! Now you just sit right here and I'll run find you something cozy to put in that ol' tummy—"

At this our hero was surprised by a feeble spasm somewhere in his middle, followed by a weak, scarcely audible whine—and Tom suddenly realized weeks had passed since he'd paid any attention to his stomach.

How's that?

After all, he was surrounded by food, the best! Why, he flourished plates and flaunted platters and paraded dessert carts all day long; flung the remains into plastic garbage sacks that by night's end were too heavy with T-bones and broiled endive and pigeon mousse for one person to tote alone. Everywhere he turned there was *food*. So how did it happen he never ate?

It wasn't as though they weren't allowed. Mitzi herself insisted that everyone eat and eat well, and would herself prepare little "specialties" for the dishwasher's toddling daughter or the arthritic milkman. Somehow, though, Tom never seemed to make it to the kitchen for his meal. There was always someone's pampered mutt to be escorted to the alley, or that dreadful Pig to plug in . . . yes, always something! His nice plate would sit on some counter, or be stuck in an oven to stay warm; and hours later Tom would find it beneath a pile of dirty napkins, or cooked to an inedible string. He would quietly empty it into a garbage pail and satisfy himself with a cold roll and, if he was lucky, a puddle of clotted sauce to mop it in. By the end of the day he was tired enough not to care, anyway.

Now Tom wondered what ever happened to that "snarling, darling mascot" that once kept him such ungracious company—and wasn't sure he was glad to feel it lurching to its feet once again. There was another, unequivocal whine, and the querulous scrabble of dull, familiar claws. Tom grabbed Ada's wrist to prevent her from jumping up.

"No! I mean—don't worry, don't bother. It's . . . I was just thinking, that's all. Of course I'm eating! Just . . . just sit for a minute. I need to tell you—that is, to give you an idea of how things work around here."

Ada briskly tossed her head. "Sure, sure. Sorry, Tom! Got a little ahead of myself, didn't I?" She paused, then added in a quick, quiet voice, "I just want to say, Tom, I couldn't be happier it's you. It's no mystery to me why you're in charge, and I intend to make you proud and happy to have me as your waitress—and, and your friend, as well . . ."

Tom stared at Ada, not really hearing her, wondering how to explain just what was at stake. "Ada—" he interrupted. "Ada, I think you need to understand that the Ruins is, well, a very special place . . . that is, uh—uh, *not* the Groaning Board," he finished lamely.

Ada, chewing her lip intently, now laughed. "My goodness, I'd hardly be here right now if I didn't know the difference, now would I?" She shook her head at him fondly. "And wasn't it me who told *you* that, Tom?"

Tom nodded. "Yes, well, I guess. But I'm not sure . . . I'm not sure you really get the picture." He scowled, frustrated by his own efforts. "Why, I'm only beginning to understand, myself! And I guess you'd allow I might have more of a handle on this than you, Ada! Or would you?"

She was startled by his tone, and immediately concil-iatory. "Why, Tom, of course you'd know *heaps* more than I! That's . . . that's why you're in charge . . . jeez, that's the last thing I'd want to question!"

Tom, still peevish, drew back from Ada's earnest face. "Oh? And what would be the *first* thing you'd like to question?"

Ada was growing confused. "What? What question?"

"You just mentioned *questioning*. I was simply asking what exactly you thought you might be *questioning*— let's see, not twenty minutes into your job?"

"Oh." Ada, in dismay, looked about the room for help. "I guess I just meant, I don't know, like where the creamers are kept, or . . . or what—for instance, how to light the chandeliers . . . That sort of thing." Something was wrong! Once again she stared at the carpet; small swallowing noises came from her slowly flushing throat.

Tom softened, cleared his own throat to gently sum-mon Ada's attention, and patted her red, wringing hands. "Of course, of course," he murmured. "Forgive me, Ada, for being so . . . protective. I've gotten awfully fond of this place, and at times I'm—ha ha!—well, convinced that I alone understand its needs. Matter of fact—be-tween you and me!—lately it's seemed to me that the Ruins is, well, let's not say *in peril,* that's perhaps too strong . . . but certainly crying out for more responsible leadership, that is . . ." Tom broke. "Oh, you can't imag-ine, not you or anybody!"

He stopped, rolled his shoulders, and continued: "I myself am only beginning to appreciate the extent to which the Ruins is, despite the, ah, best intentions, sustaining the most *frightful abuses.*"

Ada was shocked. Abuses? "But, but—"

Tom interrupted. "Now Ada, you've got to trust me on this. The Ruins is not all that it seems. There are certain, shall we say, *inconsistencies* . . . Believe me, I wish it weren't so, but—" he shrugged.

"But Tom," Ada glanced round the room. "It seems such a paradise!"

Ha! Tom also looked, with a deft, skeptical eye. Didn't he know what lay behind the illusion! How *about* that gnu-antlered *corona lucis,* blandly hanging by a thread over the hamstrung spinnet? Priceless tapestries held together with tiny aluminum staples? (The Sèvres table service diminished on a weekly basis!) He shook his head sadly.

"At such a cost, Ada, at such a cost . . ."

Ada was baffled, yet moved, by Tom's obvious suffering. "Why, I had no idea, Tom. What do you . . . what can I do to—to help?"

Tom looked at Ada now: the glistening black eyes, the fantastically sharp nose, the edges of her soft, childlike lips bruised violet as a hyacinth. He steeled himself. After all, it was not for his own sake, but for the sake of the Ruins (and consequently for the sake of everyone here) that he simply *must* take a firmer hold upon the, uh, helm. There was something at stake here! (And if he couldn't say precisely what that "something" was, surely that too would be revealed in good time?) He spoke judiciously.

"Yes, well, help *is* needed, Ada. Help is certainly needed. At the same time, there is the question of authority, that is to say *command* and—naturally enough!—*consent*. See what I'm getting at? So . . . well, think of it this way. Who's in command here?"

"Well, that would be Mr. Jones, it's his—"

"It *isn't* his!" Tom nearly pinched her in exasperation. "That is, Mr. Jones *is* the proprietor—but that's not what we mean, is it Ada? Look, think of it as a *line* of command. Is that any clearer? Now! Who's in command?"

Ada was beginning to resent this harangue. Really, she didn't recall Tom being such a pushy boy. On the contrary, he seemed gentle and humble and principled and kind—jeez, but wasn't he bullying her now! And patronizing? Her spine stiffened.

"Line of command," she repeated sulkily, "Well, I suppose you're the supervisor . . ."

"That's it, Ada! Now you're getting the picture! *I'm* in command of *you*—that's how it goes. Now I'm sure I don't have to tell you what that means, eh? Sharp girl like you. The thing is, this is a critical period for the Ruins. I've got to be able to count on you, on all my people, while things are, are developing." Tom caught his breath. "So, as I say, can I count on you? Oh! can I, Ada?"

The sudden entreaty in Tom's voice took Ada by surprise; his lukewarm reception and overbearing sermon had all but convinced the poor girl to throw up her new job and storm out—let him keep his precious "command"! But this final plea ("can I, Ada?") quivered in her ear with the old sweetness. She ran her hands (torn cuticles snagging the gold embroidered threads) over the gorgeous brocade on which they sat—snuck a glance at Tom. How tired he looked! And lonely? Her heart melted; she leaned forward to catch his eye; she took his hands.

"Shoot," she said gently, "what kind of a question is that? We're friends, aren't we? And this is our big chance! Don't you bet I'd do anything to make it work? Why—"

14—

Was that a commotion in the front hall? Ada, inured to all forms of pandemonium, continued blandly even as our hero jumped up to investigate. His hands were, however, still pressed between Ada's own, forcing him into a clumsy crouched position as she brought to a simmer the nourishing broth of her reassurance and affection.

"—there's no stopping us now! I'll work ever so hard, Tom, and you'll show me all I need to know, and exactly how things need to be! With hard work and dedication—"

Tom strained to see over his shoulder. While he hadn't the faintest idea *what,* he knew instinctively something momentous was going on out there—something that had everything to do with whatever was "next" for the Ruins, and for himself. He tugged at his trapped hands.

"Yes indeed, Ada—of course! But . . ."

"And Tom? And . . . listen Tom! We'll be friends, too, won't we? We'll help each other and, and everyone—like a family, almost! Oh I know that sounds a little chirpy, but jeez—"

Toulouse tore past them, *arf-arfing* grimly. There was an ominous hiss behind the kitchen door, followed by a brief, hollow explosion. "—the Tomster?" Tom heard his second waiter gush, "just *fabulous!*"

"Ada!" Tom tore free of Ada's fervent grip, "I've got to *go!*" He whirled to leave her and there, standing in the doorway, was the last thing he expected to see—a matchless pair of china blue eyes, and the helping hand for which he had been groping ineptly for weeks.

• • •

She was swathed in simply yards of magnificent blue tulle, from the pavonian turban exalting her broad, prominent brow . . . to the glamorous azure frock closely enveloping those surprisingly sturdy shoulders and hips . . . to the tips of her celebrated toes, just peeking from the hem of her gown and (but could it be? Tom stared) bewitching in the same glistening slippers she'd flourished that night at the Groaning Board.

"Say sweetie—"

Tom looked up, startled by the singer's sprightly drawl. Her eyes sparkled marvelously behind a translucent blue veil.

"Where do you suppose a girl might find something in the way of a cocktail? Quel parch! Well, children?"

Tom, too stunned to speak, turned to Ada, cleared his throat, and shook his head in amazement. La Stupenda, meanwhile, had swiveled into the room, the exquisite constriction of her hips, waist, and shoulders remarked by a malicious blue hiss (the provocative gossip of tulle on tulle). She stopped in front of Ada and with one fingertip lifted the girl's pale, pointed chin. "Assuming you're old enough to be working at all, honey, what say you run out to the bar and find this lady a refreshment? Hell, make it champagne." She glanced at Tom over one edenic blue shoulder. "Tom, *say* there's a decent bottle of bubbly in the house? It *is* Tom?"

Tom practically gasped. "*Yes!* I mean . . . yes, go ahead Ada."

"But Tom, I—"

"Ada, please, just—go on now. Someone will show you." Tom suddenly felt that if she did not leave the room *this instant* he would scream. Frowning, he jerked his head toward the dining room. "Go *on.*"

Ada looked from Tom to the singer and uncertainly back again. She stood up, smoothed her horrible skirt and bobbed her head at La Stupenda. "Very pleased to meet you, ma'am. I can't tell you how much I've—"

"A-*da!*"

Ada gaped at Tom, her black eyes ablaze with astonished tears, and scurried from the room. Tom looked down uneasily as she left.

"An attractive child. Close friend of yours?" La Stupenda scanned our hero's sheepish face. "*Hello?* I say sport—" Tom turned. Painstakingly reclined across the daybed, every heavenly fold in elaborate repose, La Stupenda raised an ancient ivory cigarette holder to her flawlessly polished lips, while the tip of one shoe described tantalizing circles, indicating a place for Tom at her feet.

Tom's response caught in his throat. "La, I think I may be needed in the Salon, Miss—"

La Stupenda inhaled with surprising violence, her elegant mouth set in a tense grimace as she remarked at the ceiling (through a lungful of smoke) "Such a lovely place, the Ruins . . ." Closing her eyes, she exhaled gustily, smoke billowing from both nostrils as well as from her slack, *glacé* lips. "But not for long, eh, if Jones has his way?"

Tom's stomach suddenly growled, and he blushed.

"Hungry?" She turned, and from beneath languorous, blue-varnished lids her unfathomable eyes took Tom in with lazy assiduity. "That's good. Hunger's a picnic when you know you'll be fed, don't you think?" She crooked one tulle-constrained leg at the knee, drew it up tight along the opposite shin, then straightened it again. Then drew it up . . . Tom heard the covert *whisshht* as it rose . . . then down: *whisshht*. He could not help but ogle this sinuous blue convulsion, which came and went, again and again, like waves . . . wave after wave . . . the hiss of blue water as it raced toward him, as it collapsed upon his naked feet, then receded . . . gathered to meet him again—his toes curling in anticipation! . . . *Whisshht, whi*—

"Tom?"

The blue swathed leg went still.

Tom shivered slightly. His eyes moved to La Stupenda's, and he gulped. She studied him leisurely, clicking the butt of the cigarette holder casually against one shining, exposed canine tooth. With each *tap* Tom's craven belly dropped lower, lower, lower onto its quivering haunches.

"It was me that gave him the idea of a dinner club, did you know? A place where, at midnight, one could come for bacon-lettuce-and-tomato sandwiches before the fire, and a decent glass of champagne."

(She said to-*mah*-to, Tom noted, and resolved, in the future, to do the same.)

"But Jones has his limits. Sensational in many ways, but a strict materialist—no *vision*. You, on the other hand . . ." She shook her head. "Well heaven knows, a well-fed man's hardly the equal of a hungry one! Tell you a secret, Thomas, and don't you forget it. *All* tables are bargaining tables, no matter which side you're—" With a final, breathtaking *whissht* La Stupenda swung both legs to the floor and rose from the daybed. "Jones darling!" she exclaimed, flung her arms open wide, then collapsed again upon the heap of pillows, her midnight lashes fluttering dryly. "—you *dog* . . ."

Tom spun around as Jones entered, grumbling. "Nibbling at the staff again, darling? You're so democratic in your appetite—makes our taste buds curl. *Tom-Tom*—"

"Don't bother, pet, I've ordered cham—"

"Martinis!"

Tom ventured an inquiring glance at the prostrate diva, who grimaced and mouthed *champagne* with comic desperation, her hands beseeching. He ducked his head to hide an admiring grin and turned to go, Jones crashing into a chair behind him.

"Waalll, old girl, and how's business? . . ."

•   •   •

Our hero was, we may as well admit, almost painfully excited. What a day! Was he or wasn't he beginning to get through? People believed in him! Not just *people*, either—La Stupenda herself! Who'd hinted at vision and took a dim view, herself, of Jones's limitations.

Idly stirring the gin and vermouth, Tom's gaze wandered from the utility bar to the warm green-and-black striped wall where the unrecallable painting had gone missing. He clicked his tongue. Typical! The place reinvented itself hourly! One day princely Russian side chairs line the Cloud Room walls—the next day the place is full of folding camp stools, dressed up in pillows and cheap gold paint. The menu features pink singing scallops for a week—and not once during the week are the scallops pink *or* singing. (Tom's sure it was a hoax.) On some level, he fumed, this *was* a restaurant!

Lowering two fat olives into the martinis with care, Tom admired the limpid viscosity they lent to the clear alcohol. He placed a bottle of champagne, as well, in the center of a plastic bucket (he *hated* these cheap, imitation monstrosities!), bedded it in ice and took two flutes from the upper shelf of the cabinet. Hmm, chipped. He drew two others, also chipped. Tom's eyes squeezed together tightly. Was there nothing not flawed, rigged, faithless here? All right, he knew from the start it wouldn't be easy (he'd not gotten that coat-check out of his system yet). But surely there were concerns of a higher order still? Heavens, any goomba could draw up shift rotations and decant claret. True, his martinis were superlative; but what were a few drops of vermouth and a stuffed olive compared, say, to—

"For gawd's sake, Tom!" Jones jerked the tray from his hands and was already removing the ice bucket, the flutes. "How long does it take to throw together a couple of martoonis? Really! La Stupenda's about as punctual as a cat, herself, but she does expect to be treated like a queen." Jones stopped suddenly and fixed Tom with a look of suspicion and disdain. His voice sizzled. *"And why not?* Who are you, after all, to be wasting her time, lost in some unsavory personal trance? Is that why we hired you?" He pushed Tom out of the way, spitting beneath his breath. "We expected much more from you, Tom."

Tom's heart galloped unevenly, while his breath exploded in short furious blasts—Jones had *surprised* him, that's all! He moved to put away the gin with shaking hands, then stopped.

We expected much more from you Tom!

So Jones, too, expected things from him? Well, that made it unanimous, didn't it? Tom forced a ghastly, determined grin and lifted the unstoppered bottle to his lips—gagged—but tipped the bottle again, and now the hooch went down smoothly enough. He wiped his mouth on his sleeve; with labored bravado tossed an olive in the air—and would have caught it in his mouth on the way down, but glanced involuntarily over his shoulder.

Olives were a no-no.

So, for that matter, was drinking on the job.

Well, he needed it, didn't he? He had a bottle—that is, a battle!—*ahead; one sure to demand all his crumbling . . . uh, cunning!*

Tom tittered.

The bird flies to the huntsman, he assured himself—then briefly, involuntarily bared his teeth.

Again and again and again.

CHAPTER FIVE

A Real Mob Scene

15—

"Hmmph!"

Tom tugged wrathfully at his cap, folded both arms across his narrow chest and stalked through the swarming Cloud Room, cutting stern, accusing glances left and right. Indeed, it seemed that everyone had heard about the unscheduled meeting—

Everyone but yours truly!

As you like, but Tom knew the score:

> The Maître d'hôtel of a Modern Restaurant or a
> Great Private Concern Today
> Must Be Thoroughly Familiar with All Details,
> both Culinary and Administrative,
> in All Departments of the Establishment.

Yes or no?
Hunh? Bunch of yahoos—left me in the dish scull'!

Tom knew well enough how to butt and burrow his way through a crowd, and eventually found a place on one side of the lavishly decorated bandstand from which Jones had already commenced the proceedings. And what proceedings! Distracted by a profusion of brightly painted placards, fluttering streamers and slender girls dressed in brief white tunics (complemented by beautifully tasseled gold belts), Tom paid scant attention to Jones's introductory gush.

"Halloo, halloo . . . *gawd,* what a crush! Do you really all work here? No wonder we're broke, haw! You there! Find a seat, let's get this show on the road! SIT DOWN BACK THERE! Gawd!" Jones shifted his weight onto one muscular hip and gazed at the ceiling with an air of conspicuous forbearance.

Can you beat that? A real mouth artist! Tom smirked—then spied, on a raised platform left of Jones, the arresting profile of La Stupenda. *Whoah!*

Since their brief meeting the week before she'd been frequently in his thoughts, infusing them with an ebullient if uneasy sense of provisional bliss. Impressed, as always, by her original ensemble—a stunning aquamarine caftan affair with a stiffly embroidered Chinese collar and long, flowing sleeves that concealed her hands clear to their sparkling ruby fingertips, plus a tapering violet scarf with threads of gold that encircled her head twice, its long fringes trailing snakily down her short, sturdy back—Tom's choler was tempered, for a moment, by the puppy crush of unqualified worship. As though he'd called her by name, the singer turned and gazed directly at him, her astral glance dynamite even at that distance.

By jove! She was a peach, all right! But what must she be thinking of me? The maître d'! Whose place was surely not here among these half-trained monkeys but right up there on the stage, bringing authority to bear on the matters at hand. Well, but naturally I'd been left in the dark, not even a—

"*Yasszz,* well, no doubt you're all wondering what in heaven's name ol' Daddy Jones has got up his sleeve this time." Snickers and dubious grins. "Primo, let's take just a moment to greet one another's smiling faces. Go on . . . Go *on!*" Heads ducked in embarrassment while sidelong glances slipped from the corners of shrewd, speculative eyes. Richard the cook threw back her head, snorting with exasperation. Ada, still rather new to the staff, nodded eagerly in all directions. Conchita examined her nails.

"Isn't that nice?—that's *much* better. Nothing like family, we always say. Yes or no? *Gawd!*" Jones, peering from beneath the visor of one upraised hand, waved vaguely at a stray child, crying for its mother. "Damn it, Ugo, get that rotten apple out, *out!* We simply won't tolerate that sort, not *now.* All right . . ."

As though on cue, the bare-limbed, flexible girls (who until then had been moving slowly and artfully about the stage, stopping here and there to affect postures of wonder, gravity, and delight) slipped their arms around one another's waists and drew together in a semicircle behind Jones, who himself raised both arms in the air, flung out his chest and screeched, "Now listen, you lowbrow bedlamites! In two weeks the Ruins kicks off the most ambitious event in its already fourteen-carat history. A gen-u-ine Saturnalia! The biggest blowout this place has ever seen! Our first annual *Spring Frolic!*"

Tom blinked, banked an anxious glance from Conchita—who'd taken out a little steel file and was making rapid adjustments to the nails of her left hand—to Ugo, whose blandly narrowed eyes betrayed nothing. Behind Jones, the line-up of girls began to rock back and forth with small swaying movements of their crisply pleated hips and pink dimpled knees.

"We're pulling out *all* the stops, they won't know what hit 'em! A real razzle-dazzle of events capped off by a glamorous Fool's Ball—they'll *love* it! Yes or no?"

The crowd—who'd been biting their thumbs in an excess of suspense—burst obligingly into furious applause, squeals of relief and incredulous guffaws. The swaying girls squeezed one another's waists and smiled dreamily. Jones flapped his hands and for once could not be heard above the ensuing commotion; he seemed obscurely gratified as caps and flour-clouded aprons went hurtling into the desperately tinkling chandeliers. People danced on teetering chairs, whistled through rigid fingers, and thumped one another. With a groan, Tom folded his arms and dropped his head against the edge of the stage, staggered by the news.

A what? A Frolic? Wasn't that the limit! Why not a county fair with a watermelon-eating contest as well? And who would be accountable for this three-ring circus? One guess? That's right! Good ol' Tom. (Yes, Tom-Tom, if you like!) Oh that Jones, he couldn't have picked a worse time . . .

The fact is, since Tom's conversation with La Stupenda he'd been positively itching to launch a clean reformatory sweep—a new drill, A to Z! Unfortunately not even Ada would lend herself wholeheartedly to Tom's passionate agenda. Come to think of it, Ada was occasionally downright *critical* of his proposals. Sure, she refrained from challenging Tom directly—

Well! But it was clear enough from her silence and from a certain flutter at the base of her throat—doggone if I didn't know all right!

Tom, for his part, could not help but feel offended and vaguely betrayed; this introduced a grim and diffident starch to their relations.

"Thomas . . ."

Our hero, consumed by his own dismal reckonings, only shook his head. Couldn't those knuckleheads leave him alone for a minute?

"Thomas!"

Scowling, Tom looked up; directly his eyes were met by two dazzling blue orbs, imperative, inescapable, signaling him from the other side of the stage.

Strange, the voice seemed so near.

Nevertheless it was La Stupenda, and none other, who'd summoned him. In his dim, seldom-visited subconscious, Tom found the diva adorable; full tilt, however, she paralyzed him. Indeed he liked her best as he had first seen her: blithe and inscrutable among the hokey lights and pink, acrid smoke of the Groaning Board. His chagrin notwithstanding, Tom made his way around to the other side of the stage, climbed a narrow flight of steps, bowed shyly and inquired as to how he might be of service. La Stupenda responded with a benign twang (to which our hero, despite himself, thrilled like an adolescent girl).

"*Tho*-mas, so nice to see you again! Jones has brought the roof down, hasn't he? Be a duck and keep me company—heaven knows, he's quite capable of keeping this up all day! Come on, sit down and tell me every little thing. What's on your mind, *caro?*"

Tom crouched uneasily on the edge of a seat.

You-know-who not thirty feet away! Still, he swore to crack my head for saying no to a guest. Well criminy! What was on my mind?

Impelled by chronic frustration and unprecedented ire—alas, before he could catch himself—the strictly unspeakable came bursting from our hero's nervously writhing lips:

"*The man's a criminal!*" Instantly Tom's hand flew to his mouth and his eyes popped with horror. La Stupenda threw back her head and crowed.

"I *love* it! My dear Thomas, you couldn't have said a more interesting thing if I'd put the words into your mouth myself! *A criminal*—you're too much!"

Tom (who'd really no idea where the words had come from and was understandably terrified of further indiscretions), jumped to his feet. "I beg your pardon, my mind was on other things. Actually, I . . ."

"Not a chance! Sit down this instant—sit, sit, sit. *Sit!*"

Tom sat warily, but kept his hand before his mouth and resolved to say nothing more at all if he could help it.

God! How could I be so careless! An unprofessional slip, and with her, of all people!

"Now, suppose you tell me what you mean by *criminal . . .*" Her eyes teared; Tom flounced in his chair. "Whoah, now Thomas, I'm sincere, really I am! And you have my word of honor, this is strictly between us, cross my heart." She smiled. "The fact is, *caro,* I've taken rather an interest in you—don't look so surprised, it's a thing I do now and then. Position carries certain obligations, after all. You caught my eye from the first, and I've hoped for an opportunity to meet again. And so we have! You see? It's fate. Now then, tell me more about this marvelous theory of yours regarding Jones's—" she bit her lip, ". . . criminal nature."

Above the screen of his hand, Tom's eyes were those of a penitential setter; *inside,* La Stupenda's words skidded down his spine like an arsonist's match. Nonetheless, he was guarded in his reply.

"Well, maybe 'criminal' isn't quite what I meant? In fact, I'm not sure what I meant at all." He paused hopefully, but La Stupenda only *tsk'd*. "But gee, it's the truth! Well I, what I mean is—I mean, what I meant . . . *oh oh!*" And again Tom's tongue was possessed by a gang of wildcat, intractable words that busted right through his hot, clutching fingers: "*Oh! Well! He's nothing but a bat, isn't he? A squeaking mouse with wings!*"

Now he'd done it! Even La Stupenda's eyes widened with astonishment and she clamped the cigarette holder between her teeth, her nostrils flaring at the enormity of his act.

That did it! Gone too far! Where (oh, where!) were these declarations coming from? And why now? With her!

Tom wrung his hands, but the diva's voice, when she finally spoke, only shook with laughter and a not-unpardonable measure of tender ribbing. "Thomas—oh Thomas!—a truer tag was never given. *A bat!* I'll remember that for the rest of my days. Priceless—priceless! Really Thomas, you're exceeding my highest expectations. What could you possibly come up with next!"

(Don't ask!)

"—only before you kill me out outright, I'll just interject a few words. Not in the way of advice—let's say for your further consideration? For it's obvious that you, *caro mio*, have undertaken something of great import, and it's my personal desire to help you in any way I can. Will you please believe this is true, and listen to what I have to say in light of that pledge?"

Tom stared wordlessly into the singer's vertiginous eyes, doubting, hoping . . .

It was true, after all, I had undertaken something big. Just what she meant by "help," however, was unclear, mistakable.

And perhaps even repugnant to our hero, who by now subscribed to a notion of himself as a kind of knight, tireless in the exercise, against all odds, of his lofty, solitary office. Truth to tell, he'd only (and resentfully enough) contrived this fancy as a sop to his bruised ego, having failed in his attempts to organize any practical support among his staff.

Well, you know, it was wink-wink and nudge-nudge 'til the cows came home—laughing on the other sides of their faces!

But as for La Stupenda? Tom sighed; she seemed kind.

"Okay, well, I know he's, oh . . . hair-triggered, random—but he's not a *passionate* man, is he? Though you'd think so at first. Maybe that's what feels so . . . so *sinister* in the end. Why, you never know what he's up to! You never know what he wants! And he doesn't give a, well—" Tom lowered his voice. "He calls them *bellies*. Can you believe it? But then he'll turn around and act, oh, just pathetic, trying to impress people, getting in the way. And they laugh at him, I've heard them! Then you can't help but feel almost sorry . . . at the same time you know he must have *wanted* it that way. Honest," Tom shook his head in wonder, "when things are going well you can *see* it vexes him."

How many times had Tom heard over his shoulder that heartless taunt: "It's simply running too smoothly out there!" Bang-o, off he'd go, barreling his way like a bull on a lark through an already scarcely managed bedlam. Intercepting a *crème brulée* here, terrorizing a waiter there, demanding martinis, dragging guests off to visit the Pig just as their entrees arrived, then raving about the cold vegetables. (On the other hand, Jones himself would disguise bad food without blinking an eye. "More sauce!" he'd bellow, thrusting his head between the cooks' shoulders. "You're too stingy with the damned sauce!") He thought the staff dull and fawning, "a gang of obsequious toads"—then accused them, in the next breath, of *bloody insolence* and *a plague of barbaric strivings!*

As for the latter, it was Jones himself who knew best how to cultivate strife within the crew.

"J'accuse!" cried our hero (of course to himself).

You bet, j'accuse! Give me one good reason why not?

All mischief had vanished from La Stupenda's gaze. She puffed thoughtfully on her interminable cigarette, a fine line shadowing her brow. "Of course," she mused, "no one can accuse Jones of scruples. On the other hand, I happen to know he admits and furthermore relishes the divisions of good and evil."

Good and evil?

(Tom recalled a party at which several guests had been extolling the virtues of "scratching backs" and doing "good turns." Jones, sipping a martini, turned to him and drawled with peevish disdain, "Blah blah blah. Call that 'striking a balance'? Listen, the only practical and *proven* formula for so-called 'balance' is to return good with evil. That's *balance*. Good—*evil*. Good—*evil*. Doesn't that make more sense? Period!")

La Stupenda shook her head and aimed the stem of her cigarette holder at Tom. "Never fear, Thomas, authentic norms do exist. Jones *in particular* knows this." She chuckled, though Tom failed to see the humor. "Call him impulsive, an egoist, depraved—or a criminal, why not! But you cannot reproach him for disbelief, I think. Never that!"

Tom leaned forward, his hands gripping the edge of the table. "Well, if he knows the difference, then why *isn't* he good?"

"Apropos of that, young man—and neither paradox nor even real news—the gods did not create the universe, the universe created its gods, eh? Which is to say, if Jones is vindictive, scandalous, cruel, it's simply no more—*or less*—than what people require of him. If only to give vent, you understand, to their own cruelty, envy and greed. My goodness, *caro*, have *you* ever dished up a 'no' to that skunk?"

Defeated, Tom shook his head. "Then they—oh, *we*—are all corrupt."

La Stupenda clicked her tongue. "Don't be simple. It's a question of balance."

(Tom groaned.)

"For human beings, a bit of misbehavior feels . . . well, it *feels* better. Even the Hindu, an impeccable and almost insufferably upright people, leave one corner of their temples unfinished—they trust only the gods to make something perfect. Am I making any sense?"

Tom waved one hand, refusing to look at her. "You— you're a, uh . . . relativist!"

"What in the world!"

"—like *him*, an excuse-maker!"

"On the contrary, you presumptuous little blockhead, *I* am an *archhumanist*! *You*, on the other hand, are precisely the sort of green apple that prefers a comforting lie to the uncomfortable truth!"

(Tom's heard that before.)

They faced one another, wordless above the racket of the crowd below—La Stupenda's blue eyes glittering fiercely, cold and distant as planets; Tom angry, wounded, confused.

She called me a blockhead!

The singer drew violently on her cigarette, exhaled noisily, then relented. "Thomas, I—oh, forgive me. I swear I have nothing but your best interests at heart. But my-oh-my," she chuckled and gave Tom's nose a playful tap, "you do have a stubborn streak, don't you?" Tom only brushed miserably at the end of his nose, ". . . and serious, besides. That *is* too bad." She raised the palm of one hand, and covered her heart with the other, intoning *"Thy priests go forth at dawn, they wash their hearts with*

laughter. A hymn to the sun god Ra, lovely isn't it? I dare-
say your heart could do with a wash."

Our hero—folded up in his seat, his chin hovering
somewhere near his knees—could not bear even to look
at her.

She, she called me a blockhead . . .

(The "green apple" business was still unclear to him.)

—and dirty besides!

16—

With a mollifying sigh, La Stupenda drew one of Tom's
hot, twitching paws into her own firm grasp, and began,
with weary expertise, to coax the thin, frustrated fingers
to uncurl, the knuckles to relent, the childish fist to surrender its convulsive grip. "Poor Thomas," she murmured, "poor, incredulous Thomas. It must be very hard
for you."

Well . . .

Defenseless, forlorn (his inflamed nerves chastened
by the regular, tranquilizing rake of her ruby nails),
Tom's hostility sagged, strayed, 'til finally, with a
poignant sigh, his thoughts recalled that first worshipful
night standing all alone in the Ruins' divinely blue-lit
kitchen. So dreadfully hungry, so dreadfully tired, holding a piece of pilfered bread in his mouth. Heavenly as
a little cloud upon his tongue, it was, ingenuous as a
lamb . . .

Ah, that was nice, wasn't it?

Ordinary bread, to be sure, but *inviolable*. Safe, indeed, as a snow-white bunny, tucked in a little wire hutch 'neath a green and swaying apple tree . . . He thought of old-fashioned, jubilant roses—white petticoats, blowing kisses at the sun! And finally: the familiar crest and capitulation of rakish, blue-eyed waves, tumbling about his naked feet, withdrawing, then whoah! *Whisshht . . . whisshht . . . whisshht . . .*

Meanwhile La Stupenda hummed a brusque lullaby under her breath. Its dog-eared words Tom certainly knew (recieved, no doubt, from the lips of his otherwise dryly unrecallable mother), but forgotten 'til now, wooed by La Stupenda's gruff and scarcely audible crooning.

You have the devil underrated,
I cannot yet persuaded be
A fellow who is all behated
Must something be!

You will see your castles tumble,
Chariots split fore to aft,
You will hang from one foot, waiting—
He knows his craft!

Tom closed his eyes, weary to the very marrow of his wry and misbegotten bones, yet felt his spirits begin to rise.

Um, well, you know how it is! On your toes every minute. Hustle! Bustle!

The inescapable necessity of circumstances?

And hardly a second for catching one's breath, for think-
ing an idea through front to back! Well, you get the picture.
Fella gets out of touch, carried away. And isn't that me all
over?

Tom remembered, with sudden warmth, Ada's whole-
some tips: "A nice stroll by the river! Porridge with butter!" Well, was she right?

Aww . . .

(As a matter of fact Tom would not have refused a big
helping of porridge right that minute, all haloed in curling steam—a pat of sweet butter dissembling in
streams—and cream swimming in circles around the edge
of the bowl . . . He felt his belly shudder abruptly to life;
a delirious moan, a growl of pure, anticipatory bliss, rising decidedly up, up . . .)

"That's better, Thomas." La Stupenda gave his hand a
brisk solicitous pat and leaned back in her seat, replacing
the cigarette holder in her teeth and looking around with
lazy interest. An importunate mob had cropped up
around Jones; they stood on buckling chairs, bellowing *I
have an idea, I have an idea!*

"Up the *puppy brunch*, whaddaya say?"

"Let's do wienies!"

"Tango lessons, *oo-la-la! . . .*"

Distracted, Tom frowned; they must all sit down—this
was no way to conduct a meeting! Even Ada, he observed
with displeasure, encouraged a little toothless man in
overalls, nodding her head as he jabbered away in grave

and unintelligible ecstasy. Ugo and Paulie were of course nowhere to be seen.

Those two'll find a back door in the grave!

Tom made to stand, but La Stupenda, who was blithely enjoying the scene, waved him down with her cigarette.

"Relax *caro*, there's nothing you can do. They're excited, naturally, let them flap and squawk."

"Darned shame," he muttered. "Bunch of jumping jacks! You've no idea, it's impossible—"

"Now, now," La Stupenda tapped his hand with a lacquered nail. "Heads without tails die out quickly."

"Excuse me?"

She tried again. "No man's an island."

Hunh?

"Heavens! The point I am laboring to impress on you, Thomas, is that these people comprise, if you will, a kind of 'family'—"

Whaaaat?!

Alas, our hero's just-laid hackles rose once more. "Family! You're—you sound like him, like Jones! What is all this about family? This is *not* my family! That's just a thing to say—and anyway what about Jones? Isn't he part of the family? Well, you see how he treats people! Family!" Tom choked.

How could she? La Stupenda, after all! But supposing she, too, had fallen under the spell of that—that thug? This was the limit!

Bland in the face of Tom's glowering pout, the singer continued. "All right, whatever, *don't* think of them as family if it nettles you." She chuckled. "I must say I am surprised, however . . . *Jones*—it's not exactly in his line. So . . . ecumenical."

Tom groaned and morosely bared his teeth (a recently acquired tic he was finding increasingly difficult to control).

La Stupenda drew out, from the satiny vault of her aquamarine sleeve, a delicate silver compact. She pressed a glittering jewel, springing the top, and with a tiny, pearl-handled brush touched up her serenely puckered lips, glancing at Tom over the round mirror set in the compact's lid. "Well, my point—and you'd do well to give it some thought, Thomas, given your vow to redeem the Ruins—is that these people, call them family, call them what you will . . ." She blotted her lips with satisfaction, then snapped the compact shut. "What you must remember, *carissimo*, is that an empire cannot stand fair without recourse to a principle of sorts, any sort. An *altissimo Iddio*, is what I'm getting at. Even Jones worships at a sort of altar and is not in every respect corrupt." Tom shrugged impatiently.

I know, I know, an "air of the sublime."

La Stupenda searched his face with uncharacteristic urgency. Tom squirmed. Oh, he admired her all right—a real star, no end of style, a professional! But gee, he had his own ideas about how to get things done. Surely she didn't expect him to stand around while the Ruins went from bad to worse? He'd been a timid sister all his life, well, there came a time when a fellow had to stick his head inside the lion's mouth! Besides, it wasn't as though he went *looking* for trouble. The salvation of the Ruins was not his choice *but his Fate.*

And one can hardly wriggle out of Fate. But as for an alto, uh, simidi . . . oh, a principle!—well, that anyway was in the bag. An air of the sublime! What could be more, uh . . . iddio? Listen, you can always find someone to say X, Y or Z—but I say, just follow your star!

Tom sighed and peeked shyly at La Stupenda, regretting his crankiness. Gee, but she was swell to take such an interest! And in the end she'd admit he'd been right all along. Only *must* they quarrel?

"Are you, um, going to be performing here soon?" he ventured.

La Stupenda seemed to be thinking of something else, head tilted slightly, eyes staring vacantly into Tom's own. Tom nervously cleared his throat, fingers fluttering round the danger zone of his ticklish lips. But La Stupenda merely shifted in her seat and drew hard on her cigarette, a broken smile playing across her face. "What's that? Singing? Well, if you mean anything besides this so-called *Frolic*—"

"No! Say, is that so?" Tom perked up instantly. "Say, that's great! I've been wanting to catch your show, well, ever since . . . Ha ha! Remember the Groaning Board?"

"Thomas—"

"Fact is, that was a special night for me. And it's you I have to—"

"*Thomas.*"

"What I mean is—course, I'm terribly flattered, but really you needn't, that is, everything's under—"

"Thomas!"

The singer put her hand over Tom's mouth; he smelled violets and something else, something *scorched*— and then, oh, ugh! What's *that*? Ack!

He jerked away, repulsed and embarrassed. La Stupenda frowned, swiftly withdrew her hand into its sleeve, and sat back. "You're one of a kind, *caro*. But there's something I think you should know, something—"

"For *gawd's* sake—WHERE'S TOM!"

They both started at Jones's imperious bleat. Tom's hands drew into fists; the singer glanced at him sharply.

"Listen, *caro,* don't be a chump. It's not the way it looks. There are things you should be careful of, things . . ." She leaned, and Tom ducked to listen, but his straying forelock tickled her nose and threw her briefly off course.

"TOM-TOM! THIS INSTANT!"

Tom slammed both fists into the table and stood, baring his teeth.

That destroyer, that goat! Why I—

He covered his gaping mouth. Time would tell: a champion! But for now best to avoid calling attention to himself or his plans. *And trust no one!*

Down below the mob opened to reveal Jones at its center—feet planted wide, hand on one hip—training a thick and inescapable finger up at our seething hero. "Tom-Tom, quit conspiring with that devil and get *down* here where you belong!"

Tom turned to La Stupenda, bowed furiously, and descended into the hubbub of brawling desires.

CHAPTER SIX

Tango Romantico

17—

For two weeks following Jones's cavalier announcement, there was a dizzying, high-strung *hurry up* feeling in the air. It was a time of crass, unbridled brainstorms and calculated restraint; slavish yea-saying, exclamatory boosterism, and the swapping of gleeful, backhanded odds on the likelihood of Jones "really putting it over."

The opening event—a "fashion buffet"—was thrown together with breathtaking haste and virtually no promotion; alas the models (a squad of hysterically elongated, pancake-faced waifs) outnumbered those in attendance. A colossal table was laid, about the sagging edges of which the sprinkling of guests nibbled distractedly, rubbernecking the peevish designers and their gaunt, indifferent minions. Jones himself presided in the kitchen, mincing truffles, mayonnaising lobster, booting waiters out the door with tray after tray of steaming savories and teeth-numbing sweets, until Tom dared to wonder if there wasn't already more than enough.

"The fact is—they, um—well, they're not really eating all that much."

Jones's hands froze above a tiered imminence of rose water meringues he'd just erected upon a crystal serving dish. Tom cringed. "Well, models, you know . . ." he mumbled weakly.

Jones's voice curdled like vinegared cream: "Primo! Let me tell you in a friendly way that you're a regular May basket of puerile cynicisms. Secondly, you ought to be given a sound beating! Of course they're eating! They just spent two hours ogling a pack of lurid, herring-gutted females in fur pumps and plastic loincloths skitter up and down a runway. They're *eating,* all right—in witless defense of their own incriminating bulk—and your merely necessary duty is simply to deliver the goods. Now *is* that clear?"

Tom seized the pyramid of satiny meringues and sidled uneasily toward the door. "Oh! well, way way too much is never enough, eh? Ha-ha."

Jones's eyes withered to pinpoints and he curled one lip. "Your lack of vision boggles the mind. *Way way too much is only the beginning.*"

• • •

The following afternoon when Tom went to the kitchen to ask for the firing time on that evening's Imperial Mandarin Duck (mah-jongg to follow in the Avocado Room, all got up like a swaggering Canton whore), he found the well-heeled Mrs. Shad Frick.

Marla Frick was still youngish and *suffered* from food, batting about in a manifest anorexic frenzy. She had ten or twelve dogs, a bland husband and two small oscillatory kiddies on whom she kept apathetic tabs. She and Jones publicly doted on one another; privately Jones contrived, when she ventured to dine at the Ruins, that she gorge herself green. She maligned him behind his back. Now she stood before Mitzi, her long thin passionate face white with loathing, and moaned: "He's going to kill us, you know that? Tubs of butter! Buckets of cream! Why don't *you* do something? You're the chef, stand up to him! Why don't *you*—"

Tom inadvisedly muttered, "She's right . . ."

Mitzi—whose solicitous winks and matchless *sauce suprême* had proved a reliable antidote to the sour anxiety that cropped up in our hero's troublesome middle—studied a yard-long chocolate *roulé*. Skew-jawed, protruding eyes more froglike than ever (with a malignant shine Tom had never seen there before), she carefully selected a slender bright blade for despoiling the *roulé*—then spun and slashed at Tom. She *hissed*. Tom stumbled back against the cocked elbow of Richard the cook—just drawing a cloud-capped corn soufflé from the oven. Richard yelped; the soufflé shuddered and sank with a despairing little sigh; and Mitzi leveled the point of her knife over Tom's floundering Adam's apple. "*Everyone . . . OUT!*"

Marla Frick smirked as our hero, tears blinding his eyes, clapped one hand before his mouth and fled.

• • •

He found Ugo in the back storage room with a mess of Paulie's helpers, assembling provisions for a catered Confirmation. Tom stood against the wall as they hauled away a life-sized and casually bloodcurdling crucifix. "Make way!" Paulie crowed, "Make way for the groom!"

Tom edged to Ugo's side and was dismayed to find Conchita, too, perched on the splintering lip of a plywood utility shelf, trim calves swinging like brisk opposing pendulums over Ugo's bent and shining head.

"Tom," she growled accusingly, "I underztand you've been making time with La Ztupenda, no?" She flourished an invisible cigarette holder, bent to blow a hot, impudent stream of air into Tom's upturned face—then threw back her head, exulting. "*Mira!* He's blushing!"

Tom scowled. "Yes, well, very funny, *ha ha.*"

Ugo smiled benignly at Tom's discomfort. "No disrespect! No disrespect! Stress and pressure make for mischief. Conchita?"

Conchita thrust a venomous pink tongue at Ugo and pushed from her perch, her trim doll-like body skating mercilessly down Tom's thighs, her spiked pumps straddling his wing-tips when she hit. "Zat's right, Tom," she drawled, "*is juzzee prezzure,*" then swiveled out the door.

Tom, the hair on his legs standing up, stared moodily after her. Ugo poked the small of Tom's back. "Lady killer! Well?"

"Well," Tom replied, hesitating, "well, it's just this, this lame brain circus—"

"*Frolic.* Of course! What else?"

"It's gone too far—I'm not a magician!"

"What? Why, only yesterday you came to me yourself, blazing with the light of consecrated industry, chore lists atremble in your hands!"

"You're mocking me! Every time—"

"Not true! You misunderstand! My friend, you're too thin-skinned. In fact!"

Tom sulked. "You're not the only one under pressure . . ."

Ugo reached up and patted his shoulder. "Only so much a person can do!"

"As though there aren't more important things than blown fuses and butter curls—as though this were *my* idea . . ." Tom blew his breath out bleakly. "It's hopeless anyway, Jones controls everything."

"You're discouraged. Perhaps you exaggerate Jones's influence?"

"Exaggerate! I'm telling you, he won't give me an inch! I'm trying to light a *fire* under these people . . . Oh, they nod their heads. 'You bet, Tom! Right away!' They roll over when they see me coming—and laugh in their sleeves behind my back. And it's all Jones's fault. He *encourages* them."

"They're weak, Tom, only weak—"

"And you stick up for 'em! Next you'll be whitewashing Jones himself!"

"You have to admit—"

"Great! Perfect!" Tom shook off Ugo's consoling hand. "So that's how it is? OK! The fact is I don't need you anyway. All the same, things'll change! If I have to do *everything* myself, if I—"

"That's the spirit. We all expect great things from you!"

But Tom was already drifting away, his heart wrapped like a joyless fist round the stout brandished stick of his self-conviction.

• • •

"Well, jeez—so how ya doin', anyway?" Ada mumbled shyly as together, the next afternoon, they sorted through a bushel of assorted spoons. The question was rhetorical. She'd grown wary, if not cool, in her relations with Tom. Scrupulous in her duties; deferential to a fault; eager and incurably grateful for the chance to *do for others* . . . but pointedly professional in her exchanges with Tom. He in turn was rattled by her inexplicable formality. Just when he needed a pal, a real—whatchamacallit? *advocate*—here was Ada giving him the cold shoulder. Figured! Girls! But what'd she expect? Didn't he have a job to do? (*Thought he made that clear enough when she showed up! Anyway, never asked to be tagged after.*) Still, she was worth more than the rest of his staff put together—for all the irksome plucking of her *sympathetic chords.*

"Oh, there's nothing the matter with *me,*" Tom grumbled. "Fit as a fiddle! It's all a question of balance, you know."

Ada nodded. Her voice was wistful now, and a little coy. "Didja ever—ever get that walk by the river? The ducks, the daisies . . ."

Tom stared at her. *Again with the ducks?* He snorted violently and smacked the can of polish down hard against the table. "Perhaps you think this is all some sort of a joke? Is that it, Ada? Do you find me ridiculous?"

Ada gasped and fixed her round black eyes on Tom. For one terrified moment he thought he might rip out a handful or two of that cloudy hair. She started, seeing the tightness of his jaw, and the edges of his nostrils gone white. Immediately contrite, she brushed her knuckles across his trembling wrist; he jerked away as though burned. They stared at one another: she self-reproachful and secretly appalled; he gaping miserably. He turned away and muttered into one hand.

"Whoops—sorry about that! Li'l edgy, maybe? Matter of fact, I was thinking of something else. A stroll? Why not poetry too! Ha ha, just kidding! Busy, busy, busy . . ."

"Oh Tom," Spoon in hand, Ada automatically continued to rub, "*Are* you all right? It seems to me—"

Feeling something in his middle lurch, Tom instinctively grabbed for his belly—releasing his muzzle, alas, and a headlong pack of churlish words. "I *said* I was, didn't I? It's not *me* that has the problem, anyway. The problem is *you*, you and everyone else in this stupid place! Wasn't for all of you I'd *really* be swell, but as it is . . . *Picking posies?* How dare you! How dare you! Will I go to all this trouble and be mocked as well?"

Astonished and repelled by his own outburst, Tom swept the litter of silver to the floor and stood up. The thing inside him—the thing that bucked and hammered and threatened in some dreadful way to tear loose and plunge him into an uncontrollable spin—this thing seemed to hang by a thread, an overtaxed and raveling thread that would certainly, were Ada to utter *a single word more*, certainly give way! Ada's lips trembled, parted. Tom could practically see the words hatching inside her; saw them rise to her lips, her demure little chest lift and fall, and the muscles in her slender throat open, open . . . He backed away from the prospect of these words—feathers still damp, fluttering at him blindly—cruelly seeking that final thread by which the thing inside him might yet, oh, *yet be restrained!*

Tom yelped and fled before Ada could speak. Stumbling through a side door into the dish scull', he was immediately swallowed up by founts of seething, velutinous steam.

"Poor Tom," murmured Ada; and *poor Tom* again, as she bent to gather the scattered, shining spoons.

•   •   •

In the dish scull' Robert the busboy and Paulie jumped at Tom's sudden appearance. Robert snorted smoke into one cupped hand and cocked a sable brow at Paulie in wordless inquiry. Paulie winked and pulled deeply from a haggard fag before passing it back to Robert, then pounced at Tom.

"Behold the Tomster! What's cookin', old buddy? I tell you, this place is shakin' like a two-dollar joint, am I right, brother Ro?" Robert's gorgeous copper face crumpled in helpless agreement as Paulie linked his arm in Tom's and sidled up close.

"Needless to say, we're countin' on you for a shake-down. *I know you know I know* . . . Heh heh. Natives gettin' restless, though. I says *stay cool, that's the rule!* Brother Tom'll set things straight. But as my ol' lady used to holler, *if you're comin', come quick!* So, whaddaya say, are we backin' the right horse or what? . . ."

By tugging and tickling, Paulie steered Tom to the other end of the room where they stood among leaning towers of thirty-gallon stock kettles. Tom scowled at Paulie's fatuous grin and folded his arms sternly, his cheeks hectic from the steam and from the effort to collect himself. He said nothing for a moment, then bent abruptly at the waist, his voice a passionate croak. "*Listen*, you want fair and square? I'll tell you what's fair and square. *Sink or swim!* That's fair and square!"

Paulie shoved his hands into the air as though Tom had thrust a gun at him. "My man!"

162

"Get this: I'm *not* your man! How's that? I'm not your man, I'm not your brother and I'm certainly not your—your stupid *horse!* Why should I bear the burden for the rest of you? Every man for himself! All I asked for was a little cooperation. An appreciation, an *air,* that is, of—"

"Whoa right there, ol' buddy. They'll *abolish* you, think that's a joke? You made a *commitment.* Sink or swim? Now that just ain't *done.*"

"Is that right?"

"*Zackly* right."

"Well I'll tell you what, ol' buddy, *you just watch me!*" Tom pushed Paulie aside and strode toward the door. As his trembling hands fumbled with the rust-pocked bolt, Paulie's voice drawled out cheerfully behind him.

"Ain't that easy! Not in this rat's ass, it ain't!"

18—

Tom pulled over just inside the Cloud Room, propped his back against the pink silk wall and shook like autumn's last leaf. What was happening? First Mitzi—Ugo . . . Ada! And now Paulie. *La!* There was a lump in his throat like a desiccated walnut, blunt and bitter and unrelenting, and his knees stuck him bad for the first time in weeks. He skated down his spine to the parquetry floor, eased his skewed and checkered legs out before him, and pillowed his head sideways on a carved lavender pilaster. *What was happening?*

Thoughtful, Tom's eyes automatically roved about the exquisitely appointed Cloud Room. A dozen pairs of beveled glass doors ranged like wedding couples, framed by tall arched alcoves, the apex of each enclosing a larger-than-life, yet not unnaturally rendered, ornithological tableau. There's a pontifical red cardinal, leering from the branches of a well-hung peach tree; a swaggering blue stellar's jay, one eye peeled as he plunders the booty of a black-eyed cherry; a seigneurial humming bird, his avid needle buried—to the hilt!—in the ambrosial depths of a trembling young honeysuckle. One bloodless white parrot, disemboweling an orange. One (insufficiently) swift, its heart exploding in the dispassionate talons of a great horned owl. And a humble sparrow, hung by its neck on a dirty string, dangling from the branch of a winter birch.

Hmm. That sparrow, come to think of it—

He made a mental note to rearrange the chinoiserie bamboo armchairs in the loggia and have the petit-point cushions cleaned at the earliest possible opportunity. He reckoned the platinum silk-taffeta drapes might go another month, then wondered, with a tremendous wrench, what (if anything!) might survive the next few weeks' onslaught. Things were certainly going from bad to worse.

Is Your Tropical Paradise Gone to Seed?
Is Your Ivory Tower Besieged?
Has Your Affair with Life Lost Its Zing?

Tom's forlorn gape went unremarked in the empty Cloud Room. "Now more than ever," he mourned, "now more than ever." He closed his eyes and was within a heartbeat of forty invaluable winks when he became vaguely aware of broad, soft, whiskery lips nuzzling at his neck . . . warm velvety gusts of air . . . the sudden disposition of large and importunate teeth upon the patent leather brim of his cap? Tom's lazy peek was blown wide by the glare of the walleyed malevolent pony. Flailing at the gray, bullet-shaped head, he scrambled to his feet. "What! How! *Who let this pony out?*" he roared. The sly animal promptly reared on its corpulent hindquarters and Tom backed away, cowering behind a marble pedestal. "Hey now! Settle down, you, or I—or I . . . *help!*"

• • •

"All right," snarled Tom, his thin neck conspicuously flushed, a squall of petulant curls springing from his head. The lawless pony (captured at last after a memorable romp among the lacquered armchairs and agreeably windmilling arms of the thrilled and ineffectual personnel) was banished to the loading dock. Now Tom's staff stood in a circle, the obligatory remorse on their faces corrupted by illicit smiles and outright grins. "No laughing! You were *supposed* to be setting up for tonight's Tango Lessons. What's the big idea, turning that pony loose!"

"Exercise?" volunteered someone.

"Accident!"

"Wasn't us, Tom!"

(". . . 's he blaming us?")

"What makes you so sure, Tom?"

"Yes, what makes you so sure!"

Tom espied and snatched his cap from the untidy braids of a nearby laundry-maid; then fixed an outraged and accusing eye on Ada, standing wordlessly apart, her small solicitous face an unmistakable petition for clemency. He snorted.

"Ees'cuse mee, Tom," piped a young parking valet in back, ". . . for why you ask us? Ees you in charge here, no?" The crowd smirked encouragingly; the wag continued, "so ees *your* job. Thees caballito, why *you* no get heem under your thumb? Seems like," he suggested slyly, "ees the other way roun'. *Pobricito!* Wha' else you go turn' roun'?" A chorus of delighted yelps, which no one bothered to conceal (save "Rodrigo"—the abject dancing master with badly dyed black hair and plucked eyebrows—who doubled his hands over his sweatshirted belly to curb a self-conscious guffaw).

"See here, I don't know what you're talking about," Tom snapped. "And furthermore, if you've got a problem with the management, just come right out with it." He declaimed with an automatic lift of the chin, "Direct communication—" then stopped. "Say, just who are you, anyway? I don't think I've seen you around here before."

"Mee?" the boy's black eyes seemed to contract; one shoulder lifted in rhetorical regret. "I'm nobody, *capi-*

tano. Un mus—a leetle mouse, you say? *Eee, eee . . .* Jes' a leetle squeak behin' the cupboard door, no?" He hunched his slender shoulders and tucked two elegant brown paws beneath his chin, sudden whiskers glinting as he turned into the light. The others hooted in admiration, and in a twinkling everyone's paws were tucked up and dangling before starched white tunics and greasy T-shirts. Tom exclaimed, and there was an immediate dash in all directions, a riot of long tails flirting across the dance floor like whips.

Eee, eee, eee!

"Hey!" Tom protested. Doggone it, they were getting out of hand again! He watched, dismayed, as they scampered off in mock terror, squeaking and tittering and racing each other for hideouts. "Hey listen, we've got a job to do! C'mon you guys!" But they'd already disappeared, shivering with glee beneath low gilt stools and plushly padded benches, vanishing among the ruffles of satin-slipped pillows, invisible in the guttered shadows around the long, unlit loggia.

"He-y!" He begged this time, two irreducible syllables in which one could not but catch an ancient, universal plea for justice; an appeal not only to some higher, presumably sportsmanlike power, but to the more accountable sensibilities of the mice themselves. *Fair play!* he could as well have argued. In any case, there was no response, save a few cynical squeaks.

"Look," Tom offered next, "we've all, that is, of course I appreciate the, uh, *effort* everyone's put into this, this *Frolic*—but . . ." he took a few improvident steps in the direction of a teak and ivory tea trolley—

Eee! Eee!

Tom winced, fell away, and with slow appeasing movements of his arms and hands, cautiously addressed a stack of folding tables against the opposite wall. "The problem is, *it's not over yet!* OK? Just between you and me, I wish it were, ha ha! But really we're . . . we've got lots to do here—lots! All together! You're responsible too . . ."

"We're *mice!*" shrilled a nearby laundry cart, but when Tom bent to peer into the abyss of filthy linens, the entire room broke out in hysterical *eeks* and brusque, belligerent squeals. He stopped, repulsed, and slapped one hand against his brow.

"You're . . . I can't *believe* this! What do you expect me to do?"

A peal of silvery *tee hees*.

"Look," Tom tore off his cap and ran a hand through his wayward mop. "I promise, we can play later! Fun, whatever you want! But right now—you *know* we've got this tango thing! Can't we just, can't you just stop being, uh, mice?"

He then hastily seized and, as a demonstration of his need, flung some chairs into a sloppy circle around a nearby table. "No kidding! How about, you know, laying some silver? Sure! I'm—we'll get this thing licked! And the bar, somebody stock the bar. They'll be drinking like fish! And . . . oh! *please* come on, there's still a chance if we all pitch in together!" Tom turned to a portly crystal vase and plucked with nervous fingers at the haphazard arrangement of glowering red peonies, then whirled suddenly, a sagging, long-stemmed posy clenched in his teeth. "Any of you m-m-*mice!* . . . care to tango?"

At that moment Jones barreled into the vacant Cloud Room—he bawled: "For *gawd's* sake! *This takes the bloody cake!*"

La!

Tom's knees denounced him and he nearly buckled; the peony plunged from his teeth as he gasped, clutching the vase to his belly, "You . . . oh! you startled me! Egh, if you're looking for—"

"Looking for?" Jones loomed from across the room, threw both arms into the air, and leaned forward at the waist. *"What we're looking for, Mr. So-Called Maître d',* is some redeeming glimmer of intelligent life in that feeble bulb we mistook for a brain! *Gawd!*"

He stalked with monumental ire across the glossy floor; without warning, one meaty fist punched sideways, sending a white plastic bucket of cutlery crashing into an adjacent wall. In a flash he stood close beside Tom, mouthing the lad's ear like a microphone, long threads of saliva insinuating themselves between his red, infernally writhing lips and our cringing hero's waxen white whorls. "Get it, Tom-Tom? Coming in *loud and clear?*" His voice sawed back and forth across the bleeding stumps of Tom's ravaged nerves; his scalding breath smelled of dead cats and the fetid water in which flowers have been left to rot. *"LOUD AND CLEAR?"*

Tom dully perceived the indecent butt of Jones's vast belly against his own trembling arm: pushing, thrusting, pushing, thrusting! He clung to the vase.

"GET IT, GET IT?"

Alas, poor gull. His thoughts whirled in a rising spire; his sickened blood surged, then plummeted to his feet; a black and terrifying abyss rose before his eyes; his weeping ear boomed and throbbed. In the end his own hands, suddenly boneless as bread, betrayed him, lifting in cowardly supplication before the monstrous, the unimaginable *Bite* . . .

• • •

When Tom opened his eyes he was flat on his back, surrounded by mice. There was a great deal of cheerful *tsking* and a lively wringing of paws. "Go away," he grunted, and made to sit up.

"Tom," and here was Ada crouched by his side, pressing him gently into a litter of outraged peonies. "It's all right, you've only—better lie still, though. How d'you feel? Dizzy?"

Tom stared at a tumbler of water someone thrust at him and recalled the ghastly plunge of the vase from between his faithless, renunciatory palms. How it seemed not to fall so much as bluntly subtract itself from space; his hands meeting in a hollow clap—a pucker of air—then *nothing*.

He frowned at the glass, turned and demanded of Ada, "Where . . . where's Jones? What time is it?"

"Jeez, I don't know. Nearly seven? Mr. Jones—"

"Then there's barely an hour." Tom struggled to his feet, glancing at the circle of inquisitive faces around him. "And listen. I've definitely *had it to here* with you guys. I mean it! Anyone who wants to *play* better expect . . . expect a different game! G-g-*get it?* And where's that kid, that valet or whatever? . . . that ridiculous mouse!"

There was a swift, collective intake of air—Tom intercepted a villainous wink—and Ada laid a timid hand on his arm. "Tom, don't you think . . . are you sure you're all right?"

"Fine!" he snarled, still glaring at the others. "Leave a fellow in the lurch! Very amusing, I suppose, to some people! Well, now that you've all had your fun, maybe we could get a little work done!"

Ada's sharp nose had gone white with concern, her clear brow pursed in confusion. Behind Tom's back she nodded at the others, then herself bent to collect the long pointed shards of broken glass into a prudent pile.

Tom was surprised and somewhat pacified to see the others turn and go dutifully to work. In a few minutes the tables were up and set with heavy silver and tall beeswax pillars in iridescent glass chimneys. Fresh flowers appeared (a miracle in itself!): slender, unaffected freesia with long bent backs and a stupefying perfume. The puddled floor was firmly sopped and chairs arranged in sober lines down the pink moiré walls; precise circles round the stiffly skirted tables. Silver chaffing dishes whuffled softly along a decorous buffet laden with roast pheasant, dressed in its tail feathers; truffled quails *à la moelle*; a massive Rhine carp with apocalyptic eyes; wild figs and poached Italian pears; bowls of beaten, brandy-laced cream; a moat of multicolored sherbets surrounding a fantastic ice castle in whose frozen depths starfruit, passion flowers and opium poppies, hung suspended in a transparent, slightly fish-eyed dream. There were parfait glasses of black, unblinking caviar, and a veritable Matterhorn of Strasbourg pâté.

The rosewood floor, hand-buffed with an ancient chamois, was then dusted with tiny, pearlescent soap flakes to enhance its action. The chandeliers were dimmed, and Rodrigo—mercilessly squeezed into black spandex trousers and a beaded jacket; his unfortunate hair waxed to cruel perfection; the faintly pocked surface of his skin neutralized by thick bluish powder—waited in the center of the room. He'd drawn his inelegant spine disdainfully erect; one black-swathed knee rotated out and was meticulously bent; a lean spotlight came down like a lance over his far shoulder, throwing his ill-favored visage into menacing silhouette.

Ada (a dusky moth in ruffled black taffeta from which chiffon sleeves fluttered whitely, like wings) presided over the buffet; while a battalion of cooks and servers stood

merry-eyed and ready for action, the rich red blood
blooming zestily in their tender cheeks. The band filed in
as the clock struck eight, the little china cuckoo darting
in and out with melodious ease.

Tom stood behind the bar, a polished nickel cocktail
shaker in one hand, his relief and wonder at having
brought the thing off evident only in the few and forgiv-
able drops of perspiration making their invisible way
down the pale knobs of his spine. It was, considering
their inauspicious start, rather a triumph.

19—

Forty minutes later our hero stole yet another glance at
the smugly ticking clock, and for the second time sent
Paulie skipping out to confirm that the front door was indeed unlocked, and that the doorbell (in fact notoriously
fickle) was not playing tricks on them. Naturally there
was no malfunction, except that the *carillon*, once impelled by Paulie's zealous finger, now would not stop
ringing; and as the insistent, three-toned ding-dang-
dong! ding-dang-*dong!* sang out again and again, an-
nouncing no one, Tom felt his knees begin to sicken and
shake. He tried to catch Ada's comforting eye, but at that
moment Jones, arms flung emblematically wide, barged
obscenely into the room. Rodrigo started nervously from
his studied pose, the spotlight painting a lurid portrait of
his frivolous brows and ghastly, acne-scarred cheeks.

"Kept us tapping our toes, you crazy wracks! *Waal,* let the dancing begin! We—" Jones stopped, his arms falling to his sides, and looked about with scrupulous formality, inspecting the vacant, resplendent room, the expressionless musicians, the melting sherbet, and the crabbed form of the Tango Master, mincing backwards off the floor. He seemed to smile—at any rate his lower jaw shot forward, sheered harshly; and his next words, directed at no one in particular, came out in a half-strangled simulation of casual inquiry. "Anyone got the time?"

Cu-ckoo, cu-ckoo, cu-ckoo, cu-ckoo, cu-ckoo, cu-ckoo,
cu-ckoo, cu-ckoo, cu-ckoo!

Jones tipped his head sideways, closed his eyes, "Yaz-zss, thank you." Though his voice, like an old rope, twisted and kinked ever more tightly on itself, Jones stood nonetheless calmly enough in the center of the gleaming floor. "Next question—how our memory fails us!—at what time did we expect our company?" The musicians looked at each other and began to disassemble their instruments. Jones watched them with meticulous interest as he waited for a reply, finally prompting, "*Tom-Tom?*"

Tom burst out, "Oh! . . . cocktails and heavy app.s at eight; dancing at nine—"

"Eight o'clock you say?" Jones turned to face him.

"For cocktails . . ."

"And—our silly lapses!—*what* time is it now?" As he spoke Jones clasped his hands and took one coy, deferential step toward the bar.

Tom set down the cocktail shaker and stepped out, his own hands dropping grimly to his sides; Paulie sidled away. "I—it isn't . . . *Nine.*"

"Ah yes. Nine, *and* a little change, eh?" Jones took another step, laying one finger to the side of his nose and furrowing his brow. "And, dear me, just one more time. *When* did we expect—"

"Look—"

"*Yes*, Tom-Tom? There's something you'd like to say?" Now Jones extended both arms before him as he advanced, hands rotating on their wrists, inveigling Tom forward. "By all means, *don't hold back!*"

Tom took a step; the air between them crackled. It seemed, indeed, it seemed that—

Suddenly Ada dropped her utensils with a peculiar cry, a high, remonstrative whinny, which was immediately endorsed by an equally surprising and vigorous *Yoo hoo!* from somewhere among the opulent silver draperies. Instantly the band stabbed into the first bars of *Tango Piccolo Morto,* and a short, robust elderly woman with an improbable blond flip and an enormous overbite staggered at last into the Cloud Room.

"To hell with these curtains! Where's the dance!"

Jones (who'd stood to meet Tom's diffident charge with open arms and one leg crossed before the other) pivoted smartly and without missing a beat strode forward to welcome their huffing and violently disheveled guest.

"Waalll, look who's *herrre!* If it isn't Betty Garsin-Greer herself! *Love* your hair! Ready and rarin'? Of course you are, you're the belle of the ball!" Jones laid Mrs. Garsin-Greer's pudgy hand upon his pink velour sleeve and executed a vicious turn-step-dip-and-spin, rasping over his shoulder, "*Martinis, Tom-Tom!*"

Rodrigo, sidling out from behind a large ornamental palm, bisected the dance floor with furiously swiveling hips, one powdered hand dangling carelessly from the end of a glittering, outstretched arm. On the bandstand the cellist glowered, threw back her head and let her fingers snarl over the strings of her instrument. Ada collected her wits, found her tongs and with a brave smile resumed her post.

For a moment, Tom could not move. A long tremor went through him. *I . . . Jones! Why, we nearly!* He closed his eyes and returned to the bar. "Fresh ice," he muttered automatically; then wearily reached for the gin. The party commenced.

• • •

Betty Garsin-Greer simply could not fathom why no one else had come to take advantage of Jones's "Fun Idea."

"Why," she gasped, "those bloodless old sticks haven't any idea what they're missing! Just look at all this FUN FOOD! And that wonderful young man in the FUN COSTUME!" It was virtually impossible to understand her excited speech, hampered as it was not only by a magnificent overbite, but by her gallant and forthright attempts to subdue the by now rather irredeemable quail. "*Thtickths!*" she repeated—lurching for a depleted glass of caviar on its way to the kitchen.

Jones slouched beside her, propped on a fist planted smack between a bouquet of bristling cheese straws and the disconsolate carp. "*Yazzss . . .*" he replied. "Isn't it *too* fun!" The band played with matchless condescension, now led by a lean, porpoise-faced *accordianiste,* who tossed his shoulders seductively behind the back of his instrument. Jones sniffed, turned abruptly and inquired of the wheezing matron at his side, "Madam, will you tango?" As they sallied across the room to where the Master waited, Jones leaned over and confided gloomily, "It's fabulous, really, and so *de rigueur!*"

Mrs. Garsin-Greer, an easy foot shorter than the lofty and suddenly suave Rodrigo, proved a wonder on the dance floor. She trod as though in glass slippers; she turned on a dime; she kept her neck long and her elbows high. The Tango Master pouted hopefully. Really, the *señorita* was so promising! What a shame there weren't *three* students who with himself would form two ideal couples. *Perhaps?* . . . The corner of one mascaraed eye on Jones, Rodrigo gestured at the room. Betty Garsin-Greer, delighted and embarrassed by this praise, huffed and patted her do and flapped her hand at Jones.

"Go on, there must be someone who can come and dance. It's FUN," she announced, peering nearsightedly around her. "My goodness, there's no end of people just standing around!" Motor racing, she shoved naughtily at Jones's stomach. "Go on then. *Get someone!*"

Jones parried the woman's impetuous slap, wagged a stiff finger, then turned and dourly surveyed the room.

Our hero, observing this exchange, was frankly astonished by Jones's however graceless acquiescence; and more astonished still when Jones raised a hand and snapped his fingers at the buffet, whence Ada, innocently surrendering her tools, now hurried to see how she might be of service. "Impossible," Tom murmured; and Paulie, half-swacked by the numerous glasses of brandy he'd nipped in his function as bar-back, ground an elbow into his ribs.

"Jealous, *Tom-Tom?*" he squawked with boozy satisfaction. "Green-eyed so-and-so got you by the—" Goosing Tom, he jumped back giggling as Tom whirled and swatted his hand. "Oooh! Touched a nerve? Can't say I blame you. I mean, after all you've done for *him* . . . And now he throws you over for a mousy little nobody in big white sleeves?" Paulie shook his head, belched cheerfully. "It's tough, kid."

They paired up, Mrs. Garsin-Greer with the gloating Tango Master, Jones with Ada.

Jones with Ada!

The porpoise counted off two bars and they were off—over the growl of the *chitarra* and the excited protestations of the clarinet, Rodrigo's shrill voice exhorted his students, "Slow, slow, fast-fast, slow . . ." And while our hero's nerves coiled and smoked like snapped wires, the two couples swaggered up and down the dance floor, spines rigid, feet shadowing one another like thieves. *Inexcusable! Ada! A table servant!*

It was wicked, Tom felt, to persecute Ada this way. Look how she blushed! and stumbled! and struggled to meet Jones's eye. Jones who refused to look at her at all; who glared contemptuously over the top of her dizzily whipping head. *Next thing he'll put her on stage to, to . . .*

Do something shameless?

Rodrigo flung Betty over one disdainful arm, jerked her upright and executed a savage quarter-turn, hurtling himself and his partner straight at the bar, Jones and Ada smoldering in his wake. Our hero's throat tightened and a fine sweat filmed his upper lip. He could hear Paulie laughing hysterically behind him and knew he was alone (with no idea what to do!), only sure, from the slow sick rising pressure in his belly that *something must be done!* He stepped blindly from behind the bar to meet the advancing couples. The clarinetist's eyes began to roll with premonitory alarm.

Two feet in front of Tom the music reared, staggered, and fell to its knees but for a single, deliriously prolonged *tremolando*. The first couple screamed to a halt. "Really FUN," gasped Mrs. Garsin-Greer, supine over the Tango Master's peremptory arm, as he sneered and with his free hand pulled a thin black cigarette from his breast pocket, lighting it on a match struck against the powder-caked stubble on his chin.

The clarinet's A clawed its way to B-flat, to B, to sharping C . . . Jones bore down on the bar, his gaze, like a lightning bolt, impaling Tom on the spot. *Snap, crack!* Ada flipped right, rolled left, was spun like a top, Jones cutting in to catch her by the waist and drape her, defiantly, practically in Tom's lap. It was this spectacle of Ada's upside-down face—the normally reassuring smile overturned, the round eyes oddly flattened, her hair drifting to the floor (the slender rubber-tipped pins falling soundlessly around it)—that appalled and finally galvanized Tom.

As though she were a puppet, a doll!

The clarinet player was by now standing on his chair, back arched as though he too were slung from the ebony will of his instrument, his sweating lips clenched on the merciless stick and the outrageously upward-spiraling note. Tom and Jones faced one another from either side of Ada's depending form. Our hero picked nervously at the girl's exultant white sleeve.

"Uh! C'mon Ada, you're—I need you in the kitchen."

He was ashamed to meet Jones's no doubt withering gaze, kept his eyes on the naked, fluttering pulse at the base of Ada's throat, and longed for the dreadful, demented music to stop, *just stop!* And for Mrs. Garsin-Greer to stand and pat her flip and oh, go finish the caviar! For Rodrigo (whose real name, Tom suddenly recalled, was plain old Roger) to change his clothes and dash the powder and rouge from his dissolute face; for Ada to collect her hairpins and retire to the buffet. And for everyone, everyone to just go away, go home, *just leave him alone!*

"Um, uh," Tom plucked again at the white chiffon, "So listen, Ada? Ada!"

There's abrupt mayhem on the bandstand as the clarinetist's chair collapses, plunging him directly into the outraged brasses (a predictable cacophony of crossed french horn and coronet, music stands and metal folding chairs . . .). Servers dashed to the scene, laughing madly. Paper-capped cooks hallooed through the doorway, pointing their long dripping ladles. Mrs. Garsin-Greer yelped to be up, both hands paddling ineffectually at the air until her partner flipped his cigarette away, set the old woman on her feet and slunk off to cadge a sherry from Paulie behind the bar.

Jones's lip curled in disgust. He dryly withdrew his hand from the small of Ada's back and she dropped to the floor: "Oh!" she exclaimed, the wind knocked from her in one astonished *pooff.* Tom's mouth twitched in protest.

"Way to go, Tom. Broke our concentration—don't speak! Your lack of timing is flawless. *Gawd!"* Jones made a face and flapped his hand at the melee gathering hysterical momentum around them; when a stout brown sausage tore across the floor, he stuck out his foot and Toulouse went careening into the bandstand. He quite

ignored poor Ada, still hiccoughing for breath. "Just what *is* this ado about? You call this Tango Ro*man*tico? Do you? Well, guess what—we call this an unqualified *flop!* Get the picture?"

At the buffet table, Mrs. Garsin-Greer (practicing her steps round the puddling ice castle) went down with a shriek and a twisted ankle, clutching at the tablecloth as she foundered. Brandied figs, pyramids of canapés, and the untouched platter of Strasbourg pâté were scuttled along with her. Jones didn't blink; his voice pierced the commotion like a poisoned auger.

"What IS the big idea, Tom?"

An eager crowd gathered. Tom's face was fishy and damp; his forearms pressed against his middle where a terrible batter and wail was swiftly undoing him from the inside out. Still, he tried to speak. "*I—*"

"Save the excuses! You just don't have what it takes. *Sorry to tell you.*" Jones simpered and rolled his eyes and the surrounding faces approved the farce.

Tom flinched. "No! I—"

"*You* . . ." Jones sniffed. "*You* don't know chalk from cheese, you bootlicking little table hag. Whatever smarts you had got used up finagling a place here at all."

"That's not . . . I do too! I know—"

"*You know nothing!* You stand in the pantry and play in your pockets! You put carrots down your pants! You ogle the candle-butts and drink off the pickle juice and slick your lips with clarified butter! You'd *fancy* a firm steamed pudding, period!"

Jones was raving now, and Tom would have happily accepted an ally. But even Ada (still on her back, though breathing normally) did not speak, her rapt, acquiescent gaze skipping mutely back and forth, as a sparrow hops from twig to twig and back again. Tom gripped his belly where dogged claws gouged and tore; his throat burned from some caustic reflux. *All right, he'd show them! Right to Jones's face! He'd*—

"Who the *hell* do you think you are, Tom? A *nobody*. What's worse, you don't know enough to stay where you belong: *on your knees!*" Jones smirked. "There's a thought! Did you hear us? *Down on your knees . . .* NOW!"

And that, as they say, was that.

Tom's head snapped up; his arms fell to his sides. "No," he croaked. Then again, a broken whimper, "*No*—"

"No?" Jones repeated with interest. "No?" The crowd around them took a judicious step back.

"HOW DARE YOU!"

Jones roared; the champagne flutes literally rattled.

"Now hear this, you insubordinate, greedy little goose egg! YOU are asking to be DISMISSED!"

There was a gasp of genuine horror all around, and Ada bore down on her lower lip so earnestly it bled. Jones folded his arms and yawned at the ceiling. "Now then, Mr. Too-Big-for-His-Britches, is that what you're after? *Is* it? Yes or no, Tom?"

Oh! Our hero could not see for the tears scouring his eyes; could not hear for a howl that echoed somewhere beyond the burst and swinging gates of his ribs, *the black and smoking vacancy of his once and for all empty belly!*

"*Yes* or No!"

"I, I—" Tom was stunned, astonished by and unable to control the surging, unspeakable grief that broke like a storm against the empty fortress of his heart. "I . . ."

"YES OR NO!"

"I . . ." Tom reeled, then lunged unseeing at the linked arms gleefully encircling him; recoiled, trampling Ada's outspread skirts. He lurched forward and back, back and forth, 'til at last he fell to his hands and knees and, weeping, crept between the legs of the merry, remorseless crowd. *Away* from Jones and his infernal buffet (his own bloody cocktail shaker)—and oh, from his bright and perilous Salon! From everything, *from it all!*

At the edge of the dance floor Tom pulled himself up on the towering folds of gelid silver drapery; turned—

"You—I . . . *I quit!*"

And at last broke, sobbing, from the one place in the world he'd ever savored the ripe and divinely swollen fruits of glory.

CHAPTER SEVEN

Mortificatio

20—

The massive front door fell to with a reverberant clang; Tom was, in a word, shattered. Outside, the air was a rancorous broth of congealed smoke and fog, desolate as a week-old pudding; but our hero flung himself into it heedlessly, his only desire to *get away!* from this bear garden of ridicule and betrayal.

How dare they!

He sputtered, swiping at fat salty tears. That's right, how dare *they!* Jones was a monster, a real predator—that was one thing! But the others, the others! Unnatural, appraising as alley cats, they'd watched and laughed. After all he'd done for them! To be sure he adored the Ruins— the Ruins, first and last! But he'd labored as well to elevate *them*, to raise their expectations, to *inspire* them. It was their Big Chance too! They didn't see that! Selfish and arrogant, lazy and lecherous and greedy and bad-tempered . . . they were jealous of him! Yes! And he'd only tried to set a good example!

Tom stumbled on a litter of broken bricks and went again to his knees, double bolts of pain firing straight to his annihilated belly. He bit his lips and rocked and ultimately could not contain the rude sobs slugging their way up from his lungs. *Pbuh, pbuh, pbuh.* His frowzy head bobbed blindly back and forth like some decrepit pony; his raised hands insensibly beseeched, wrists bared to the rain streaming down the inside of his cuffs.

Never fear, fret, or bemoan your fate!

Impossible! To whom might he appeal? It was over, *over.* His "promising future"! He writhed in an apprehension of grief and shame and inconsolable loss. *His lily-scented paradise, his ting-a-ling of knife on fork . . .* The air around him soured and wet his clothes like a spiteful cat. Burying his face in his hands he caught a whiff, already, of the blight and putrefaction of the streets. *His fate!* He sobbed and retched and struggled to his feet, slipping on the rancid offscum of backed-up sewage and random shit.

Hours later, ravaged by the the horror and sheer havoc of his reversed fortune, and wasted by hours of hapless staggering through streets aloof and disobliging in their terminal camouflage of fog . . . Tom stumbled at last through the plank door of his old abandoned hut.

Two walls of wattle and mud, another of corrugated fiberglass, the last of stuffed lath. The thatched roof moldered and smelled of mice; a torn sheet of dirty plastic bellied out over the small, unglazed window. He shared the yard with half a dozen hogs and a gang of malevolent hens, and when they all got going it sounded like hell's own *ee-yi-ee-yi-oh*.

Now, with a sob, he flung himself down on the musty straw pallet that made his bed. There was a furious squeal and two lean rats skipped reproachfully across Tom's shins to wriggle beneath a heap of blackened rags in the corner. This was Tom's work kit, his "outfit": a couple of steel picks, a few soft brushes, four or five tins of rich, redolent polish. He stared at these things through the predawn smut of light. Curled on his side, laced fingers pressed against the blight of his once-immaculate tunic; his hand-boned shoes now caked with mud and corruption . . . still he winced at the worse memory of the *old* days, squatting for hours against a pissed-upon wall, tirelessly wooing impervious passersby. Oh those stupid, humiliating jingles!

Then painfully, almost twitching, Tom recalls the Ruins as he first saw it. Wandering alone in a predawn trance from the Cloud Room (erubescent, lilac-shadowed dream) into the humming, stainless steel mysteries of the kitchen, illuminated by a host of tiny blue pilot lights (an everlasting combustion—a scarcely audible, antiphonal chorus!). And finally the Salon itself, its silence broken only by the murmuring pink fountain, trembling waters laced with gilded carp, black-and-silver samurai, and corpulent orange guppies. Remember? The way the table silver collected and multiplied the lambent yellow flames of tiny votive candles scattered across the ecru linens like so many fallen, flickering stars . . .

He'd rambled, that first night, like green Adam in the world's first garden, not daring to touch—blushing, at times, just to peek—so blandly bared, so *unconcealed* were these infinite delights. What a dope he'd been! Innocently addressing a Louis XVI raspberry taffeta duchesse: *Chair*. And the barbaric, velvet-tongued mug of a vituperative purple orchid: *Flower*. Why, he'd known nothing! He was ignorant, then, as a . . . well, all right, as a plain piece of chalk! But swelling with an almost painful desire, a *will to rise*.

So he shirked nothing. Listen, he couldn't count the times he'd crept, at some idiot's command, among the wizened teats of the smug, sartorial Pig, groping for its frayed cord! And *was* it all in vain? Had he really learned nothing, as that snake Jones maintained? It wasn't so! For how about his martinis? None finer! Furthermore, La Stupenda herself had alluded to *vision!* How about that? Was that chalk from cheese?

La Stupenda!

Tom's face flamed. For it was La Stupenda, more than anyone, who'd believed in him (as he'd believed in himself!). What would she think? Would she . . . was there any hope she might *defend* him? Alas, this notion perished quickly in the deadly climate of Tom's ripening despair. After all, what was he to her? A polite young man, an unobjectionable table servant; in short, a nobody. He whimpered. Those fluttering, azure-slippered feet, paddling the pink and impressively high clouds above the rheumy eyes, the outstretched hands of the masses! Could one so eminent as she still take an interest in one so low, so certainly lost, as he?

Tom groaned and lurched to his swollen feet, stood in the middle of his godforsaken hovel and glared, first in one direction and then another. In truth, he saw nothing—not the tilting, three-legged stool, nor the battered tin bucket he'd filched for a pot, nor his old, bump-toed sneakers gone green beneath the dripping window. Only . . .

Only *mice!* Agh!

A whirling ring of impudent, red-cheeked mice, their black eyes bulging, and not a hair out of place! And right there among them—the blowhard, the rat!—his wind-big belly gassy with malice, his broad flat nose a blizzard of exploding capillaries, his wicked lips always just-licked, always wet! Was it? It *was*—

Tom bent one leg and kicked ineffectually at the crooked stool. Made fists, grimaced, and flailed at the air. He shivered in the inadequacy of his rage. In the end he spun on one heel and tore at the curtain of a little blue cupboard; thrust a blind hand among the unlabeled tins and blackened fruit jars; dumped half a sack of barley into a splash of rusty water and set it atop a little gas burner. For the next thirty minutes he paced the dirt floor, flapping and wringing his hands, exclaiming under his breath, and occasionally breaking into shocking paroxysms of stripped down, inarticulate sobs. Eventually he smelled the gruel burning. Poking the pot to the floor he squatted beside it. With two bent fingers he began to shovel the scorched, half-cooked grains into his mouth.

"Mmm, mmm," he assured himself, delirious with anger, remorse, and self-loathing. "Now *this* is what I call food . . ."

Alas, for as long as he'd been at the Ruins, he never did find time to sit down and eat a proper meal. And now?

Well now, ha ha! If nothing else one could eat! No black cloud without its silver lining! Eh? That's the spirit!

Gagging a little, his fingers traveling with grudging obedience between the can and his joylessly gaping mouth, Tom laughed and wept and stopped up the terrifying abyss that was his belly with a great sticky mass of indigestible chuck. When he could eat no more he crept on hands and knees to his meager pallet, collapsed and continued to reassure and congratulate himself on his change of fortune.

"Ah!" he cried. "What luxury to lie here all unbothered! A regular lazybones! Suits me to a T!" He chuckled and belched fire, the poisonous green bile lapping at the back of his throat. In fact for several hours poor Tom was thoroughly wracked as he waited for his meal to relent, for his knees to leave off their caviling and his head its jeremiad of ignominy and woe. In the end he submitted gratefully to a twitching, troubled sleep.

Thereafter, the pattern of Tom's days was more or less the same. He gobbled—giggling, or *pbuh pbuh*-ing in sheer bathos—on colossal, half-cooked messes of gruel, or pink wrinkled beans that conspired in his middle for hours, organizing shameless collusions of gas and bile that detonated haphazardly like terrorist's bombs. He gorged himself 'til he groaned and then, still groaning, collapsed on his pallet and slept; his dreams were vile.

He saw himself naked, bent over his own outstretched leg. A fat greenish vein ran up his thigh to a small, inexplicable hole. Again and again he drew his index finger firmly up this vessel to its outlet, from which issued a copious goo of little round worms, plump white O's suspended in a gluey, transparent mucus. Tom—annoyed, repelled, and yet determined to discharge the mess completely—continued to run his finger up the swollen vein, forcing its contents up his leg and out the mouth of the little ragged hole, wherefrom it dribbled inconveniently down the inside of his thigh.

He dreamed he was working at the Ruins. The Salon roared with people furious to be served, while Tom stood frozen before a whalelike fellow in a rumpled suit. The man gazed down at the menu in his hands, dicating with interminable deliberation. *Well, he'd have the pressed duck, the éclairs, the collared eel à la royale, and a pink gin—and the rice croquettes, plus mushrooms in Madeira* . . . the man never looked up from his menu . . . *apricot flan, cassoulet, then crayfish bisque, and coffee* . . . Tom gazed desperately about him. So much to do! *Celeriac puree, macaroons* . . . Without even pretending to take down the preposterous order, Tom was nonetheless riveted by his office— mute, paralyzed, in a perfect agony of dire and conflicting impulses. Convulsed by the need to *do*, he could not stir an inch.

Well, what morbidness! And what preoccupation with the soft white underbelly of his own carnal existence! He had an unsavory fascination with his daily "b.m.," which was vehement (if of an unwholesome tint), plunging between the cheeks of his windy white bum into a thick slippery coil round the bottom of the bucket. Pulling up his trousers he'd turn and stare at his issue with satisfaction and disgust, relishing its noxious vapors—actually kicking the side of the bucket to see how inflexibly it held its ground! But how, he sneered, could anything so explicit and rude and resolute come from one so trifling and incompetent as *himself*? Huh? A *goose egg*!

Clearly our hero felt not only dashed by his recent misfortune, but bluntly betrayed by life: a *victim*, even, of Fate. It was impossible, of course, for Tom to undertake the cat's cradle of deeds and tokens leading to his disgrace; to consider, even as a simple exercise in plain reasoning, that, for example, he might have had a hand in his own unmaking. No! He could only feel, to the very nadir of his being, that something really *wrong* had taken place; something that, until it happened, was not merely unthought-of, but literally unthinkable. "How could they?" he raved, and "It can't be!" Alas, that the unthinkable in fact occurs with breathtaking regularity up and down the course of any given day, had not yet made itself clear to our hero, who for all his hard knocks was still, after all, rather fatuous and inclined to dote on Life. The sophisticated reader will marvel at poor Tom's blindness to these salient and certainly well-advertised facts of existence; indeed, there are those who would say he *had it coming*. That's as it may be.

That Tom experienced the annihilation of this world, *his* world, in the limp sinews and wasted marrow of his very bones, was indisputable. He certainly looked a wreck. Right off the bat he'd shucked his white tunic and checkered trousers for the frayed green leggings and burlap blouse he'd sported as a shoeshine. "Much better!" he growled, and swaggered across the room on gladiatorily spread legs. But the coarse shirt quickly chafed his wrists and the back of his neck; his gummy, unattended hair matted like beach kelp; and it wasn't long, either, before he began to smell himself.

He wished, in the beginning, for company. Some other to whom he might unbosom himself; some other with whom to bawl out loud: "The fiends!" and "How could they?" In short, sympathetic and enlightened fellowship. To be sure, he went so far as to steal, one drizzly afternoon, back to the Groaning Board. What a mistake! Immediately he entered, his knees dissolved and his voice cracked and stammered. Trembling before the plank and barrel bar he could not get over the feeling that he was being deliberately ignored; he was certain he heard a waitress titter. "Huh!" he pronounced (more or less at the sawdust floor, but with as much contempt as he could muster); then turned and fled the place, arriving back at his own door wheezing and moreover sopping wet.

He shivered and exclaimed for a moment outside his hut, then turned and slunk along one wall to the back where the pigs and hens were kept. He barged in on them, roaring "My friends!" and spent the next quarter of an hour stumping back and forth across their beds of straw and manure, discoursing incoherently, choked by intermittent sobs, finally prizing off a couple of the rotten planks that separated his own interior from their dark, fetid stalls. "Come in, yes of course—do!" he urged, staggering with a gasp into his cold little room. He turned and tore one knuckle on a nail, beckoning them hopefully through the ragged gap, and was granted a few dismissive oinks and clucks. "Of course," he replied, stung by their indifference, "As you wish! Don't mention it! As you wish!" Tears pricked his eyes, and he surrendered himself once more to his lonely pallet, one arm crooked beneath his cheek, both knees tucked against his desecrated belly, his foregone heart awhistle with cold, reproachful winds.

"Little brother," he finally, weepily confided to a small blind potato bug trundling up the wall before his face, "*thou art myself.*" And so saying, Tom collared the tiny creature between two fingers and placed it solemnly upon his own extruded tongue, gagging only slightly as the dry and tasteless "pill" was fetched (with understandable resistance) down the back of his throat.

• • •

After that Tom could eat no more. Indeed, following his debauch of gluttony and sloth, vengefulness and stellar pride (the last couple of which, if nothing else, were fizzy and empowering emotions), Tom found his passion abdicating to a potent lassitude that dripped like a slow IV, diluting and anaesthetizing all trace of personal consequence, of subjectivity, of *stead*.

Sipping indifferently from a can of brackish water, Tom sprawled, gazing at the underside of his disintegrating roof, his mind utterly blank, his body a drearily lit, conspicuously empty hallway. *Nobody home.* Overhead the sky reeled with constellations turning in a vast, inexorable wheel; with the weeping colors of a small and furiously squalling sun in the throes of its own unremarked rising and falling; and with the massive, implacable moon, her powdered jowels obscured by insoluble carbon veils, by nightbirds swarming in vast cryptograms, and by high, guileful clouds.

Down below, in the city of backed-up sewers and baleful cats, at the end of a narrow, unkempt lane, tucked in the mucked-out corner of a dilapidated shed, our hero lay dry-eyed, motionless, mute. His mind creaked like the swing of an empty cupboard's door. Waiting?

But for what?

Perhaps not waiting, then; perhaps something else. Who knew? Ah, how could one tell? He stared unseeing, he breathed not a word, his slack jaw hung askance, bestowing on him the half-dazzled look of idiots, and those meeting death. And yet, perhaps not overtly, something was afoot. As a matter of fact, his expression was rather that of someone *falling*—unfathomably falling!—plunging through the stark and durationless ether of being. *Just falling.*

It was in this peculiar state that, two days later, Tom, finally sought, was with lively interest found.

21—

"Oh, is he dead!" cried Ada in a tiny, horrified voice; and she tumbled to her knees in the dirty straw.

"Pshaw! Too many novels, my girl." Ugo shooed a venomous hen from the lid of a splintered crate and, in breezy holiday humor, took a seat. He gazed around the little shed with sympathetic delight. "What a hole!"

Conchita stood fast in the center of the room, rebuffing a goat come to whiff at the savorous hem of her woolen cape. "Ugo! You don' do zomzing, we'll be 'ere all day!"

Eager, uncertain, Ada pit-a-patted Tom's lifeless hand. "Tom, Tom dear? . . . Tom?"

"Tom-Tom!" sang Ugo, borrowing Jones's serrated treble and chuckling with grim satisfaction as Tom bolted upright in the straw, turning on them an astonished, stricken face. Ada caught her breath.

"Nize plaze, Tom," observed Conchita through courteously clenched teeth. She was all business, as usual, and going straight to the point announced, "We've come to collect you."

But say, who were these . . . these others?

Poor Tom could only gawk, his long spare parenthetical fall abruptly arrested. Saved? He struggled to grasp the material significance of these faint, disorienting shadows shifting about his room—these distracting cries interrupting a lengthy and increasingly restful tenure of silent, disembodied vacancy—these vaguely obliging modifications in that pure suspension in which he'd dangled (no, plunged? no, *soared!*), well, for who knew how long?

Finding himself upright (and disagreeably sensible of a cold draft upon his back and the riddle of straw through the seat of his threadbare britches), he peered at these others through the wrong end, as it were, of a badly focused telescope: tiny and indistinct, they might have been insects, or mere imperfections in the glass. He squinted at Ada's distant, anguished face, and whispered "Why you're . . . aren't you? A fig—a fig—"

"Tom!" Ada pleaded, poking his shoulder doubtfully; but our hero recoiled violently from that outright contact with his own dismissed and oblivious corpus. He drew against the wall and bit his lip at length. She turned and bawled at the others. "He's—there's something wrong! I think he's . . ."

"Malingering!" confirmed Ugo, shaking his head with elaborate regret. "Too bad, too bad! My friend, leave off this unbecoming little drama."

Conchita marched to the edge of the pallet and leaned over, scrutinizing Tom; her terse, throaty growl was cautious with complaint. "Is zat right, Tom? You getting puzzy-catty wizzus? Hmmph . . ." She looked skeptically about the wretched hut. "But now, 'ow about offering your guezts somzing—dat is . . . a little refreshment?"

Ugo snorted. "A cache, no doubt, of vintage cognac? No doubt! Fortunately," he drew a magnificent silver flask from the inside pocket of his greatcoat, "A little something! Ladies first—Ada? No?" Ugo shrugged and tipped the flask with balmy complaisance.

Conchita swiped at him. "Give me zat!" She tossed back a quick one, then kneeled hastily at Tom's side. Supporting his head with uncharacteristic charity, she placed the flask against his lips and murmured, "A drop of dis may greeze your wheel. Zlowly, Zlowly . . ."

And in fact the little snort did not go amiss. Tom was transfixed by a long caustic trickle of something diabolical and bright, which cleaved a path straight through to his middle, tickling his disenthralled flesh: he came to, shuddering and a little sick. Raising his hand to steady the flask he grasped Conchita's warm, well-knit wrist (to be sure, seemed to hang from it!), her pulse so firm and regular within his trembling grip. When she withdrew he wiped his chin with a blush, reassuringly eloquent of his old bashful ways. Ada grinned to hear him stammer.

"Oh! It's, well . . . As you can see! I haven't been quite, that is—not myself! Not exactly, no, not lately."

Alas, the mortal extremity of his earlier straits—his near-fatal disenchantment with life's inscrutable *huff* and *puff*—came over him suddenly, as though he stood in the wake of *whooshing* air left behind a barreling and narrowly side-stepped bus. Despite the brandy bracer and his own customary restraint, Tom turned and hid his face against the wall, sobbing in a backlash of retrospective terror.

The girls, embarrassed, sat back on their heels; it was Ugo who unexpectedly came to the rescue. Pushing the others aside, he hooked both elbows under Tom's sagging shoulders and muscled him up from the straw, reviving him with friendly shakes and reassuring words as they shuffled together—Ugo's little arm encircling Tom's waist—back and forth across the dirt floor.

"In fact, my friend, in fact! Best to get it all out! That's it! Get it out, get it all behind you . . ." Tom blubbered gratefully. "Yes, yes, and when you're finished we'll discuss the future—"

Huh?!

Our hero sniffed.

He might have seen it coming: The Future! And just look at him! Was this the time for tasteless gibes? Barely, *barely,* he'd managed to dodge, oh! he didn't like to *think* what he dodged! And anyway, who said he even *wanted* a future?

Tom scowled, cheeks stiff with interrupted tears, and could almost have wished to be left alone with his "little drama" after all, so loath was he to *discuss the future.* Nervously he eyed his rumpled pallet, wondering if a modest relapse might discourage his friends from further intervention. Instead, Ugo sat him briskly down upon the wooden crate; then, giving the lad a final, affectionate shake, he took up a post beside him, arms folded across his chest like two cudgels. Conchita stood at Tom's other side, and Ada pulled up on the little stool in the event further nursing should be wanted.

"So," began Ugo with a knowing wink, "where have you been hiding these days?"

Tom's jaw dropped with a last-second, disbelieving click of his tongue. What sort of a question was that? Did they mock him? He replied stiffly, indicating with a wave of his hand the desperate little room. "As you can see, I . . . egh! That is, just keeping more or less to myself."

"Charming," interrupted Conchita, narrowing her eyes to imponderable gray slits. "But zelfish, Tom." And when our hero exclaimed, astonished and uncomprehending, she repeated, nodding her head with indisputable conviction, "Very zelfish."

Ada patted Tom's hand helpfully. "The thing is, Tom, you haven't come to work in ages, and naturally we wondered . . . Well, you should see Mitzi. Flapping around like a hen short one chick!" Ada chuckled, then lowered her voice apologetically. "Course, she would have come too, but there's a really key event tonight and—" she shrugged. "Guess I don't need to tell *you* how it is!"

How it is?

Tom recalled with abrupt and poignant clarity those evenings he thrilled to the opening ding-dang-*dong!* of the Ruins' front doorbell. His cocktail shaker at the ready, his serving tray poised, polished 'til it matched his own hand fingertip for fingertip, palm for quicksilver palm (by the end of the night it seemed almost alive, an indispensable extension of his own insignificant flesh; cool and imperturbable and . . .)

"Yes," he grunted, "I know how it is."

"Zo if you *know* 'ow it is," Conchita broke in (really she was in a waspish mood!), "why inzist on dis hide-and-zeek? You were 'ired for a reezon—"

"Hired?" Tom yelped, having now had quite enough of this pretense, "—and fired! At least, that is to say, I *quit.*" How dare they treat him so, so . . . and Ada too! And in his own home! He opened his mouth to say more (indeed, to show them the door, that was more like it!) but Ugo held up one hand and regarded Tom with grave surprise.

"Again! That last bit?"

"He said, oh! He said he was—" Ada gulped and turned her wide, appalled eyes on Ugo, "*fired.* Can that be?"

"Nonsense! Fired? That's—"

"Not fired," averred Tom, looking daggers at the floor. "*Quit.*"

"Equal nonsense! Fired, quit . . ." Ugo considered; then coaxed, "Come, my friend. You're sensitive! And even—"

"I know when I've been fired—*quit!* Oh, must you torture me!"

At that moment Tom hated Ugo, hated them all. What did they want from him? Suddenly Conchita snapped her fingers.

"*Aiee!* An intrigue, Paulie zaid. Unrequited pazzion! And . . ."

Ugo slapped a hand to his shining head. "In fact! The Tango Lessons!" He looked at Tom, one brow describing an innocent question mark. "There was . . . an incident?" When Tom only slumped lower on his crate, Ugo turned, "Ada, you may elaborate."

Ada, who had ever been weak, if earnest, in the memory department, now tipped her head to one side. "Well, uh, there might have been some confusion at the end . . ."

"Look," Tom was decidedly spent. "I—Mr. Jones and I . . . there was a difference of opinion and he . . . There was no alternative and I—I quit. That's all."

"*That's* all?" Ugo planted his hands on his hips. "A difference of opinion? My friend, a sow's ear from a silk purse! You *deserted*, for a difference of opinion?" He struck his hands together. "Enough! Collect your essentials and we'll be—"

"I'm not going back. You don't get it." Tom sighed. "He was going to *fire* me, and so instead I quit. I can't go back." Tom shook his head.

"Prozper Gozzling's asking for you," Conchita menaced.

"Mrs. Gosling," interrupted Ada, puckering her brow. "Jeez, now is she? Did she come in that time—"

"Shuddup, Ada," Conchita snapped, then added distractedly, "zilly idiot." She fixed Tom with a challenging eye. "She inzists you return. She's throwing hors d'oeuvre at ze ozzer waiters."

Tom closed his eyes. "It's not my beeswax anymore." He was by now longing to creep back into his straw. It honestly pained him to think of Mrs. Prosper Gosling. What was he to her? And as for the others, let food be thrown at them. They were hooligans and probably asked for it.

"Shame you missed the Puppy Brunch," Ugo remarked.

"Mmph." (Really! he couldn't have cared less.)

But Ada chuckled and shook Tom's arm. "Oh Tom, you should have seen Toulouse! All bathed and brushed and perfumed up—he wore a little red jacket!"

Conchita snorted pointedly. "Why mus' you bring zat up? A cataztrophe!"

Oh?

"So there were . . . complications?"

Ugo jerked his head in vehement agreement. "Complications!"

"Well, I—"

"You predicted! Don't say it! *And you were right!* Now you're thinking we got what we asked for? Just desserts! Well, you're right again. Still, one speculates! Had *you* been there . . ."

"What, um—" Tom could not resist, ". . . happened?"

"Go ahead zen, Ugo, tell 'im." Conchita's voice was tantalizing. *"About ze animal trainer."*

Ugo blew out his breath and began to explore Tom's little room, sticking his nose into corner after corner with evident relish, smacking his lips as he went, "In fact! The abominable woe-man! The one-eyed misanthrope! The tightly buttoned Cyclops!—"

What was he talking about?

"Recall the plan! A professional dog trainer to work the crowd, *create a mood*. Biscuits and gravy, then Wanda makes her entrance." Ugo bent over the cache of filthy rags in the corner. "Heavens, don't tell me?" He glanced over his shoulder at Tom, who quickly looked away. "You don't say! *Anyway*. Enter Wanda, brow beetling over two mad eyes so narrowly set they seemed, at first glance, to be one. She was . . . *portly*, and sported a short red tunic, some kind of sausage casing woven of sequins and gold military braid. A glamorous whip and helmet! And high black boots . . .

Tom was bewildered, intrigued. "And? What?"

Withdrawing his head from the breach in the wall that opened onto the hoggery, Ugo shrugged. "Imagine! Parents and their pooches! Each the incontestable center of the other's universe. Muffin, Rex, what-have-you."

Ada cooed, "And weren't they *good!* And even—"

"She make a *zpell!*" Conchita interrupted. "Dat Wanda—"

"In fact! She conjured! Cracked her whip, 'volunteers!' Poor Junebug, poor Sparky, one by one they trotted off, proud parents left behind." Ugo stopped, one hand laid protectively upon Ada's downy head. "Tragic! God knows how many were lost."

"What!"

Ada's mouth began to blur as her pupils widened with abruptly recollected horror. "Oh," she whimpered. "They—oh, *Tom!*" and she burst into tears, her little face dropping onto Tom's bent knees.

"A little 'owz, like a tower," Conchita hissed. "One by one dese doggies go in. Wanda marches roun' and roun'."

"Versemongering!" frowned Ugo.

> *Hippity-hoppity into the pot*
> *Day's not done 'til the rabbit is caught!*

"But—"

"Oh Tom!" Ada's fist surprised his tender ribs. "*They never came back!*"

Ugo threw up his hands. "We passed it off! A brilliant sleight-of-hand, what else? Skipped the peach melba and shooed them out the door." He flicked a careless finger against the plastic-covered window, then turned and pointed at Tom. "But that's when Mrs. Gosling complained. Her bald bitch Missy? Wouldn't miss her. But said it was all in savage taste and threw a squeak toy at *me!*"

Tom had to ask. "Um . . . Toulouse?"

"Toulouse? Popped up later. In fact!"

Of course.

"Few survivors. A schnauzer or two, one resourceful Yorkie. The rest, I'd say, are gone for good."

The room was silent, then, but for the melancholy honk of Ada's nose. Ugo coughed apologetically. "So you see! Heaven knows what could happen next—and this Saturday, well!" He nodded at Tom, knowing he need say no more.

The Fool's Ball!

On the one hand, Tom had a hard time believing their story. But would Ada? . . . Never! Not even to coax Tom back to the Ruins? He shook his head and had to wonder what was on the menu the day after the brunch.

"Tom."

Fluffy arrosto? Ruffles Royale?

"Tom—"

Better, an enormous *cassoulet.* That way, they'd all—

"Oh Tom!"

Tom would not meet Ada's imploring eyes, but stood and moved determinedly to his pallet. Ugo followed, squatting down beside him. "This tiff between you and Jones? A mere nothing! Less! People get excited, they say things, it's perfectly natural! Life moves on. And the Ruins needs you." He added shrewdly, "And what's good for the Ruins is good for you, eh? Can you forget that now, my friend?"

Conchita scolded, "You know, Tom, Jonz didn't zend us. It was de ozzers, de ztaff." Her laugh was quicksand and amber. "All lef' feet wizzout you."

Ugo whistled. "The old place doesn't look itself."

"And Mitzi," Ada chimed in, "she's ready to scratch our eyes out. And swearing? Jeez!" Ada's cheeks went pink, "I don't like to say."

Tom gazed at the ceiling. Oh, how little they knew him! *The staff in a shambles! Prosper Gosling in a snit!* Next they'd announce it was raining, ha! But he wasn't heartless, and guessed he felt a little sorry for them. After all, the big Ball! One last chance to make up for the torturous recitals, unattended hobby nights . . . *and catastrophic dance lessons.* It was always the final impression that counted most; yes, he could appreciate their urgency.

On the other hand, they should have thought about that earlier, shouldn't they? He turned to face the wall.

"Well!" declared Conchita, after a moment of shocked silence. And she drew her cape around her and marched to the door.

Ugo rested his hand on Tom's shoulder. "My friend?" he invited. Then, "I regret to say, not all your oars in the water!" He joined Conchita at the door.

Ada dropped to her knees behind Tom's back. "I guess you must have thought this out pretty clearly, but I—oh, Tom! Won't you reconsider? Of course, I'm sure you'll do the right thing, whatever it is."

Tom's gaze nervously panned the wall as his will threatened to waffle. *Sort of a shame to treat one's friends so coldly.* Assuming they'd come in good faith, was it strictly necessary to send them off without a word? An appropriate gesture of regret? On the other hand it was true that, not to mince matters, he owed them nothing. *A clean break*, he told himself—it was best for everyone.

"Well," Ada was left to say, her bewilderment transparent, "so long, I guess." Tom heard the straw rustle as she turned, then, "Jeez! I nearly forgot!" and a pale blue envelope dangled before his nose, began to rise. "La Stupenda asked me to give you this. I'll just—" Quick as a flash, Tom snatched the envelope from Ada's ascending fingers. "Hey! Well, I guess that's it, then." A last, disconsolate pause. "Good luck, Tom . . ."

Tom waited for his friends' footsteps to die away, then sat up quickly in the straw, tearing at the sealed envelope. Inside was a single sheet of folded blue paper, and this Tom held in his fingers for a moment, not daring to proceed.

La Stupenda, his only real regret. Forgetting their several differences of opinion, Tom rubbed one finger softly over the stiff blue paper. *She'd* touched this paper, and what's more, she'd been thinking of *him.* He brought it to his nose; there was the scorched, faintly acrid scent of violets he associated with her, with her cigarettes and flamey eyes and the slow-burning fuse of her central core (all the more bewitching under cool blue wraps).

Tom's fingers shook as he unfolded the note and read what was written in a casual, back-slanting hand.

There's no hurry.

He frowned and turned it over: nothing. It wasn't even signed.

There's no hurry?

What was that supposed to mean? Tom sat back against the wall. He felt disappointed and obscurely provoked, and reached absentmindedly for a dish of stale millet sitting on the floor. What *was* the big idea? One minute he was petitioned, pestered, beseeched to resume his post. And then? A blithe blue *there's no hurry.*

Puzzling, he scratched loose and one-by-one nibbled the hard grains glued to the sides of the bowl. Well, was there a hurry or wasn't there? Did he matter or didn't he? Tick, tick, tick, the dry grains fell to his chastened belly like loaves from a blank blue sky. Outside, the sun went down behind a bank of gray clouds, and two ecstatic swallows chased each other over roofs and crumbling chimneys into the high broken windows of an empty warehouse. The steel lid of a nearby dumpster fell with a crash. And a bored young sow came wriggling through the broken planks into our hero's room; Tom passed her his bowl.

His decision was made: back to the Ruins.

Clearly there wasn't a moment to lose!

CHAPTER EIGHT

The Ball
(About Which Please See Explanatory Remark) *

22—

Three days later our recalled hero stands tall and incontestably presentable in a freshly laundered tunic and pressed checkered trousers. Guests are expected at any moment. If young Tom waits with doughty, not to say insensible, composure, on the other hand his silver tray flashes like the rolling eye of an overwrought heifer. His hair (he considers, belligerently) is, for once, flawless.

*What follows—the whole of the bizarre and unaccountable evening, to be sure, but in particular the really sinister dénouement just after midnight—is surely the most disquieting and painful part of our story. One could, for the sake of discretion, write the whole affair off to "the inevitability of circumstances." Just leave it, and our hero's fate, at that! It is not, however, our business to write off anything at all. Having introduced our tale, and our earnest, uneasy hero, we must see them through to their mutual end. A debacle? So be it. Though for this, admittedly, words may serve at best as but the frailest of sticks on which one nonetheless stumps, eyes bulging with disbelief, across the torn and smoking field of battle.

Tom's return to the Ruins was unflinching and strictly business—he felt neither obligated nor inclined to enlarge upon the already prodigal drama of his leave-taking. And for once Jones, consumed by last-minute preparations for the Ball, was willing to let sleeping dogs lie, only throwing up his arms from across the teeming kitchen as Tom quietly reentered and all heads turned.

"At *last* and not a moment too soon! Don't speak! The place is bloody bon ton central! And why not? First, and *immediately* . . ."

Tom stood impassively in the doorway, but his bashful glance panned the room with swelling emotion. There were at least a dozen people toiling breathlessly at one thing or another. Mitzi, at the butcher block, blew a kiss from her sticky cleaver; Ada stuck her head around the door of the walk-in and they exchanged tremulous smiles; even Richard paused in her furious mincing to look up and, with a curt nod, acknowledge Tom's return. He smelled shallots melting in hot yellow butter, and the fresh rude brine of pink crabs still waving weakly from their sinking beaches of shaved ice, and the sweetly needled scent of ripening strawberries. A violent stream of water hammered the bottom of the sink behind him, and he reached back to hush the thunder as Jones continued, one fist braced against his aproned hip, the other brandishing a leek at Tom across the wary, wordless kitchen.

". . . just where this young firebrand ever picked up such *ways*, such adorable defiance! You minx! *Waall*, new discoveries are always—"

Wham! Toulouse charged in from the Maisonette, wheezing authoritatively. Before the door fell to, Tom had a glimpse of azure-slippered feet, the provocative curve of a silk-hosed gam, and a clinging storm of sky blue feathers. Two veiled, imperturbable periwinkles squarely met and transfixed Tom's uncertain glance. He caught his breath, she winked, that was all.

("Dammit, where's Ugo! *People!* Tom-Tom, get Ugo to give you the drill," Jones whirled and flung up his hands, "oh for *gawd's* sake!")

Tom, mesmerized by the dwindling wig and wag of the door, nodded. *Soon enough,* he thought.

• • •

Arrangements for the Ball made a hash of the next two days, and our hero, back at his celebrated helm, had to content himself with mere fleeting glimpses of the elusive diva. It was naturally his desire to consult with her directly; he was keen to know what she *really thought,* wished to justify, to speculate and accuse. He wanted to know if, in her opinion, he'd done the right thing. Above all, he hoped she might remark with pleasure at his return.

That is, if she *was* pleased?

(What did she mean by that note!)

Alas, though La Stupenda was daily at the Ruins, ostensibly preparing her act, she'd spoken to Tom but once, and this in virtually heedless passing (at that, he'd been down on his knees, attempting to shim a perilous side table). Rushing past, trailing smoke, arm in arm with the unctuous Ugo, she'd raked bitter fingers through Tom's trailing locks, then bent and blew into his immediately flaming ear, *"you won't regret it!"* He started, braining himself on the edge of the marble table, but she'd already gone, calling at Jones across the room to get her floor-to-ceiling blue satin, *or the show, darling, was off!*

•   •   •

Tom's sensitive fingers press delicately, now, on that still tender nob; and he wonders, resentfully, how it is that little Ugo had time to sashay La Stupenda hither and thither while he, Tom, toiled round the clock. Stuffing olives and trimming wicks, tuning the mechanical Pig's innards; detailing, detailing! Things certainly *had* gotten out of hand. Tom discovered brandy bottles in the pony's manger; the glass chandelier in the Ladies' had a luxurious gray fur upon it; and the coat rack . . . the infernal, never-to-be-resolved coat rack! Confronted, his staff hung their gleaming heads, twisting their fingers and exchanging perfectly senseless allegations, innuendoes and smirks. Tom merely sighed (twice shy!), turned and began to put things to rights himself. Immediately they leaped to his side, plucked urgently at his sleeve and swore in chorus that at any rate *now* they were unconditionally at his service—whatever Tom wanted!—they *promised*.

And for a wonder they seemed to do just that! And for two days were on their best—indeed, never-before-seen—behavior, bounding upstairs and down for cases of swizzle sticks and frilled paper anklets for the lamb. They *oohed* and *ahhed* at Tom's distribution of cocktail napkins, nodding with approval, as though there were no conceivable alternative, when he shifted the ebony ashtray left, the silver filigree matchbox right, on the low table before the saffron velvet *chaise longue*.

"What next! What next!" they caroled, and tumbled after him, pointing and exclaiming while he inspected the premises. They elbowed one another aside to hang on his neck and peer at his hastily scribbled notes, at which times Tom felt besieged by a flock of importunate crows, and would shake his shoulders roughly to open a little space. At this they would fall back, and eye each other accusingly, and even flap their hands, complaining loudly, "Get back, you. Can't you see he's trying to work!" Periodically Tom would tear off a square of paper and look doubtfully at his candidates as they bounced up and down, thumping their chests, or stood by licking their lips. "Me! Let me this time, Tom! I'm the one!"

There seemed no end of volunteers, and as the day wore on Tom observed, quite to his own astonishment, that in fact these commissions were being carried out; and, what's more, with something approaching his own lofty standards. Rags and water and baking soda were lavished on tarnished grates and the ornamental knobs of tea carts. Pillows were pounded and vigorously perfumed. Salt cellars were filled, burned-out bulbs replaced.

Furthermore, no sooner was a task accomplished than its executor would be back panting at Tom's side, dizzy with dust and scent, knees crusted with patches of paste, petitioning for a new assignment. Frankly disbelieving, Tom would double-check each job, his disciples literally breathing down his collar as he bent to scrutinize the work—which invariably, incredibly *measured up*. "Well done," he'd grumble, straightening in embarrassment, "well done, actually." Then followed a chorus of enthusiastically echoed "well done's," whistling and the patting of one another's cheeks. "What next!" they demanded, "What next!"

Tom was naturally reluctant to put any faith in these zealous exhibitions; hadn't they always been a clever, deceptive bunch? He remained on his toes. But gradually, grudgingly, he had to admit things *were* getting done; and he did not frown or squirm with quite such evident distaste when, at the end of the day as they sat down to a sumptuous meal prepared by Mitzi herself, his helpers snuggled up on all sides, plying him with tidbits from their own outstretched forks.

Out of habit, Tom took only a little bread and a small glass of weak ale. At one point, certain he'd heard La Stupenda's voice in the next room, he struggled to rise from the mesh of anxious, encircling arms. Perhaps he might catch her as she left (a moment of privacy among the blooms and marble haunches of the Florentine sculpture garden!). But they laughed and pulled him down again, patting his knee. "What a worker, our Tom! But now it's time for a snack!" He heard the front door slam and re-signed himself to another comfortless day, having not yet managed the longed-for commendatory word with the one person for whom he'd *really*, albeit frowningly, returned.

"Welcome back, Tom."

Simpers and a hasty shifting of hips as a place was made for Ada at Tom's side.

"Jeez, we're all so excited and relieved to have you back." She beamed loyally, her slender back rounding, her small head stuck out at the end of her neck, her fingers playing idly in the crumbs of yellow cake trimmings heaped on her plate.

"Egh," Tom allowed, remembering with a prickle of guilt the cold shoulder he'd offered Ada when she knelt beside his dirty pallet. "Yes? Ahem! Well, I wasn't really doing anything so important at home. It seemed like . . . a good idea! I mean—"

Ada wagged her fingertips vaguely. "You really did us a favor, Tom."

"Yes . . ." Tom repeated. And then, more sternly (because he did not know how else, in his shame and embarrassment, to behave), "Ahem! Well, we'll all certainly have to buckle down before the big night, won't we! Ugo wasn't exaggerating when he said the place—that is . . ." He broke off again, strictly loathe to remind her of that unfortunate conversation. "Anyway, we made a dent in it today." And he recounted with gruff and yet unfeigned approval the remarkable results of his staff's labors over the course of just one day, while they wriggled and puffed their chests.

Ada nibbled her bits of cake and listened appreciatively to Tom's account. "They *are* wonderful, aren't they?" and she looked about the table with a grateful smile.

Tom snorted. "Wonderful?"

There was an abrupt, begrudging silence; and Tom, realizing he'd hurt their feelings, relented a bit. "The point is, they're taking some pride now. This is how things *should* go, don't you think?" He put his hands on the table and looked around, eyebrows pointedly raised. Feelings assuaged, they nodded back at him happily, knocking their knees together beneath the table and chewing their dinners with wide, self-laudatory smiles.

• • •

The following day was essentially the same, a high-strung fuss-and-ruckus stew. An extra shift was called to assist with the banquet, and the kitchen resounded with the metallic chatter of wire whips on spun copper, steeled blades snipping through crisp vegetables, deep fat snapping, sauce foaming, the lugubrious chug of the enormous mixer as it ploughed the heavy dough, the shrill whine of the electric blender that drowned out everything else—and of course the ubiquitous and rarely justified thunder of water assaulting the stainless steel sinks. From other parts of the Ruins came the demented wail of the vacuum cleaner, the fidgety tinkle of glass, the powdery, concussive *boom* of blown electrical circuits. In the midst of this Jones swished and stormed and threatened to "cheese the whole damned thing, and to the other side of hell with *all* of you!"

La Stupenda closeted herself in the Maisonette, and Tom was periodically obliged by Jones to inquire at the door as to her possible needs. "Not a thing! Not a thing!" she'd call back in a thick, unfamiliar voice; and Tom, transfixed on the other side of the door, struggled against a desire to knock more urgently, perhaps even to slip inside and cadge a brief audience, "a word or two, between old friends, er, well!"

The problem was, ever since he returned to the Ruins, and despite the exceptional duties of the past couple of days, Tom's felt . . . well, neither hot nor cold? Oh, on the outside he may manage a reasonable facsimile of his old uncompromising rigor; but inside he's thinking to himself: *whatever!* He called his shots half-heartedly. When a sweat-drenched laundry miss came to him wringing her hands because she could not locate six hundred hand towels for the men's and ladies' washrooms, Tom longed to reply "Could it possibly matter?" When humble Ada denounced herself for accepting shipment on forty instead of forty dozen yellow orchids, Tom rolled his eyes and hummed. *So what!* But this was surely "not him"; and what could have become of his previous ardor?

Naturally he could discuss this with no one on his staff, not even Ada, who, though admittedly a loyal booster, was *still* an underling. He could hardly risk his own authority, so recently recovered, by confessing to an inexplicable and untimely ennui. Nor could he, for obvious reasons, confer with the likes of Ugo, Conchita, or even Mitzi. He had a position to maintain, after all; it would do him no good to undermine that position now.

But La Stupenda, *that* was different. Tom believed he might lay anything upon the altar of those smoking sapphire eyes. Strangely enough, he *wished* to confess, to open up to her. She'd understood so much already; surely her sympathy might see as far as this?

Unhappily, Tom could never find her alone. She was surrounded by an entourage of lackeys and hangers-on who hovered and buzzed like obsequious bees about their eminent queen. She was busy.

A fanned stage was erected to her specifications in the Cloud Room. Two acutely intersecting planes suggested a mammoth, seemingly fathomless "flue," where the afore-haggled blue satin panels hung, from some invisible place high among the rafters, like gleaming scrolls let down by heaven itself. The effect was highly sculptural, breathtakingly simple, and (it was agreed all around) perfectly *stunning*. But when the last gorgeous fold had been hung and La Stupenda summoned for approval, she stood at its foot for a long moment, not saying a word while her crew murmured anxiously.

At last she dragged deeply from her smoldering cigarette, leaned toward the curtain and released the smoke in a long, languorous stream. The impressionable satin received and disseminated the force of her breath. An exquisite tremor, emanating from where she'd blown, quickly flared up—then out, sensationally, in all directions—until the entire spectacle shimmered and seethed: a looming, apocalyptic grotto of royal blue flame. Those standing by gasped at its splendor. *"Right, then,"* muttered La Stupenda; then strode away and locked herself in the Maisonette, wherefrom she refused to be lured for the remainder of the day.

• • •

At the risk of laboring the point, we repeat: Tom would have given *a lot* for just a word or two from those solicitous lips before the commencement of the Ball itself. In truth, he feels uneasy in a way he cannot put his finger on, and does not look forward (la, quite the contrary!) to the unavoidable excesses of the evening ahead. With characteristic chagrin, he recalls the girlish fainting spell to which he'd succumbed his very first night at the Ruins. It seems a hundred years, at least, since that fraught and perhaps ominous first night. Tom sighs and shakes his head. Well, here he is again. Smarter, he hopes; at least better dressed. But what else has in fact changed?

An earsplitting, broad-minded curse announces the kitchen, which door flies open as Toulouse rockets past (*splat* into the wall, with a stunned skid to the floor, like a pigeon colliding with a plate glass window). Again! More shabby monkey business! Glumly Tom nudges the dog with the toe of his shoe; it lifts its head, rises and trots off in the direction of the Cloud Room. Tom rests his forehead against the cool plaster, then jumps as three yardmen in coveralls lumber blithely behind him with a forty-foot palm. As they pass, Tom bites his lip. Is this the time for last-minute landscaping? Jones always wanted something rearranged even as the guests were ringing the bell! It was just the sort of thing that drove Tom mad . . . *and would it ever be any other way?*

Suddenly our hero is unspeakably (indeed, he suspects unrecoverably) tired. So tired, so utterly tired, that a warm and importunate pressure precipitates a mist before his eyes; and he lifts his hands and covers his face, a testimony to powerlessness and finally to plain resignation.

Dear.

Oh dear.

Alas, the poor lad gives himself—impractically, and all at once—to a brief despairing fit. As a matter of fact, he's never felt quite so alone in his life; nor, he realizes with a violent start, so . . . well, quite so *terrified.* He blinks, he pinches himself, he whimpers. Poor Tom; a *world* surrounds, contains him. A world of backed-up drains and overstuffed gullets belching up indigestible lumps of truth; of cupboards where the half-baked cakes of hopeless or forfeited dreams sit languishing. A world where behind every door, doomed, ruby-eyed bunnies hang by their ears from the rafters, innocent noses quivering. In this world's every pantry rats bored holes through colossal wheels of moldering regret; gallant rainbows dimmed on the ice-bedded flanks of dying trout; silverfish wriggled along the walls of elegant sham—and half the cooks were consumed by scabies, head lice, and ringworm.

Lord! Tom can practically hear the chorus of gnashing jaws swelling around him: tiny hooked mandibles and pink-gummed molars, smacking lips and snapping beaks and god knows what else! And who was eating whom? And who, in the end, would be left? And who (did he?) had the stomach for such inexorable, omnivorous zeal?

Well, did he?

Ding-dang-*dong!* Ding-dang-*dong!*

The bell tolls. The band strikes up a churlish march. The Ball, for better or worse, begins.

23—

Polk and Pansy Datzenbach as Beauty Chased by Tragic Laughter! J. J. Jacobs as Old Probability; his wife, Cindi, A Transient Madness!

Hot blinis with carrots, cold blinis with caviar, Lithuanian blinis with sour cream and butter; fois gras croquettes à la reine, with truffles; oyster croquettes and rissoles and bouchées . . .

Martinis—of course!—but also Manhattans, Rob Roys and daiquiris, side cars and flips . . .

Ding-dang-*dong!* Ding-dang-*dong!*

Jack Niagra as a Six-Foot Carrot . . .

There is no telling how, in the haphazard exigencies of arrival (of champagne cocktails and brusque, enigmatic

kitchen dispatches; of eel—jellied, collared, and cold—
and an immediate insufficiency of coat hangers) . . . there
is simply no telling *how*, inside of thirty incredulous minutes, our hero could have found himself farcically
sprawled, effectively disemployed, and in all respects
aghast upon the saffron velvet divan; with thick slabs of
pecan roll and small pâtés *aux duxelles* pillowing each
elbow, and an overfull martini wetting his cuff. His cap
was gone; a strange bosom cleft to either side of his vir-
tuously hackled neck. His consternation may not be over-
stated.

It's! But! What the—!

He sputtered in the redoubtable candlelit crush.

Marla Frick (the first to show, with her cabbage-
headed husband and two butterflied children, as *Paradise Lost*), flung her mink at the grinning dwarf attend-
ing the door and catapulted herself at our waiting hero,
hooking his silver tray with a whoop. Tom, his
weltschmerz unruffled by even this brash and portentous
prank, could only stare as she scampered around the corner, his filched tray perched on the consummate pitch of
her soaring filigree bouffant.

Without skipping a beat, the front door burst open
and a flood of illustrious Fools overran the front hall. It
was like nothing poor Tom could ever have imagined,
not in his worst nor his wildest dreams.

Archie de Bonaventura—*A Boy, Beguiled*—shouldered
him from the bar to tackle a fleet of gin rickeys.

Betty Garsin-Greer—a stout blond *Rabbit*—having peremptorily summoned him to the *chaise longue,* then razed him horizontal with her bulldozer bosom and a crafty hassock behind the knees.

"Rog" Beemish *(Natural Piety)* thrust a fat Havana between Tom's teeth and loudly solicited his angle on the latest securities scandal.

•   •   •

Our hero's eyes popped. What had gotten into these people? Like an overturned beetle, Tom thrashed to no avail. Where was his tray! His cap! And what would Jones say if he saw Tom flopped here! And—but what a crush!

•   •   •

Tom lost his drink to a vaguely familiar *Maiden* in a white pleated tunic, now drowsily commandeering his tray; brushed "Rog's" cigar ashes from his own smoldering hair. He meant to sit up; he was quickly straddled by a *Hapless Grasshopper.*

> Finished your drink? Have another!
> Tried the curried tartlets?
> Met my *Colleague?* Met *The Wife?*

(But did they mistake him for *Someone Else?*)

He proposed, "Need to make a quick round, back in a sec!" Apologized, "Actually, I'm due in the kitchen." Desperately cajoled, "Say, folks, you-know-who'll have my head on a platter!" No use.

All right then, what *did* they want?

Dame Cynthia Tilt showed off her new choppers while Horst Dinwiddie squeezed his buttocks with a damp pink wink and an apologetic whinny. Voices *hallooed* from across the room, clamoring for cocktails, declaiming toasts, bawling for Tom to come on over, what the hell! Get a load of the *Girls!* Shake hands with the *Most Powerful Man in the City!* And say, here's *Mom!*

Mom?

Ada staggered past under a load of coats, curtseying and bobbing her head, tripping over trailing scarves and umbrellas and fur stoles. When Tom threw up a hand to get her attention, that hand was seized and cheerfully pumped by a sociably dripping *Man Overboard*. He endeavored to call out and was nearly asphyxiated by a passing *Noxious Miasma*. Still, couldn't Ada see what was happening here? And where in this unnatural hurrah's nest was Ugo? Where was Conchita? (He looked suspiciously at the well-set thorns of a *Rio Samba Rose* in gathered yellow satin.) Could no one see he needed help? Our hero, for all his strenuous protests, was subdued by a barrage of pink gins and toffee peanuts.

My cocktail shaker, my cap!

When Mrs. Prosper Gosling hobbled by, our hero, in desperation, clutched at her sleeve. "Mrs.—Ma'am! I uh . . . *help!* Why is everyone, you know? Oh, I'm *Tom!* It's me! But what's going on?"

Mrs. Gosling narrowed her shrewd, dryly hooded eyes. "Of course you're *Tom*. What do you take us for, idiots?" She sneered. "Yes, we know you, we know you very well." Then she moved on into the crowd, boring a path with the head of her barbaric silver cane.

At that moment Tom felt the floor plunge beneath him as the band changed tempo for a rollicking polka and his saffron barge was hoisted, dismayingly conveyed, and deposited in the Cloud Room (grounded with a mortal, sepulchral groan, deep inside the ancient frame; a cry our hero echoed, sure the priceless divan was wrecked, and that he, as always, would be liable for the crime).

The motley of Fools swarmed in after, and again Tom was captive; mortified, besieged; and rapt with disbelief as one by one the revelers staggered and weaved before him in a bawdy mockery of their regular Reception Line, wagging their heads and dandling their jewels and having one hell of a time, oh you bet!

Boogie-woogie? No, rumba!

He writhes, angling for what? a way out? a friendly face? But aren't these droll, importunate faces friendly, after all? At a signal from the glowering cellist the band lurches into a genial two-step.

• • •

"I don't believe this!" groans our hero.

"Don't believe what, *carissimo?*"

Tom, floundering in the opulent squalor of tasseled cushions and chips, beer nuts and evening bags, can't—

quite—get . . . oh, to *see!* But he'd know that ravishing twang anywhere, and that indisputable perfume. La Stupenda!

Bodiless fingers tease Tom's unnaturally tamed hair into a reckless *capriccio*; in objection to which (despite his thrill at having *her,* in any event, near) Tom fidgets like a kid. "My dear Thomas," the voice whispers intimately, reassuringly into Tom's ear, "you ain't, as they say, seen nothin' yet!"

And then she is off, *again!* Leaving our hero to his own scant resources, a solitary pea on a saffron raft, in the pitch and tumble of a preposterous, unnavigable sea.

CHAPTER NINE

Sacrificio

24—

There's a fanfare of stridulant brass, a throaty, unintelligible roll of timpani, the menacing chatter of a tambourine . . . as the band assembles one outlandish and pretentiously deafening chord, which hovers—glowering, senseless, aggrieved—over the agreeably cringing crowd. Tom squirms and is at last allowed a perch on his knees. Indeed the Fools, for the moment, have forgotten him.

The Show! The Big Show!

In a flash all voices are hushed, all eyes trained upon the stage and the monumental intersection of royal blue silk. The great orchestral chord dissembles, disintegrates, but for one querulous note from the clarinet, which circulates like a pesky wasp above the crowd until people shuffle and mutter and look around, frowning, for Jones to make it stop.

Meanwhile Tom is recalling, with a tender, anticipatory thrill, his first glimpse of La Stupenda's *Artistry,* remember? The teeming public house; the unforgettable stench of wet wool, rancid beer, and unheeded diapers; the bare bulbs popping overhead; and the cutthroat rustle of vermin trafficking beneath one's feet. And finally, fatefully, across a sea of tousled heads: an ineffable pink cloud, and an azure-mantled form that rose like a feather on a incidental updraft. The distant illumination of a pale, auspicious face; and a voice (so refined! so remote and refined its source!) that lapsed and wandered, despite the slavish hush of the crowd. Obscured, equivocal; still our hero *knew* that this distant beacon, this exquisite coincidence of heaven and earth, this *Sign,* was, without a shadow of doubt, for him. Called *him,* summoned *him.* Raised an illustrative question meant for him and him alone, the answer to which he'd been after, ever since.

Perhaps it was revealing itself at last?

Tom gazes at the cryptic blue curtain and feels sure, come what may, it is his destiny staring at him from the other side. Not a vision in the offing, as at the Groaning Board (virtually indiscernible); but right here, front and center. Tonight he has the best seat in the house, and he knows *it was meant to be.* No buts about it, this is the moment he's been waiting for!

Finally, and to everyone's explicit relief, the clarinet is mollified by the low repeated *boom* of a libidinous kettle drum, and it looks as though the boundless blue veil is up to something. There is a single bewitching convulsion along the shimmering hem, like the swift lap of a lake upon its shore; but no, it happens again! And is met with an appreciative chorus of *oohs* and *ahhs*. On the third go a nimble arpeggio skips part way up the curtain, then turns, rippling to the floor. After that there are no false moves, and an exotic life seems to possess the blue satin, and to animate it in ways both beguiling and unmistakably lewd.

The drum *boom-boom*s; the clarinet squeals indecently.

The curtain seethes, flourishing itself in waves that rise from its foot, shiver from side to side, coyly plumb the unplumbable (that arresting vertical crux!) and lose themselves in the remote entanglements of high invisible rafters . . . Tom is uneasy, but the guests around him chuckle and nod, rock their hips in time to the guttural sob of the drum, and wipe the gin from their lips. Eventually the drum and clarinet are accompanied by other, less menacing instruments; and soon there is a conciliatory bolero in full swing.

Reassured, Tom lets his toes tap and his mind wander, but keeps his eyes riveted to the now-innocuously swaying curtain (from behind which, he is thrilled to imagine, La Stupenda is no doubt preparing to emerge).

There is a final, frivolous racket (really, the musicians seem exceptionally unreliable!), and at last the curtain furls. Oh! But—

There are no pink clouds, Tom observes with disappointment, his eyes anxiously sweeping the stage. In fact there is nothing much up there at all. A few folding chairs unrecalled against the wall (Tom flushes—a housekeeping oversight), dust bunnies . . . and a filthy rope which, initially flat upon the floor, now pops up and is drawn taut from one side of the proscenium to the other. It wobbles a bit, and jerks, and edges oddly across the stage until, to Tom's surprise, a swaybacked and barely upright piano appears, tied to one end. And atop that spavined nag: *La Stupenda*, at last!

A savage *h'ray!* goes up from the crowd.

Tom applauds as eagerly as the others (who also stamp their feet and whistle in what strikes him as an unseemly manner). At the same time he is taken aback by the shabby, unvarnished aspect of the production.

In no time at all he is appalled.

25—

Scrambling down from the top of the buckling instrument, La Stupenda simpers like a seasoned burlesque bawd. She is joined onstage by a grinning accompanist and they launch, with a regrettable lack of ado, into a scandalous medley of hits from around the world. It would be ungallant to observe that she sang with no evident musical sensibility whatsoever, not to say a great many farcical asides in unreliable foreign accents. And if she forgot the words, which happened with coquettish frequency, she merely strode about the stage with one hand churning the air above her head while the pianist shot maliciously ahead, leaving her to catch up as she might.

This first travesty is a marvelous success with the crowd, and without a moment's hesitation she reprises the last number. ("C'mon, *sing* it with me! . . .

> *Flyyyy me to the moooon*
> *And let me plaayy among the staaaars . . .")*

At a surly jab of his neighbor's elbow, our hero nods and gloomily mouths the words to the final chorus. But what, Tom frets, can be the meaning of this, *this spectacle?*

A hastily rigged sound system corrupts the music with cheerfully interruptive feedback. The lighting is haggard, La Stupenda showing up a pale, poisonous shade of green, with no eyes to speak of, but a frankly dazzling roll of flesh billowing over the snug elastic waistband of her shiny turquoise "cocktail pajamas." Topside her solid, broadish chest is chapped an uneven red, arms slung from meaty, sloping shoulders. She sports an intrepid turquoise camisole, plus two grimy rhinestone "cuffs" that skitter up and down the snagged nylon evening gloves ensheathing her heavy forearms. Her face and neck, bereft of the usual veil, are lurid beneath the merciless lights; her make-up dripping, dogged and yet insufficient to camouflage a suspicious shadow about the chin and upper lip.

What, our hero may rightly exclaim, can account for this inconceivable and dismaying transformation? Where is the glamorous siren, the sublime *provocatress*? And who is this husky, stubbled impostor!

And yet, it *is* La Stupenda. It must be! For who else could whip these bigshots, easily piqued and resentful as a rule, into a comparable lather of delight? Indeed, while their glamorous star looked to have been around the block any number of times (check the unhealthy pallor of her gums as she throws back her head to roar at her own jokes), still, everyone in the room (save Tom) roared with her, spewing gin and maraschino juice, choking on peanuts and stuffed olives, wiping delirous tears from their eyes with the hand-turned hems of oversized napkins.

Who else could have done all that?

•   •   •

"And now it's time to tell you about an old and very dear pal of mine—a real carouser, know what I mean? . . ."

Oh, Tom doubted not that it was La Stupenda sizzling up there in the lights; but never, *never* could he have foreseen this shameless perversion of what he, anyway, had for so long and so reverently regarded as her *Art!*

". . . wouldn't you know it? After a life-long bender, when he finally gets off the sauce, well! His body just goes to pieces! One nasty indisposition after another. At the same time he finds his accountant's been buggering him for years! Poor Dougie, things certainly looked black . . ."

Our hero shifted rebelliously in his seat. La, was it for this he'd calculated and dreamed, piously pledging each thought, while beseeching prickly dishwashers for unchipped dinner plates? Or swabbing out the Ladies' each time the plumbing refluxed? Or daily dusting the mechanical trotter's irksome cloven hooves?

"*. . . next thing his teeth fall out, the fate of every reformed tosspot! And the accountant's off to Rio with half Dougie's cash and the wife he'd always (sort of) fancied. I give up! he hollers, and a cagey dentist puts him down to yank the lot, uppers and lowers, and set your man up with first-class dentures. Oh, said the rat, he'd do it for a song . . .*"

Plus, sputtered Tom, he'd thrown over a thriving—well, a reliable—well, his *own* business. And left his baby sister in the lurch! And all for this?

"*. . . course they knocked him out. The old laughing gas! (Five-to-one he begged for it—no one prized a laugh like Dougie.) But it was the wrong juice, or too much. For my dear disreputable mate, all splayed out in the dentist's chair, his savage mouth open as a whore's—ahem! . . .well the thing of it is, he died! That's right! A mortal overdose, at last!*"

(Tom is distracted by a scuffle over in the corner. Tertz Wanning and I. M. LeClerq?)

"*. . . which only goes to show you, as it bloody did old Dougie, in the end there's no eluding Destiny. But that ain't all!*"

The two men are furiously clenched, crouched with elbows hooked round one another's fat, glistening napes; lurching this way and that against a stanch, grinning circle of people who flatter and provoke them. Tom stares forlornly.

"*. . . they laid him out leering like a wolf, looking properly à la with his gaudy new dentures—only double the rate! . . .*"

Oh, those faithless winks and nudges, and the way they'd all so casually betrayed him. And Jones (that villain!) with his flagrant contempt for virtue and his inexcusable voice!

"*. . . you won't believe it, though I swear on Doug's own squandered eyeteeth, but the very morning of his, uh, interment, there happened a whacking earthquake, and a chasm big as a—ahem!—a regular gash opened up beneath the funeral home, and into it tumbled our man's coffin! True! Swallowed him whole, and with a will!—for never were they able to fish ol' Dougie out . . .*"

All for this—this mockery, this sham!

"*. . . and that was the end of the gay dog Doug, and a more distinguished end he'd never have mustered if he'd stayed respectable all his days. So there you are, drink up! This one's for Dougie!*"

•   •   •

The band is moved to yawn, then lashes into a scathing dirge. The pony, mad eyes rolling, highballs into the Cloud Room with Toulouse on its back. But our pensive hero doesn't blink.

And even when the guests are inspired to storm the stark, bewitching stage, shouldering silk trains and popping satin cummerbunds to haul themselves over the front lip; Tom merely notes, with no particular interest, that actually these well-heeled, elderly goats were far more limber than one might suppose.

Meanwhile La Stupenda throws her lusty arms wide, and bawls over the commotion, "That's it! Don't hold back! C'mon up, every Jack Fart of you!" while the pianist abuses the ivories for all he's worth—and a caustic spotlight comes up like a blister in the center of the teeming Cloud Room—and all the people *(every Jack Fart!)* open their hearts and their ravaged throats to the memory of poor old Dougie.

> *He waltzed about the belfry while*
> *The bats danced with the moon . . .*
> *He'd saved a single nickel*
> *So they played a single tune—*
> > *(they played a single tune)*

It was a vast and unimaginable chorus.

Arm in arm they stood linked and swaying: Tattooed Hoyden with Venomous Hen, Dancing Master with Obstinate Stick, Plaster Saint, Swaggering Jay, Cardboard Cow, Brightly Feathered Hope . . . Prosper Gosling and Richard the cook are dancing cheek-to-cheek. There's the rakehell pony gnawing placidly on the corner of the rattling piano, and over there, Toulouse making dashes at the winking, lip-smacking Pig. And baying or blubbering, each to his abilities, they all roared out a last hurrah for *Dougie of the Ill-Omened Molars! Dougie and his*

Treacherous C.P.A.! Good ol' pore ol' rotten ol' Dougie! (who was, for all his flaws, after all swallowed in a rather incomparable fashion by the sweet earth's providently gaping mug).

> *Stealing sweet nothings but in the end*
> *Can you blame him for a dream?*

The big spot—a leering, lidless eye—careened this way and that, disclosing the halo of a gilded headdress here, the sanguine wink of a ruby cufflink there (a cracked glass slipper, a candid tear!). Plus innumerable uncorked, incarnadine maws, taut throats pitched like black bottomless wells. Holding back? I should say not! No more than the uncompromising cellist holds back, her right arm sawing with exquisite fury across the ecstatic gut!

> *JUSST . . . A . . . DREEAMM!*

Our hero shades his eyes against the exterminative glare; feels an old familiar tickle in the region of his belly; and struggles with a private and implacably mounting sense of dread.

The fact is, you see, *no* one is holding back.

26—

"You're not singing, Thomas."

La Stupenda collapsed upon the disheveled *chaise longue,* leaned back and casually lit a cigarette.

"It's my usual pinochle night, I can't think how Jones managed to lure me away. But it's turned out a creamy do, if I say so myself. A regular scream." She poked Tom with the tarnished toe of a silver lamé mule. "You're awfully quiet—didn't much fancy my sob story about ol' Dougie? I drag it out every show, brings the house down." When Tom would not reply she shrugged, "course I stole it," then laughed and waved her cigarette dismissively. "Ah well, everyone's a critic."

Tom leaned forward, clutching an abandoned feather harness to the tensed muscles of his belly. "It isn't funny!"

La Stupenda stared, her stubbled chin lifting in mock reproof. "Why Thomas, of course it's funny. Look around you, *caro*. Aren't these people laughing?"

And Tom did glance swiftly round the teeming Cloud Room, and observed the fit of hilarity that in fact possessed the crowd, so that everywhere curved fingers clutched at swelling throats, tears sloshed from the turned-up corners of incredulous eyes, bosoms and bellies quaked, desiccated old ladies doubled over hiccoughing. Blushing, he shook his head. "It's, it's not . . ."

"'Thy priests go forth at dawn,'" reminded the singer. "'They wash their hearts with laughter.' It's *antiseptic*, dear boy, and like any antiseptic, it often stings, or tastes bad. Nevertheless, it's very good for discouraging certain undesirable complexes." She nudged him again with the toe of her shoe. "Like I said, you should try it yourself." Tom drew back offended, and La Stupenda pressed a knuckle between her eyes with a frown of contained impatience.

"Look, I'm an *artiste*. I have a message to deliver, and strategy is everything. Believe me! I've been in the business a long time and tried a lot of gimmicks, many of them against my better judgment. Why, I've been grim as the grave itself, but where did that get me? No, take it from me, there's nothing to gain by estranging your audience. Whet the sauce with a little salt! Go with what works, the indestructible Ha-Ha! That's right, make 'em laugh, unhinge their jaws with laughter! Without even knowing it, they'll stagger that much closer to the truth—that is, to see what I see, love what I love . . ."

"You call yourself an artist," Tom hissed. "What exactly is this so-called message of yours? What do you see? What do you love? What is this *truth?*"

"Well naturally there's more than one, and damned few of them very pretty!" La Stupenda leaned over the prow of the padded divan and collared an unfinished bottle of champagne. She swung it butt end up and Tom watched the sturdy muscles of her throat *contract* (and relax), *contract* (and relax), his own belly involuntarily following along; and he felt both absolutely knackered and that this night—this perilous, compulsory night— would never end. The singer watched him from the corner of one eye, winked reassuringly, then lowered the bottle and smacked her lips.

"Me, I like surprises. Truth's perversity! Perversity's truth! *There* lies the jelly in the donut, agreed? The question is, where does the line of perversity exist for you? Where do desire and repulsion, *Yes* and *No*, rear up and defy one another? There's the truth I love, and to which I would entice you. Yes, and especially you! All unhinged, unfettered by laughter."

Tom caught his breath. "What do you mean? Why would—I just want to be good, to better myself! I only meant . . . I always thought of you."

"Flatterer! I sense, however, that you now feel of two minds on the subject? You're confused, no? Your vision was clear, and now, too bad, it's gone all muddy. Well, let me tell you from experience, one does not become enlightened by visualizing figures of light, but by making the darkness visible. That, by the way, is why Jones is so important—indeed, the most important of us all," she shook her head affectionately, ". . . the old hooligan."

"Jones! But he's . . . he's the worst! Why, if it weren't for him!"

"—*he's* your best ally."

"He's a monster!"

"Yes."

"He—he trips you up at every step. He humiliates and interferes! And besides, he's sinister, he lures people into doing the wrong thing, he traps them. He has no conscience!"

"Yes."

"Yes! Well—but then . . . how can you say he's my ally? Why, black is perfectly white to him—you call that helpful? I tell you he's a double-crosser! A snake in the grass and a gobbler!"

"Now you're beginning to understand."

"*What?* I don't . . . you're not making any sense!"

La Stupenda shrugged and bent to examine a vicious run laddering the heel of her stocking. "Listen, you want to be free or not?"

Tom's belly lurches. "What do you mean?"

"I mean go ahead and *be* gobbled. If you want to be free, that is." She spit on her finger and dabbed at the run.

"But . . ." Tom was incredulous. *What kind of freedom is that?*

"Look, Thomas, and listen carefully. *You'll only ever be as powerful as your most powerful adversary.* Get it? The wolf at the door happens to be man's best friend! Will you open that door?

"I ask you again: at what, *caro,* do you draw the line? Is it mortality, the blind worm gnawing at the back of the eye? Is it some 'Dougie' scuttled in his own vomit? A hair in your soup? Is it ghosts? From what in the world do you most violently recoil? And to what, my sweet sweet darling, my precious, well-intentioned ass, to what *will* you consent?"

Tom paled and turned away, plucking distractedly at the feather harness. *Consent?* It was then he noticed an exceptional thrill in the crowd. People no longer milled and yodeled, but stood on their toes, lips stretched tight in anticipatory smiles. La Stupenda raised her bottle in salute. The cooled sweat left a glaze on her cheeks, and she shoved a savage nail under her skewed blond wig and scratched luxuriously.

Tom winced and bit the inside of his lip, struggling to revive his perishing first impressions of the now-sprawled and frankly yawning diva. Genius? Yes, in part. Virtue and breathtaking finesse? He *guessed* (now shaking his head). The dark stubble shadowing her ravaged make-up saddened and confused him; the sullen red rash granulating her stout upper arms and chest seemed, well . . .

What a brute! he thought helplessly, with love and timid horror. Cigarettes and pinochle, broad jokes and vulgar ditties. How . . . why, she!—oh, I can't!

Consent? To this?

In the end Tom's eyes fill with tears of loyalty—no less tears of grief and unrecoverable loss; and then, for just a moment, through the warm bright glittering veil, La Stupenda appears just as he'd first seen her: exalted, ineffable, a luminous and surely providential Star.

He blinks—the tears are dashed from his eyes; and she is gone, leaving in her absence only a mawkish blond wig and the wistful, bitter scent of her smoldering cigarette.

27—

There's another roll from the timpani, the obligatory fanfare of brass; and the lights are struck completely but for two hectic spots that pan the stage with questionable design. People blink and exclaim, fumbling at their dominoes, their plumes and fans. In a flash (having made himself inexplicably scarce thus far), Jones himself sallies out onto the stage, advancing with quick mincing steps. The two roving spots hastily collide, then merge, Jones's illuminated hair branding a platinum halo in the air around his head. He glares out across the sea of upturned, expectant faces; the spotlights shift and flutter on either side.

"Gawd, will you *look* what the cat dragged in. We LOVE it! Kiss KISS! Let off some steam, did you? Yes or no? Period! But now it's time to get down to business." He flapped one hand in the direction of the band and a low, boding, undulant rhythm began to prowl the room: Boom, boom-boom-*ssssss!* . . .

Tom struggled up. *La, what time is it? Time to go?* That struck him as not a bad idea; for to tell the truth our newly shattered hero—wrung out, obscurely wounded, and downright rattled by the wig—had quite lost track of his professional obligations. *Was he? What was the drill?* He admonished himself, *c'mon! get this thing over with!* Indeed, managed to stand for a moment; then twitched once and violently swayed, forward and back, as though having seen over the edge of a thundering precipice. For a fact, he rather frightened himself (*no fainting!*), and cautiously sat down on the edge of the divan, head between his knees, to wait out the extravagant wobble and plunge.

Boom! The thump of an abysmal drum came up through the soles of his shoes, convulsing his knees, his hips and belly. *Boom-BOOM.* A rousing, rhetorical goad. All the same, he felt so . . . so *creaturely*, so anonymous and overlooked. Curiously (he had to admit), *it wasn't bad.* Nose tucked comfortably between two momentarily well-behaved knees; why he was almost invisible! It comforted him to think that this latest and as yet poignant letdown might confer its own not-to-be-sniffed-at allowances; a secretly satisfying isolation, for one. And so he hunkers down a little further, relishing the unlit, fugitive respite, into which one might spool backwards like a snail into its shell, tucking in its tender, offended horns. To do nothing, see no one!

Boom, boom-boom . . . Boom, boom-boom—*sssss!*

Down here Jones's voice is, if not completely dismissable, at any rate relieved of its characteristic virulence. "*And* so, without further ado, the Grand Fool for whom we've all been waiting! Officiating wizard of the double-barreled martini! Bland pantry despot! Illustrious overlord of winekeys and kitchen matches . . ."

Tom listens wearily at first, and then with growing apprehension, ". . . *crackerjack fussbudget!* . . . *gallant old maid of the prudent simper* . . ." gradually realizing that the entertainment, far from being over, may have only just begun. "Well, have you guessed it? *Gawd*, you asked for it! Fool of the Hour and furthermore of the *highest* rank!—"

The crowd, in an agony of impatience, erupts, drowning Jones's voice. Both spots sheer off to rifle the room; and all heads swivel—yaps unstoppered, roaring—in search of their exalted, delinquent prodigy. Jones stands with both hands propped against his lower back, braying into the microphone, "*Tom!* Where is that little flirt? Come out, come out this instant. *Tom-Tom!*"

With merciless delight the spotlights cut to and impale our cowering would-be mollusk, obliviously adhered to the lee of his saffron raft. Automatically looking up at the lash of Jones's voice—not having grasped the significance of the announcement—Tom visors his eyes, intending to take hurried stock of the mob determinedly howling his name. Only now, as it happens, they've turned their backs and are gazing as one in the direction of . . . that is? Of—

What in the world??

Hastily, instinctively, the spectators open up a wide and unobstructed path between our dumbfounded hero and, and—

But . . . you don't say!

Broad as a barn at its base; rising in tiers to a tapering peak nearly tickling the rafters; and literally swaying with urgency, with the riveting absurdity of inescapable kismet. It was a thing which . . . To be sure, it could only . . . Well! The fact is, *it was constructed entirely of food.* Jones skipped to the lip of the stage as the blue curtain descended in a single shimmering glissando behind him.

He spread his arms, rose to his toes and cackled over the extravagant *oohs* and *ahs* of the crowd—

> *"We Give You The Purely Gratuitous Acme*
> *of the Gastronomical Sublime!"*

Smoked joints, watermelons, and huge waxen wheels of cheese (by the hundreds!) formed the undercarriage; cabbages, fruitcakes, and whole suckling pigs buttressed it further, with some mostly decorative breastworks in sculpted pumpernickel. Truffled turkeys and roast squab perched on scrolled ledges of nougat and nutted fudge. Elegant moldings in asparagus and artichoke puree were a sophisticated complement to well-placed parquetry panels of butter brickle and zwieback. There were slender quivering palisades of orange gelatin and processed cheese, and little faux galleries of fish sticks, cheese straws, and licorice whips. Ramparts built of meatloaf, cold porridge and matzoh balls gave the thing a stolid air at whimsical odds with the numerous pistachio mousse rosettes and trefoils, cornices of sponge cake and crab *au gratin.*

And oh! the gay swags of veal sausages and interlocking sugar donuts! The artless sprays of peppercorns, caviar, and Jordan almonds! The droll borders of Latvian sprats, dancing on their tails among marshmallow peanuts and deviled eggs!

At the top, the incontestable zenith of monstrous overmuchness: a blinding, twelve-layer white chiffon *gâteau suprême,* fully six feet in diameter, with an apical bower of yellow marzipan roses high-hatting a chaste white dais.

It was grotesque.

It was spellbinding.

It had an air, yes, of the sublime!

Stunned (in extreme cases, streaming) faces gaze in worshipful silence, moved by the lofty, preposterous monument to milk and honey, gilded lilies, and the over-running cup. No two ways about it, Jones had strictly outdone himself this time.

Three additional spotlights were required to fully illuminate the thing; and under their collective 10,000 watt glare, what didn't glisten, smoked; and the frank proximity of ill-met odors stewed woozily into one vast miasmic dream; and Tom himself, despite his natural and swiftly accruing shock and embarrassment, found himself—with scarcely any hedging—bewitched. Indeed, as the band struck up a saucy triumphal march, our hero found himself creeping on hands, on eagerly truckling knees, toward the irresistible, half-cooked palace. High above his head Jones played his dreadful voice like a barbed-wire violin.

> *Because you counted swizzle sticks,*
> *And counted on fortune's wizened grin,*
> *Because you scrubbed grates, dreamed of roses*
> *Tippled gin . . .*

Only, why *was* Tom crawling? After all that had happened—the straws he'd grasped at, the chickens he'd counted, the spilled milk he'd mopped—after all his rising stars and sunken ships . . . Why go through with this suspicious drama? Why not just stand up and call it a day? What more, after all, could one expect?

Knowing there are puppets
(and then there is the puppeteer)
Fearing gorgons, hydras, and chimaeras dire

Tom trundled on. He kept his head down and aimed for the great overturned cornucopia. He did not ask himself *why?* Neither did he lend an ear to Jones's interminable (and, from what little one could catch, unintelligible) oration. He went—in a tidy, true line—for perhaps no other reason than that he could not imagine what he would do were he to *stop*. Some things are that simple.

And because you're tired
(And your feet, like anyone's,
Smell when they're tired)

Tom paused, sat back on his heels and tried to look around. *Ack!* could they not bring these lights down a bit! He winced and batted like a kitten at the dazzle. It would be reassuring, he felt, to catch a friendly eye. Perhaps Ada, even Paulie! Yes, but where had they got to? Disappointed, chin sinking, he consequently failed to notice a tall, childish cylinder of stiff paper and dusty red velveteen—with an ink-stippled border of cotton wool and a saw-toothed crest—approach and deftly be settled atop his head. Tom started, lifting his hands. What? Oh dear! What now?

The crown weighed virtually nothing and gave Tom a perilous feeling, as though he balanced a plate of peach *flambé* on his noggin. *One more thing to take care of* . . . His chest squeezed, pumping his eyes full, which lent a weird underwater effect to the swarming overhead lights and the forms darkly refracting around him. Meanwhile the *boom* of the bass, the bongos (and an intermittent, strangled cowbell), pulsed and throbbed in his ears.

He blinked; tears tumbled to the floor; and the tower reared, vehement as a lightning bolt and inconceivably perverse, before him. Tom caught his breath, leaned close. There were boiled crawdads, still alive, their legs waving dazedly from chuckholes of congealing sauce . . . slender eels kinking in dismay beneath the blistering lights . . . bogs of terrine, and alcoholic babas soggy as old sponges in puddles of turning cream. Some of the game, haphazardly butchered, and despite scorched and even smoking flesh, continued to bleed unsavorily from the joints. And in certain, admittedly bizarre cases, creatures unfortunately not yet expired made pathetic (and thank goodness unsuccessful) attempts to prey upon their more prostrate neighbors; or instinctively munched, with touching optimism, upon whatever might be within reach: a limp parsley sprig, a pretzel.

Tom cast a dubious glance about the lower fortifications, eventually spying a kind of porthole through which, it occurred to him, one might handily enter. For-

getting for a moment the mob whooping at his back—
still careful of his horrible crown—he stuck his head inside. *Hmm.* There was a low crawl space leading to the
center of the tower where a ladder rose up a narrow central shaft, presumably to the very summit. Impulsively,
Tom wriggled into the passageway, lost to the appreciative thunder of applause from the crowd behind him. At
once he felt he'd been transported to a world unlike any
he'd ever known, and his heart danced nervously against
his ribs.

My, but it's quiet!

Indeed, the silence was profound, shaken only by the
regular *boom, boom-boom* of the distant, sonic bass, now
muffled by the surrounding walls of food (yet unmistakable as a change of pressure within one's own sinuses).
Tom crept to the bottom of the ladder and looked up; it
was as though from the bottom of a very deep well: dank,
a bit airless, very dark.

But look, a little light!

He craned his neck, squinting at the high, mild unruffled light, so cooly aloof after the ruthless strafing of the
big spots; but his tall crown jostled the wall behind him
and forced him to face straight ahead. The air inside the
tower was virtually unbreathable, hot and ponderous
with the collective, imploding odors of encompassing
food. Again Tom's chest tightened, and now he pressed
his forehead to a dusty ladder rung. He gulped and
breathed through his mouth, but the tears glided swiftly
down his cheeks anyway, wetting his wrists.

Oh for pete's sake! one might well exclaim at this point. For what, now, does our inconstant hero weep? Is he not at last precisely where he schemed (in good faith!) labored (hammers and tongs!) and indeed shamelessly *aspired* to be? And does he not stand, furthermore, at the center, the focal heart, of a monument created for the sole and conspicuous purpose of acclaiming those very labors, dreams and machinations? Really, it's quite clear Tom himself has no idea, no idea at all! Can he really not understand what's at stake here?

Oh, must I go on? Can't I . . . ?

Goose! Though our stickling hero be deaf to it, there's a mob out there working itself into an opulent lather, for him! Moreover (if not vouchsafed to his tightly pinched, terrified eyes), way high above them all, and as though waiting for this moment, the jewel-encrusted vestments of heaven swirl, gather, and with the tenderest of obliterating blows, at once ravish and exalt the tawdry Ruins and all whose hearts beat within it—and Tom's too! And perhaps *especially* our poor Tom, who quakes at the foot of his own colossal and monstrously ripening throne, blubbering like a stubborn kid and wishing to be anywhere but *here*, going anywhere but *up*!

(But anyway, what was it he always said? *Could be worse!* So buck up! It's not enough to want to "go home"; one way or another, the show must go on!)

Well, I'm . . . I guess—

Wiping his nose on the back of one hand, our hero braces himself and begins to climb the ladder, pausing for a moment on each rung before proceeding to the next. *Boom, boom-boom!* The walls of the shaft convulse perceptibly around him. When his paper crown clears the top, Tom takes a deep breath and peeks out over the glistening white dais.

Oh! but one's quite high above the crowd now! Tom cranes his neck, catching the tiny flash of diamond signet from a far off salute, the twinkle of an upturned sequined mask. *And every eye in the house trained on him!* But say, this wasn't so bad after all! Top of the world! Above it all! And best of all, nobody but him! Okey-doke! Why not see this thing through to the end, if that's how it is? Why not—

Clambering onto the small round platform, Tom peers over the lip and is immediately aghast, his gaze skidding like a tiny, incidental pebble down steep and tumbling pitches of stacked partridge galantines, malodorous grottos of Limburger and Stilton, unlit thickets of wilting, impenetrable greens, plunging spires of tired pâté, fondue wallows, blackened crab . . . *down, down, down!*

Whoah! Tom reels backward with a gasp, recoiling instinctively from the view; sitting on his heels, his hands fly like a giddy girl's to abruptly bloodless cheeks. He closes his eyes, struggling to compose himself. *Whoah!* The air up here is even hotter than below, and at alarming liberty, sweeping in vast unbridled currents. The sheer exposure saps the marrow of our hero's bones; indeed, if some bodiless hand stretched out and with one finger poked at the base of his spine, he was sure he would topple. And yet, conscious that his crown was about to slip, he raised his hands automatically to secure it. *Boom, boom-boom!*

Only, mustn't kneel!

Ever sparing of his unreliable knees, Tom (defying his natural cowardice), gingerly crooks one leg forward and plants his foot flat on the white dais, hands still palming his crown. The second foot warily joins the first; and from this awkward squatting position, Tom slowly, painstakingly begins to rise, his eyes still squeezed shut, the little dais tipping like a great pie beneath his feet, a few marzipan roses parting company from their rickety arbor. Never, never have his legs so begrudged their un-kinking.

At last erect, our hero opens his eyes and, without thinking, looks down again upon the crowd. The lights have opened up now, and hundreds of well-known faces can be seen grinning up at him; he moreover (and even quite naturally), grins back down at them. Not a word is spoken; the lugubrious beat of the drum and bass have ceased as well. Indeed, a sonorous hush fills the Cloud Room. Tom feels a cold nose thrust chummily against the walls of his belly, hears a familiar whine. Licking his impulsively stretched lips he savors, timidly, the pungent salt of his own previous tears. *Whet the sauce with a little salt . . . it's antiseptic, my dear boy . . . consent, consent! . . . a Champion—*

Tom feels the crown topple once more down the back of his head and makes no effort to catch it.

A champion at last!

A voluptuous shudder goes through him, unseating every particle of his singular, misshapen being; followed by a gasp that sucks deeply at his heart as though upon a straw. A broad, buzzing prickle, a fizz, rolls in waves from the effervescing hairs of his head to each taut, curling toe—and back—setting the protons and neutrons of each humble cell spinning at the double. He is ultimately possessed by a brief, peculiar spasm, something like those little mounted dolls whose limbs, strung on an elastic thread, explode, uncoupling at the joints to fly chattering together again. He drops to his knees beneath the yellow marzipan roses; a tiny blue flame dances about his pale, amazed brow.

Where, where is the line?

Tom gazes down on the crowd, eyes streaming with tears of plain recognition and incredulity. *Pbuh, pbuh, pbuh . . .* His voice fails him; and what, anyway, could he possibly say? In the end he can only lift his shoulders, and with the artlessly curved fingers of one hand, indicate his heart.

· · ·

And that, for all practical purposes, was that.

With a deafening collective roar, the company hurled itself upon the last bastion of the *gastronomical sublime.* Our hero felt the first impact vibrate up through the tower's inner shaft and (abandoning the flickering blue flame) immediately dropped to all fours, blinking uncertainly. Far below, contenders whistled and brawled, vaulting right over one another like stampeding game. Weaker guests fell upon the periphery where preserved lemons and potato gnocchi mingled in pools of whisky-laced cream; while others ranged the lower slopes, breaking off slabs of Belgian waffle, sucking the cloves from the swelling pink flesh of glazed holiday hams. Sticky fingers filched the pralines from puddling custards, and cronies stood on one another's shoulders to claw down jugged hare, chitterlings, and veal *quenelles*. When Candice Topping crowns Marla Frick with a mammoth lamb shank, practical Shad borrows his wife's crumpled form as a step to reach his favorite mincemeat tarts. Betty Garsin-Greer has hiked up her skirt and is scaling a particularly steep slope, her overbite snapping at a high cornice of truffle mousse. Toulouse yaps happily atop a hill of Russian cakes; and there was Ada—

She too!

—helping I. M. LeClerq extricate a pheasant as she gnawed contentedly at a butterscotched apple.

Tom felt a second drastic tremor as a sugar rose shattered on the crown of his head. Whole terraces were shearing off now; ornate balconies, their mostly decorative supports jerked heedlessly out from under them, went pitching down upon the diners below. People gobbled and bickered and inevitably choked on the fistfuls of food crammed practically whole down their gullets. But all of them—stowed on their hinies in wallows of sauerkraut, or spidering up a cleft face of nougat, or beating their chests from collapsing pastry battlements—*all* had their shiny eyes fixed on just one thing: the as-yet-untouched summital white cake, itself crowned by a bower of yellow roses.

Three massive blows aft and Tom was pelted by sugar posies wrenched free of their overhead wires. The sound itself was concussive, like the hubbub of thunder, as the mob stormed ever higher, bucking every hurdle in its path.

Mesmerized, Tom watched them advance, licking their lips, gobs stretched with desire.

They're coming for me

—he thought, as a triumphant *hrrg-wack* finally snapped the dais beneath him like a thin sugar wafer and he felt himself cant forward, his outstretched hands plunge, into the fathomless buttercream frosting of the sublime and divinely unlayering cake.

They are!

They are coming for me!

CHAPTER TEN

Kee-kee-kkiree!
An Epilogue . . .

When Tom opens his eyes the first thing he sees (through an intervening screen of tousled yellow straw) is a white porcelain dinner plate, artfully cowled by a not unfamiliar white brocade napkin.

The plate is parked on the pitched seat of a staggering three-legged stool. Tom's sprawled across his own rumpled pallet, sneezing at the faint spores loosed by the old and moldering overhead thatch, while the morning sun maneuvers in the plastic window with the cheerful insistence of a well-intended busy-body. *Kee-kee-kkiree!* insists the cock in the yard, while under the table his distraught coppery hen tacks her head at the clamor of ten identical dollops of dazzling yellow floss. Tom rub-a-dubs, with one unthinking foot, the primrose belly of a dusky young sow writhing in bliss at the other end of the bed. With a yawn he rolls to his back, then sharply turns his head and stares again at the plate. At last, reluctantly, he pushes himself to a sitting position.

His elegant shoes are gone, black silk socks laddered with runs; and moreover he's caked—from knees to toes, cuffs to collar—with a stiff white paste. He starts automatically to pick at the stuff, then stops; shyly he reaches instead to lift one corner of the napkin from the plate. Underneath: a mangled lamb shank, a cluster of squashed grapes, a gelid wedge of coconut-banana cream pie.

Tom gets up and moves the plate to the table; he looks down at it and yawns again, still absently picking at his sleeve.

Phew, am I beat!

At least (if on the other hand) it's an exhaustion he feels on-the-other-side-of? The *sabbatical* fatigue, as it were, of achievement?

Oie, he affirms, *now I'm resting*.

As if to illustrate Tom leans over the table, forearms crossed on the top rung of the laddered chair, eyelids gravely lowered. Even so little sun as manages to pierce the mildewed plastic window is indulgent, succoring; and the scuffed and overstrained places within our hero are assuaged by this mild green sap.

At the same time, even if he happens to recall the previous night *(even if,* before he knows it, a fugitive tear slips from the corner of one eye), he can and does nonetheless say to himself, and know it to be true: *Done . . . now I'm done with all that.* He opens his eyes and repeats very softly, gazing at the wetness of the split grapes seeping up through the distended napkin. *"That's all over now."*

Turning, Tom strips off his soiled tunic, his shabby checkered trousers; finds a pair of old sweatpants and a clean flannel shirt and digs in a cupboard for his duct-taped sneakers. Glancing curiously, once more, at the white-tented plate, he pulls open the door and walks out into the squalid, shining lane.

The very air is blue, clean as a whistle and full of beans after all that rain. In the small plot across the open ditch behind his hut, Tom sees his neighbor has been tilling: long tender hillocks of steaming black dirt run up and down; starlings and dingy pigeons with mother-of-pearl throats peck practically at the overturned soil. Further on, the high bright panes of factory windows blink like squares of flung confetti. And further still, a parking strip, poetically planted in ornamental plums. The trees have already begun to bloom; tiny pink rags explode from twigs still black and spongy with rain.

Tom saunters on, stopping to peer in a department store window where eager mannequins gather round a plaster watermelon, paper plates gripped in rigid hands. Dandelions bristle emphatically from the cracked asphalt of a freshly painted crosswalk; and glancing over one shoulder Tom is astonished to see the river *Q—* blazing at the end of the block like a sheet of stretched aluminum. And, heavens! Can that be a duck?

A truck honks to announce itself; as Tom jumps aside to let it pass, the driver, in a natty pink polo shirt and sunglasses, smiles and waves.

• • •

Without "exactly" meaning to, our hero finds himself in the neighborhood of the Ruins. But is he going back, then, after all? Oh, perhaps only to have a word or two with Ugo, say hello to Ada; make sure, at any rate, that someone managed to corral that witless pony.

Goodness, and wasn't he something last night? Up on that stage! Ta-da!

(That is! He meant the *pony!*)

But now (as of course, eventually, it must) the whole scandalous, unaccountable Ball comes rocketing back at Tom in brisk uncompromising detail. The rampant daughters Frick, like trained circus terriers, back-treading a huge and implacably turning wheel of Gruyère . . . A half-devoured lobster *in situ* atop Ax Axelrod's head, its surviving claws goosing the air like a lewd, predatory crown . . . And then—straddling a massive smoked goose—Midge Sprain Wilson ablush in black rubber, a myopic dominatrix in tortoiseshell pince-nez . . .

And don't forget the ultimate plunge of two cocked arms, two braced knees, that splay on impact, wallow engulfed. Or no, not engulfed! Exalted, surmounting—yes, or as though borne aloft! A placid, omphalic buttercream cloud! Sticky-feathered-happy-ever-after kiss!

(It was Toulouse, of course, who dug the lad out, himself no stranger to the bombshells of the sublime.)

Our hero bites his trembling lip, grins sheepishly, then slows his steps at the recollection of La Stupenda. That unspeakable wig! Still, credit where credit is due; the crowd adored her, didn't they? Ha ha! That tired old tale of desperate Dougie! Tom's heart flutters with pride and with the small blue flame of an inextinguishable crush. Well? *Wasn't* she something? And even if things did get a little out of hand (his shoulders tense, then relax)—heck, a party was a party! And what's a bit of rough-and-tumble anyway? A little hoorah among, uh . . .

Family?

Tom's eye is caught by a long glittered plume lying across a sewer grate. Oh, they were a "bunch," all right! Richard the cook, the Datzenbachs . . . why, only think of Ada! He'd never have pegged her for such a sport (just the *sight* of her, dimpled knees twinkling up a tricky bank of pheasant in aspic; nostrils flaring, cheeks flushing with effort).

Tom is met by an empty bottle of gin standing outside the entrance to the Ruins. He bends to pick it up; looks over one shoulder; takes careful aim with his taped-together sneaker and sends the bottle caroming down the sidewalk, ringing like a sturdy bell as it banks a brick wall. The front door, normally closed, today stands blandly on its hinges. Our hero (who'd only ever entered from the loading dock) considers, shrugs, then ducks in with a good-natured *Haallooo!*

Tom's rubber soles slap the bare cement. He stops. *Huh?* But, where's the yellow paisley runner? Arms akimbo, he looks up. And say, what about those notorious portraits—the aristocratic giraffe, the woo-able pooch? Sure he never liked them; still, *where were they?* The walls, flatly whitewashed (formerly a warm chocolate brown), suggest the unappetizing pallor of unglazed pastry.

Tom hurries along the hall, glancing with a gasp through the high exposed portals of the conspicuously vacant ballroom. The platinum silk-taffeta drapes! The lavender pilasters! And the walls themselves, denuded of their pink moiré silk; they too a vapid, lackluster white. Where . . . ? Oh, but hurry! *What if?*

Prepared for the worst, his braced heart nonetheless lurches at the spectacle of the former Salon, his darling, his pride. *No!* Tom exclaims at the gaping hole where the pink marble fountain once flirted and foamed. *For god's sake where are the fish!!*

Hardly breathing, sneakers catching on the smooth, unfamiliar floor, our hero slowly explores his harbor, his heaven, his bower of bliss. *La!* Cold grates where once pranced perennial flames. Ghastly white walls where once shimmered the limpid greens and yellows of spring. The birds who (only yesterday!) winked from the painted alcoves over the paired french doors? Flown the coop! From the center of the ceiling dangled an enormous violet ribbon, twisting in a desultory draft. But besides all that, Tom senses . . . there's something . . .

He whirls on one heel: the Pig! The mammoth Pig is gone! Nothing could impress our hero more profoundly than this.

For a while Tom simply drifts, stunned, through what was the "Maisonette" (recalling the matchless celestial clamor of a Sèvres breakfast service tripping down the once bright wall); across the echoing loading dock; in and out of indistinguishable offices; what *was* the laundry, the florist . . . He arrives, ultimately, at the kitchen itself.

Stainless steel refrigerators, convection ovens, ramekins; rubber scrapers and coffee urns; candy thermometers, soup tureens; fish kettles and various presses; steamers and fryers, ice troughs and pastry brushes—everything, down to the last jelly mold, gone! Indeed, you'd never have known it had been a kitchen at all, but for the bank of (strangely silent) sinks, in the last of which a dented saucepan loiters. Tom *tsks* in awe and, tugging at a stray forelock, shuffles thoughtfully back to the Salon.

Well! What to think of this? All gone?

Well yes, as it appears, quite empty.

But where? What does that mean, *gone?* How is it a thing can be here one minute—vociferous, ablaze with life—and the next minute be *gone?* Vamoosed, whitewashed . . . kaput!

Yes.

In the Salon Tom's eye nearly misses a quick spasm of light astride the spine of an overlooked spoon—there, in the corner! He picks it up, twirls it between his fingers:

the scant dazzle fills (then empties), fills (then empties), its round pouting belly.

Hello, what's that? Steps in the hall!

Tom takes the spoon and hurries to the front gallery. Too bad, no one here! But what's that again? The slam of a dryer door in the laundry room? Hurry!

Egh! Again he finds no one. What nonsense!

No, but listen! . . . Now *sure* of a voice mumbling to itself somewhere near the kitchen, Tom races down the utility hall, nips across the Salon and bursts into the Maisonette, the spoon clutched in one hand like a left-over stub of wand.

Not a soul, and (outside the not quite regular thump of his heart) not a sound. He sags, slaps the back of the spoon idly against the heel of his hand . . . and literally yips when Ada rushes in—she, too, exclaiming in surprise.

"Why Tom!"

"Ada!—"

"What are you—"

"Ada, what's happened, where—"

As usual, they are eager, abrupt, stepping on the heels of one another's words. They both stop, Tom at a loss; Ada, too, surprisingly demure, smoothing her hair. But when she spies the spoon in Tom's hand she laughs, soft lips parting over small, childish teeth.

"Jeez, I've been looking for that everywhere! Jones won't leave without it, you know? *Every spoon accounted for!* Well, that's to be expected, that's just how he is! But now it's found, and none the worse for wear, I guess. So, uh—can I?—I'll just take that, why don't I?" And she thrusts out her hand, faint pulse quaking at the base of her throat, though her black eyes hold Tom's steadily enough.

Tom, bewildered, hands her the spoon. "Sure, of course, but . . . Ada, where's the crew, what's going on? Where is everything?"

Ada's brow furrows. "But, I thought you knew! We're leaving—that is, we're *moving on*. The thing is, uh, Jones had this idea—"

Tom breaks in. "Moving *on*! Moving on *where*? What are you talking about? I don't understand!"

"Jeez, I'm saying!" Ada raps the air between them with the silver spoon. "Jones says we need a new image. He won't say what exactly but everyone's got a new contract. We're *all* going. That is . . ." She stops; then, with a catch in her voice, "Oh Tom, sure you won't go too?"

Tom by now has turned and nervously paces, hands milking the tail of his flannel shirt. Can it be as she says? That Jones! What can he be up to this time? Anyway, the point is . . . Tom mutters painfully at the floor.

"But I don't . . . no, listen Ada—uh . . . how about the pony? No! That's not what I mean! I mean—" He stops and wails, "Oh, but I can't believe—and you too? But Ada . . . sure, I know I didn't listen. Ducks! Porridge! I thought I was after—oh, it doesn't matter. I was wrong, you were right! I know that now! I made a mess, did I hurt your feelings? Well, that's all different! *I'm* not different, but I'm *changed*. Oh, I can't explain!" Ada's eyes glisten, as ever, with affection and approval.

"But Ada, I don't see how you of all people could sign up for this, this surely harebrained scheme. *Move on?* With Jones! What can it come to?"

Ada chuckles. "As for all that, Tom, you simply mustn't worry. Goodness, don't I know what I'm doing? Didn't I pin my wishes to a star? Just like you!" She throws out her arms—"this is my Big Chance!"— then siezes Tom's hand in her own, the spoon cruelly bruising his knuckles. "But Tom, it won't be the same without you!"

There's a terse *honk-honk* from outside the window, followed by a breezy "Yoo-hoo, kids!" Tom catches his breath and glances out to discover a sleek chauffeured convertible coupé drawn up beside the sidewalk. La Stupenda (swathed and snooded in powder blue chantilly lace) waves from the capacious back seat. "Ada darling!" She blows Tom a cheerful kiss as Ada pulls away.

"Oh, the pet! Isn't she something? Jeez, I just gotta run! But say, I'll be looking for you, all right? And you look for me, Tom, don't forget! I'm the one with puffy white wings!" And with a final, excited little wave, she hurries from the room. Tom stands at the window, hears her footsteps slap down the hall; now she's tumbling into the car beside La Stupenda, and with a powerful *fwooosh*—they're off.

• • •

For a long time Tom remains at the window. Ada, in her haste, had run off quite forgetting the fugitive spoon still clutched in Tom's hand. This he absently twirls, taps, and rubs against the front of his shirt (even, remembering a cute trick of Rosie's, attempts to hang from the end of his nose), as he gazes with shining, unreadable eyes, out into the street.

Finally placing the spoon on the sill, he wanders once more through the vacant Salon, the gallery, the hall . . . On his way out of the building he stops to inspect a sheet of white foolscap scotch-taped to the back of the drab metal door.

THE RUINS
(Now in a New Location!)

Has Your Bed of Roses Gone to Seed?
Is Your Ivory Tower Besieged?
Has the Spice in Your Life Lost Its Zing?

Never Fear, Fret, or Bemoan Your Fate!

The Ruins . . .

Imagine . . .

Join Us and Leave Your Troubles Behind!

Tom brushes pensive fingers across the embossed, back-slanting gold script. Above his head, on the ridge of a steeply pitched roof, two pigeons are taking turns gagging each other—first one and then the other plunging its beak into the other's craw, snatching a grain of corn back and forth between them. Tom flexes his knees and whistles; steps nimbly into the empty street and strikes for home beneath a blue, line-dried dream of a sky. *A bun,* he muses amiably. *Or a cold bottle of ginger—that's what the doctor ordered!*

Behind him the silver spoon boils like a shaft of broken lightning, quietly blistering the liverish brown sill beneath a small (and ever smaller) winking casement window.

ABOUT THE AUTHOR

Trace Farrell currently lives and works in Seattle.